When Breath Is Taken

Morgan Hadden

Paperback ISBN: 979-8-9887910-0-3

eBook ISBN: 979-8-9887910-1-0

Contents

For my Brother,
Thank you for giving me hope

PROLOGUE

LUCAS

I never thought I would die young.

I mean, I had everything going for me. I had the classic family with supportive parents. We lived in a nice home in a wealthy neighborhood. My little sister, Brinley, was finally old enough to start dating, and I was stoked to take on the protective older brother role. I'd been going to the gym for years, building muscle and fantasizing about that moment when the doorbell would ring. Brinley would be stuck in the bathroom fretting about her makeup, and I would be first to arrive at the door. I would've opened it slowly and looked the guy over, smirking at his over-gelled hair and strong cologne. Then I would've raised one eyebrow, making it clear from that very first moment—that very first second— that he wasn't good enough for my sister. And before

Brinley showed up, I would've made certain he understood his place.

But, like so many other moments that never come for the dead, I never got to live that experience. By the time Brinley went on her first date, I was irreversibly six feet under. My body suffocated in a tight coffin, my spirit loose and completely lost. Every connection I had—to my life, to my identity, to everything I cared about—was severed the day I died. And now, all that's left for me is to drift along with the wind, always watching but never participating in the lives that go on without me.

ALEX

I never thought I would die young.

But when my mother entered my hospital room after the eighth and final surgery, the first thing she did was burst into tears. She took one look at me, her daughter, lying pale and exhausted behind the oxygen mask, then started to cry. For almost an hour, she couldn't stop. Despite the grog from the anesthesia, I knew the procedure hadn't gone well.

And sure enough, later that day, the doctor informed me that it hadn't. He came into my room and said that despite his best efforts, the cancer was too rooted. He removed as much of my lungs as he dared, but it wasn't enough. My cancer had spread. It's an integrated part of my body now. And like most stubborn weeds that refuse to be uprooted, it will eventually choke me out. Despite the surgery and everything I've been through, I am going to die.

But it's not like I was unprepared to hear that news. Not entirely, at least. When we first discovered the cancer three years ago, we knew, even back then, that my chances weren't great. Myelofibrosis is a rare type of bone marrow cancer, especially in teenagers, and it was already well-established when we found it. We hadn't questioned my growing fatigue early enough. We didn't assume, like we should have, that my night chills, bruising, and joint pain were symptoms of a deadly disease. All we thought was that I was a growing fourteen-year-old girl, not a dying one. And now, three years and two months later, I am paying the terminal and permanent price for that mistake.

We all are, in fact—me, my mom, and her longtime fiancé, Craig. I've wondered all this time what's kept them from actually tying the knot. But now, lying weak and listless in a hospital bed, recovering from the removal of blood-producing tumors in my lungs, I have to wonder if it's been me. And if, after I'm gone, they might finally decide to move forward with the ceremony. After all, when I'm dead, Medicaid will no longer be so important. My mom can move up in the salary bracket and live as unrestrained and free as she's always deserved.

The idea of my mom's freedom is happy, but it is also deeply painful. Perhaps it's the pain meds swirling in my system, confusing my emotions and jumbling them together. But I desperately want Mom to be free with the same breathtaking desperation with which I want to remain alive.

It's just too bad that because of cancer, Mom's freedom and my life can never coexist again.

BRINLEY

I never thought I would die young.

I mean, I ruminate about it daily now, but the thought never occurred to me until Lucas died. Before then, I was always vibrant, enthusiastic, and full of life. The kids at school seemed to think I was part of the popular group or something, but that wasn't an image I intentionally put on. I didn't try to make people like me; they just did. I was fun, I was cheerful, so naturally, everyone wanted to be around me.

But all of that changed on the cold, brutal night that shattered everything. The night an ambulance drove off, taking my brother's corpse with it. After that, I felt deep inside myself that something more than Lucas had died. A part of me, somehow, had died with him. From that moment on, I would never again be called happy. I would never again be known as Brinley, Lucas Prowley's bubbly little sister, or Brinley, Carrie and Jared's lovable second child. No. When Lucas died and left us, he ripped a piece of me away with him. The vibrant piece. The lovable piece. The happy and joyful and enthusiastic piece. The piece that kept life worth living.

And now, months later, I am just...Brinley. Brinley. The pitiful, empty, and lost single child.

The girl who became a murderer that night. The girl who became a loner. And the girl who I know, irreversibly, no longer deserves to live.

CHAPTER ONE

LUCAS

I don't know why, during our lifetimes, we obsess over watching so much TV. Why we lounge around on a couch, watching a screen, observing event after event float by without having a say in what happens or being able to influence the outcome. Television is mind-numbing. It is an impersonal experience. And it is the closest analogy I have for what it is like to be dead.

The only difference is, while the things that happen on television aren't real, the things that happen after death are. And those first few days, even weeks, of being dead were some of the worst of my existence. Even now, I shudder to remember the deep, intense, ripping sensation of my spirit rooting itself out of my body. I don't like to recall how disorienting it was to find myself standing over my corpse, looking down, gasping to see the pool of blood that surrounded me. Because in that moment, my flesh was still *me*. My sense of existence was still tied hand-in-glove to the person beneath me. I didn't know I could continue beyond my body. And so to see myself bleeding—*me*—hemorrhaged to death on the car's hood and jutting through the jagged windshield, was more than just a nauseating or gut-wrenching experience. It was soul-splitting.

From there I stood by and screamed in panic at the EMTs and first responders, pleading with them to do something. But the moment they saw my body—the slice in my carotid artery and the unreal, glassy look in my eyes— they walked away from me. *Me*, who was standing right next to them. Me, who was screaming that I wasn't yet dead and to stay put and fix what was broken. They didn't hear me. Of course they didn't. They turned their backs and rushed over to the next victim, the drunk driver who had drifted out of her lane and hit my vehicle straight on. The perpetrator who, miraculously, had nothing more than a concussion and a superficial gash in her hairline.

That night, it was me who died. Saige, as I later came to learn was her name, lived. Though after peeking my head into her hospital room to confirm that, I've never bothered to visit her again. Her presence was then, and still is now, too emotional for me to handle.

I understand now, though, that there are some angry

spirits who choose differently. Some souls who, fevered by the unfairness of their death, choose to linger around whoever caused it—purposeful or not. I've seen those spirits. I've crossed paths with more than one in my drifting, and I've seen how dark their souls have become. It's a tangible thing, the light, or goodness, that a spirit does or does not radiate. And after seeing the light-sucking aura of those who choose to stay bitter and linger, I know that haunting is a fate I will never allow for myself.

So instead, I purposefully and wisely give Saige a wide berth. And the people I choose to linger around are the people who, though I can no longer influence, still bring me a shadow of joy: my family. And most especially today, Brinley.

It's a Monday, and she is struggling. She's standing in front of the mirror, trying hurriedly to apply another layer of mascara, but it's not wanting to stay. The problem is, her sad, blue eyes are filled with tears. They well up, brim over her bottom eyelids, and snag in the top row of her lashes every time she blinks. The mascara is clumping, gooing together in blobs, and I can see how distressing this is to her. I sit on the edge of the tub, watching and aching with a desire to help. Yet, like always, there is nothing I can possibly do.

"It's all right, Brin," I murmur to my sister, though more to myself than to her. After four months of floating around with no tangible vocal cords, I've more than learned that it's pointless to speak. But still, I can't help but try. "You look great. I mean it. You really do."

But Brinley doesn't respond. She just desperately uses the wand to smooth out the clumps, trying to fix the mess without smudging it further. Then she looks at the clock. With a grit of her small, perfect white teeth, she jams the wand back into the tube and screws it on, giving up.

I see the pain in her face as she reaches down, grabbing her backpack from the floor, then looks in the mirror one last time. Because I know Brinley so well, I understand that it's a multilayered pain etched across her face. One with so much depth to it. I recognize the pain of her frustration—the frustration of not looking the way that she wants to. The pain of humiliation—worrying that others on the bus will notice the wet shimmer in her eyes or the red splotches on her face from crying. And then there's the real pain, the deep and unrelenting pain, that I'm sure is the real reason for her misery: the hurt of my absence.

It's the first Monday in March and there's supposed to be an assembly. The cheer squad, *my* cheer squad, will be performing today. And in honor of losing one of their best bases (one of only two boys—best friends—who dared try out for the team and make it), they will be dedicating the performance entirely to me. But I know, and Brinley knows, that the flyers won't be flying as high. The spotters won't be as focused. The stunts won't be as swift or impressive. Not without me there, flinging and catching and spinning. Brinley sees the loss of me everywhere. And she's not looking forward to the gaps I'm bound to leave in this performance, or the grand finale when the team will end in the formation of a pyramid with the top, pointed tier left empty, symbolizing the spot I once held with them.

No. Four months later, Brinley is still struggling. And there is nothing that I can do about it. With a sigh, I push myself up from the tub's edge and rub a hand wearily down my face. But though I'm touching what should have been skin, I don't actually feel myself there.

The loss of me is everywhere. And although my presence doesn't choose to haunt, my absence involuntarily does. It's agonizing how painful it feels for both Brinley and me alike.

BRINLEY

I stare out the bus window, my forehead pressed against the cool glass as it bumps along, weaving through the newly paved roads that make up Western Albuquerque. The landscape outside my window is a long stretch of desert— there's brown dirt, dead clumps of sagebrush, and piles of volcanic rock. As the bus weaves around a curve, a new development comes into view—expensive homes that, though on the outskirts of a barren wilderness, hint at even bigger and better neighborhoods to come.

Western Albuquerque is growing, and there's no doubt it's for the wealthy. It's far enough from the downtown slums that families like mine, who can afford the finer things of life, are drawn here. After all, my dad makes plenty enough money as a nuclear scientist to keep my family afloat. Not to mention the added income from my mom's successful fitness center. Like so many of our neighbors, my family is pretty rich. But unlike so many of them, we are anything but happy.

I pull my face away from the glass and look down at my hands, fisted on my lap. My eyes are swimming with tears again, but I won't let them spill out. Not here, on a bus full of people. To force myself to get a grip, I clench my jaw and try to take a deep, shaky breath in. I pull the air inside me and, once it's there, I beg it to fix the horrible, crushing ache I feel inside my chest.

But the thing is—the stupid thing is—the breath doesn't help. In fact, it never does. No matter how much I cry, or scream, or try to breathe like people tell me to, the pain of Lucas's death never leaves. Some days it weighs on me like I'm drowning. Other days, it's like I'm being strangled. And today, the agonizing pain of his death is making it hard to even think.

My eyes well up more and I know, from other mornings like this, that my only option is to ignore the pain. I have to if I want to make it through the day intact. So I yank my earbuds out of my pocket and jam them in my ears—my signal to the world that I don't want to be disturbed. But once they're in, I don't turn anything on. I close my eyes and lean my head back against the window, listening to the high school bus as my backdrop. There's the sound of cheerful voices greeting each other, the occasional snore from a sleep-deprived nerd, and the hum of sleepy chatter. Everyone is so...whole. So ok. No one else is on the verge of breaking apart.

For the next fifteen minutes, I reign in the grief. Because once we get to school, I know I'll need to put on my everyday perfect-Brinley facade. Like always, I'll take out my earbuds and return them to my pocket. I'll groan and appropriately sigh when the bell rings, then find myself trudging along in the herd of other faceless students, all of us making our way to our first period classroom.

In the past, I would have sought out my friends to walk with. Probably, I would have been late to class from talking with them too long. But I won't do that this morning. And I won't do that tomorrow morning either. In fact, every morning since Lucas died, I have been deliberately avoiding them. I'll simply duck my head and press on, doing whatever is necessary to make it through one more morning intact.

Then, when the assembly hits, I'll ditch. I'll sneak into an empty classroom on the second floor, sit jammed in an unseen corner, and actually listen to music until the bell rings and I'm free to get on the bus again. I'll be a forgotten face that no one will notice is missing. One of many who, honestly, the world would probably be better without.

ALEX

It's been seven days since my lung surgery. Seven days since we were told I'm destined to die. And not once during those seven days have I been left alone.

Not once, that is, until now.

"Ok, sweet girl, I promise I won't be gone long," Mom says, bending over and planting a gentle kiss on my forehead. My hair—at least, what little is left of it—is plastered to my skin with cold sweat. I've had a nagging, persistent fever the past few days, one that keeps me chained to this bed rather than being released back home. The doctors say I should get over it quickly. Minor fevers like these aren't totally uncommon following an operation, and I'm getting pumped so full of antibiotics that this infection doesn't stand a chance. But until my temperature stabilizes, I'm stuck in the hospital a little bit longer.

"I know, Mom." I want to smile at her, to reassure her, but I'm feeling really tired. And the burning pain in my chest isn't helping. They cut out a significant portion of my lungs to remove the tumors, and I can feel a decrease in my lung capacity. At the same time, I'm kind of grateful for it. I may not be able to breathe as deeply anymore, but at least I'm no longer drowning and coughing up bloody mucus every hour.

"I probably won't be back until after dinnertime, but if you need anything, I'm only a call away. I promise. This client knows you just had surgery, and if the tax deadline wasn't coming up so soon, they wouldn't have asked me to come. It's just..." Mom sighs heavily, running a hand through her brown, lightly graying hair. "Oh, you know. They aren't reconciling their accounts right, and they need me to compare their paper trail to their digital trail. I'm going to try my best to get out of there quickly."

"Don't worry about it," I tell her, then grimace as I weakly cough. For as long as I can remember, Mom has been running her own one-person accounting business from home, dividing time between homeschooling me as a single parent and meeting the needs of small, local businesses. "Your work is important. Your clients need you, and I'm used to it. Besides, it's not like I'm going anywhere."

She smiles wryly. "Yeah, you better not. Not on my watch."

I roll my eyes, but that's about all I can muster. It's been a week since the operation, so I'm not doing as poorly as I was several days ago. In fact, a lot of my strength is coming back. I can now hobble to and from the restroom without help, and I hold my own during most conversations pretty well. But in this case, Mom is kidding and I don't need to give her a pity laugh. Those still really hurt.

"Well, ok. You rest up, and when I come back, I'll bring Craig with me. Maybe the three of us can all watch a movie together or something, all right? Be thinking about what you want to watch."

"K, I will."

"All right, sweetie. I love you."

"I love you too, Mom."

And with that, she turns and heads for the door. Most of my life, when leaving my hospital room or leaving my bedroom, she's always just closed the door behind her with a click. But now, ever since getting my prognosis, she lingers a little. She steps outside, turns over her shoulder to look, and just kind of stares at me for a while. Then she smiles sadly and slowly pulls the door closed.

But I know that once that door closes, her expression falls and her steps get a whole lot heavier. I know, because I've heard the tears she cries at night when she thinks I'm fast asleep, and I've heard the whispered conversations she has with Craig. We've been fighting this cancer for over three years now, going on four. Miraculously, we beat it the first time, after massive amounts of chemotherapy, removing my spleen, and an allogeneic stem cell transplant when I was fifteen. We thought I was in the clear then. I even went to public school for a while, just to try it out. But unfortunately, a little over a year later, we were told I had relapsed. And this time, with much smaller chances of survival.

And sure enough, this second round of cancer isn't responding well to chemotherapy or radiation. The clinical trial drugs are failing. And even this lung surgery wasn't entirely designed to save my life. Mostly, it was designed to make breathing more comfortable until I die.

So, yeah. For the past three years, my family has been hounded by bad news. Because of it, my mom has learned to master the brave face. Or at least, when she's around me, she's learned to master it.

But when I'm gone, and it's just her and Craig all alone, I know that's when she finally crumbles.

And when she's gone, and it's just me all alone, that's when I finally crumble too.

CHAPTER TWO

LUCAS

I'm not sure whether to be grateful for Mr. Buchanan or angry. He's the vice principal of the school and, like most administrators, must have been prowling the halls during the assembly, looking for ditchers and dragging them back to the auditorium. Or, if they refused to follow, writing them up for truancy.

It's Mr. Buchanan who eventually finds Brinley huddled in the corner of an empty classroom. Her eyes are closed and a strand of blonde hair is wrapped around her finger, her head bobbing rhythmically to her music. She doesn't hear Mr. Buchanan open the door. She doesn't notice his presence until he's standing over her, looming with his lips pressed tight. I'm in the room, of course, watching Brinley, and I want to shout at her to open her eyes, to pay attention and take the earbuds out. But like always, it would accomplish nothing. So I don't. I just shove my hands into my ghostly jean pockets and stand by.

I watch, then wince, when Mr. Buchanan clears his throat, finally capturing Brinley's attention. She gasps loudly, reflexively covering her face, before reality catches up and she realizes what is happening. Embarrassed beyond measure, Brinley yanks the earbuds out of her ears, then stares at Mr. Buchanan's feet, blushing.

"Hello there." Mr. Buchanan's voice is high-pitched and pleasant, though he's still staring Brinley down.

"Hello," she mutters back, not raising her gaze.

"And what do you think you're doing here? There's an assembly going on, you know."

"Yes, I..." Brinley hesitates. Then after biting her lip, she sighs deeply. Slowly, she gets to her feet. "I know."

"And you also know you are required to attend, don't you?" Mr. Buchanan presses. "If not, you'll be counted truant. I don't expect you want me to call your parents this afternoon, do you?"

"No." Brinley's answer is immediate, forceful. Then she seems to catch herself. Her lips turn down in a sharp grimace as she realizes how desperate she sounded. Looking at her feet, she adds more quietly, "No, Mr. Buchanan. I don't."

"All right, then. I'll escort you back to the auditorium. If you stay put until the end, both you and I can forget this conversation ever happened. Deal?"

Brinley doesn't answer. Not with words, at least. But she does nod, and she does begin to follow as Mr. Buchanan leaves the room. He holds the door open for Brinley to sulk past him, then the two of them head down the hallway. To his credit, Mr. Buchanan is trying his best to be stern yet friendly. He even attempts to make small talk with Brinley. But for her own reasons, Brinley doesn't offer much more than one-word answers, her eyes still glued to her feet, her earbuds bulging in her front pocket.

I can see the way Mr. Buchanan's eyes narrow with worry each time he looks over at my sister. After four months of only watching, never interacting, I'm getting incredibly good at reading body language and facial expressions. I can almost see the internal war he must be waging with himself. He isn't sure, I'm confident in assuming, whether to bring up my passing. He knows exactly who Brinley Prowley is. He can see that the girl is struggling. But he doesn't know whether it would be helpful or hurtful to mention her dead older brother at this precise moment.

So instead, he settles with asking Brinley how she's been doing, to which she responds by muttering, "Fine." Then he asks how her classes are going, to which she responds, "All right." Finally, he asks whether Brinley has been enjoying her first year as a freshman at Volcano Vista High School, to which she only shrugs.

By this point in the conversation, the pair reaches the auditorium. Still concerned for Brinley, but also trying to be stern, Mr. Buchanan tells her to go take her seat. As he reminds her to stay put until the entire school is excused, Brinley grimaces. Still not meeting his eyes, she shoulders her backpack and slowly drags her feet into the auditorium. She sits as far back from the stage as possible, hiding herself alone in the shadows, and shoves her earbuds in at full volume again. The cheer squad hasn't performed yet and, judging by her expression, I know that both she and I are in for an excruciating hour.

BRINLEY

It's stupid. So stupid! If I weren't such a timid goody-goody, then I wouldn't be here in the auditorium. If I had any more of a spine, I would have accepted the truancy for what it was and let Mr. Buchanan call my parents. I mean, if I had explained the situation to them, they may have understood. Possibly. Or more likely than not, they would have taken it as a sign that I need therapy. They would have shoved me into the first couch they found with a therapist hovering over, glasses perched on their nose and clipboard in hand. My parents have been threatening me with that for months, watching me under a microscope, ready to leap at the first indication that I am, in fact, the emotional mess that everyone expects me to be. I've barely been able to hold them off this long. But if my grades start slipping or my behavior gets even a toe out of line, then it's game over. And I cannot, *will not*, end up shrinked. If word got out that I was in therapy, that I was one of *those* people, then I don't think I could ever show my face at this school again.

In fact, I know I couldn't. So instead of standing up to Mr. Buchanan, I did what I was told to do. I lived up to the expectation of Brinley-the-good-girl, just like I've been doing all year. I followed Mr. Buchanan. I took my seat. And out of that stupid goody-goody fear, I *will* stay here until the assembly ends, come rain or shine.

I mean, I guess from a distant perspective, it is a little bit sad. I used to really enjoy assemblies. I used to get together with my group of friends, all of us looking really cute and fun, and we would sit as close to the front row as possible. If the assembly called for audience participation, we would immediately volunteer. In middle school, I was even chosen to participate in the annual pie-throwing competition. And after decking Principal Saunders really good in the face with a whipped-cream-and-banana pie, I had won. To a peal of cheering and clapping, I had personally led the students to victory over the administrators. For at least one week straight, I was hailed as the champion of the school.

But now? Now I just sit alone. In the back. Headphones in ears, music blaring, and eyes squeezed shut.

To the outside world, I probably look too cool for assemblies. I make sure that my expression comes across that way. And if people misinterpret my closed eyes as me being asleep or something, then so be it. That's fine too. But what I can't handle are the looks of sympathy that I know are coming. The craning heads. The whispered comments. The expressions of sheer pity. And everything else that will follow after the cheer squad's performance and the absence of Lucas Prowley, the good-looking hunk who actually made male cheerleaders seem cool.

So, no. I deliberately don't listen. I don't listen when the student body president stands up with the microphone, trying to whip the crowd into a frenzy of excitement for the upcoming basketball playoff. I don't listen when the band performs. Or the choir. Or the dance crews. And I most especially, *especially* don't listen when near the end, Ms. Beck, the cheerleading coach, takes control of the microphone and says that the next performance will be dedicated to the memory of our very own Lucas Prowley. A more solemn hush falls over the crowd when she says that— that much I do recognize. I also hear when Ms. Beck gets choked up talking about him. But gritting my teeth, I make sure to block out everything else after. The music. The sound of back handsprings thudding across the stage, enthusiastic calls, and then, at the very end, a loud, "L-U-C-A-S-P...*Lucas...Prowley!*"

The crowd is silent for a moment, then erupts into cheers. There is whooping, there is calling. And then, from somewhere out in the crowd, someone yells out, "We love you, Lucas!"

Furious, I rip the earbuds out and shove them into my backpack. Whoever said that is a liar. They don't love Lucas. No one in this entire school who is whooping, cheering, and clapping their hands at his death really, truly loves him. Not like I do. If so, they wouldn't be beaming or celebrating. They wouldn't call out and cheer. No. They can't love him. Because they aren't paying the price of emotional agony right now, the price that it really costs to say with sincerity that they love Lucas Prowley.

I am about to stand up and leave, spitting in the face of my deal with Mr. Buchanan, when something stops me short. Principal Meyers, a middle-aged woman in her early forties, grabs the microphone and claps against it with her free hand, causing low, electronic thuds to echo across the auditorium. On the stage next to her, a pyramid of cheerleaders is clambering apart. The top tier is, of course, empty, and the second tier is quickly following suit.

"Wow," Principal Meyers says into the microphone, still

clapping and looking over with gratitude at the cheer squad. "Wow. Thank you so much for such a beautiful performance. Your art has expressed what so many of us have been feeling. This school will never forget Lucas and his legacy. And thank you, cheerleaders, for taking the time and putting forth the effort to honor him in such a magnificent way. I think I speak for all of us when I say thank you. You have truly touched our hearts."

There's more cheering, more whooping, more calling. Some of the cheerleaders on the stage are even wiping their eyes. I keep an eye out for Rory, scanning the squad for him. Now that his best friend is gone, he's easy to find. He's the only male left on the squad, the only one wearing white shorts and an athletic tee in the school's shade of ashen black. He isn't crying—Rory is too tough for that—but he is swiftly walking over to Melissa, his girlfriend and fellow cheerleader. Melissa's face is buried in her hands, and she's crying so hard she can't stop. With a smile and a distracted wave from Rory to the crowd, he slings one arm around her shoulders and quickly ushers her off the stage, followed by the rest of the cheer squad.

The sight of Melissa coming apart like that almost has me feeling...smug? Not exactly. But I do like seeing that at least one other person in this crowd of strangers actually has their head on straight. Melissa, if no one else, loved Lucas. At least she and Rory understand that Lucas's death is not something to celebrate. They aren't cheering or whooping like the rest of the idiots around me.

"All right, all right," Principal Meyers continues, trying to quiet the crowd. "Like I said, what a marvelous performance we just watched. It is always a tragedy, a true tragedy, to lose one of our own. Every single one of you students is an irreplaceable piece of this high school. Each one of you is a part of the lifeblood that makes Volcano Vista High the magnificent place that it is. When one of you leaves us, we are all forever changed. Forever weaker, forever a bit sadder. And it is up to the rest of us who remain to band together and press onward in a way that will honor the memory of our deceased loved ones. To each of you who still mourn, I offer my sincere condolences. I, and the rest of the administration and teachers, mourn with you. Each of your lives matters to us. Lucas mattered to us. And each of you still with us today is irreplaceable.

"Now, with that said, it is with deep regret and sorrow that I must tell you about another student who is missing from our school today. Her name is Alexia Ahmed. Many of you may not know her; she was homeschooled for much of her life and only chose to attend Volcano Vista two years ago as a sophomore, after overcoming late-stage cancer in her bone marrow. She attended here for a total of four months, but unfortunately, the cancer relapsed. Since then, she has been fighting for her life, too sick to join us. We recently got word–" and here, Principal Meyers actually chokes up a little, having to pause and clear her voice. "We just got word that her most recent surgery did not go as well as hoped. She has been told by doctors that she might have as little as six months to live.

"Now, Hawks," she says, referring to the student body by our mascot, "I know that regardless of whether you know Alexia personally or not, your heart goes out to her. Your support is with her. And to show that support, we ask that each of you find time over the next week to sign the banner that will be placed on a table near the school entrance. It will be our gift to Alexia and her family, a symbol of our care for them, and nothing would make me happier than to know that each and every one of our students made the small sacrifice to write their name next to hers and pledge their support. So please, I ask you, make time for that within the upcoming week. Now again, this has been a wonderful assembly. Each and every one of you is a wonderful gift to this school and to this world. Do not forget it. And with that, you are all excused to go home. Have a safe and marvelous day."

LUCAS

I don't follow Brinley after the assembly ends. She's in a

rotten mood, one turned sour by seeping too long in sadness, and there's only so much of it I can take. I don't like watching the people I love suffer, and I especially don't like it when they suffer because of me. All I can do is stand by, watch them hurt, watch them cry, and miss them like crazy, just like they miss me. It hurts to not be able to help them, and death, it turns out, is maddeningly painful and lonely. Not just for the living, but for the dead too.

So rather than follow Brinley, I stay standing in the auditorium row where she sat—thinking, aching, and watching. The sea of students is swarming into the aisles, flowing like a current towards the back doors. I watch as faces flood past, smiling and talking, flicking friends with rubber bands, and enjoying the company of one another's physical presence. To distract myself, I tick off names as they go by, identifying the faces that are familiar to me.

There's David Adams, who recently got his braces off and is looking better than ever.

Jacie Gwen, the quiet girl from English class who no one ever talks to.

Jerrick Jones and Alesha Jones, twins, who never stop bickering.

And so many other faces and people milling by—each of them clueless about how lucky they are to be alive.

If I wanted to, I could, technically, walk through the flowing crowd of people. I'm a ghost now, so I can pass through objects as easily as a spray of water through a mesh screen door. My molecules seem able to slide through any substance I please, as long as I'm willing to put up with the sensation. Because although it's effortless, passing through solid mass is extraordinarily unpleasant. There is this bone-deep sense of wrongness about it, almost like a chill down my spine or a grotesque clench of my gut. It leaves me gasping every time. And if the thing I pass through is *living*, the sensation is especially, overwhelmingly worse. To walk through an endless crowd of teenagers like this, all with living bodies, would be the equivalent of shoving a finger down my throat. Deeper and deeper and deeper. Every part of me would immediately and violently recoil.

So, having nothing better to do, I bide my time. I don't put myself through that torture and instead stand in place, watching as the crowd thins out. Once there's enough room to dodge bodies, I step into the carpeted aisle and stride towards the stage, looking for Rory and Melissa.

I find them like I anticipated I might: in a secluded corner backstage. Melissa is sitting on a large, black chest used by the theater department to store costumes. Rory is seated next to her, his arm slung over her shoulders. He's murmuring kind things like, "Hey, it's all right, Mel," or "Don't be sad," all while she buries her face in her hands and sobs.

The depth of Melissa's response to my passing was

honestly a surprise at first. She and I got along well enough, and I suppose we did hang out a lot in life. When she and Rory started dating two years ago, she naturally slid into our friendship. Rory would come over to my place to play video games, and he would bring her along. When we went to the gym together, she would often join us. In fact, it was Melissa who convinced Rory and me to try out for the cheer team, telling us it would be fun. She coached us through the moves and gave us a real edge when it came time to try out.

But it's not like I had a friendship with her independent of Rory. It's not like if they broke up, I would still seek Melissa out. So the fact that she's been crying like this for so long and so hard is really unexpected. And it's kind of, actually, given me a new appreciation for my best friend.

Because just like he is now, Rory has sincerely and consistently tried to comfort her. This isn't the first time he's had to talk Melissa through her grief, and it definitely won't be the last. But what's really impressed me about all of it, is how noble he's actually being.

Because, sure, Melissa may show it more, but Rory's grief runs deeper. I know, because I visit him every so often when the loneliness is driving me mad. I walk over to his house, pass through his front door, and meander into his bedroom. More often than I want to admit, I've found him there furiously punching his pillow or gritting his teeth as he pulls at his hair and tries not to cry. Rory may be more private about his pain, but it's way more intense than Melissa's.

So as I watch my best friend comfort Melissa while hiding his own grief, I experience a sensation similar to my eyes filling up with tears. None spill out because, well, spirits can't cry without tear ducts. But that doesn't mean I can't feel the need to. And that doesn't mean I like the feeling.

With a quick turn on my heel, I force myself to leave. Grinding my teeth, I take the stairs leading off the stage two at a time and head for the main common area of the school. But it's not much better. The school buses have all left by now, and the only students still milling around are people I don't know. Nothing interesting is happening. There are no conversations I feel inclined to listen to. Feeling agitated, I'm suddenly unsure what to do with myself.

I suppose I could go to my dad's office and watch him work for the rest of the day. But that's always boring. Most of his time consists of meetings filled with technical jargon, sitting in front of a computer, and muttering to himself. I could go to the women's fitness center and watch my mom. Around this time, she's probably starting one of her spin classes. But after long enough, watching a group of moms sweat together gets a little old. So I don't necessarily feel like going there either. I quickly run through other options, like watching the basketball team practice or trailing one of the janitors—or actually going home and praying that Brinley is watching something other than *The Bachelorette* on TV. But based on her current obsession, that is very unlikely.

Feeling more than a little lost, I grimace and continue meandering. Near the door, just like Principal Meyers said it would be, is a large banner draped across a folding table. I walk over to it, noticing it is made of the same material as most of the advertising banners strewn across our gym. It is white vinyl with a deep red border. Black, slanted words are printed across the middle reading, *Keep fighting, Alexia! Volcano Vista High School loves you!* Already scrawled throughout the white spaces are countless student names, written in a rainbow of colors and a splatter of different handwritings. I take my time searching through each, looking for people I know, but most importantly, looking for Brinley's name.

And sure enough, after two minutes of looking, I find it. The letters are cramped, the writing much sloppier than her usual perfect swirls, but her signature is there in the bottom corner, trying to be unobtrusive. I am surprised yet pleased to see that she signed it. Then, just because I'm painfully bored, I lean over the banner myself, select a green marker, and reach out to pick it up.

The pen, of course, passes right through my fingertips, leaving them tingling as if they're numb. I try again, then again.

It isn't going to work. It never, ever works.

With a clench of my jaw, I step back and stare at the banner once more.

Keep fighting, Alexia! Volcano Vista High School loves you!

I suppose...I suppose I could do something different today. The hospital Alexia is likely at—the one with the good cancer wing—is downtown. I would have to take the city bus to get there. Then if I stayed long enough, it would get dark and the buses would stop running. Walking home from downtown would take a lot of time, probably a couple of hours, but at least it would give me something to do at night. I can't sleep, so usually I just sulk around our dark house, watch my family drool, and get stared down by Misha, our creepy cat.

Going to the hospital is a new idea, if nothing else—one with the potential to break up the monotony. I haven't been to a hospital since visiting Saige that first night. And maybe, just maybe, it's time I do some exploring.

CHAPTER THREE

LUCAS

I hop on the city bus and stand in the aisle, people-watching as strangers embark and disembark at each stop. It's a long ride to the hospital, so I try to amuse myself by guessing at the names, careers, and hobbies of the people around me. Since I don't have a phone anymore, it's about all I can do to entertain myself. But after a while, even my tedious game gets boring.

In time, I start to eye an empty seat and decide that I want to sit down. I approach it and try to, but as often happens, my butt passes right through. Groaning, I straighten and look down at the seat. The cushioned chair is bolted into the bottom of the bus. It is a set fixture, so technically, I should be able to sit. Wrinkling my forehead in concentration, I take a deep, airless breath and try to change the way I perceive the chair in front of me. Rather than being a freestanding object, it is a piece of the floor, like a hill on a landscape. The seat is just a wart that sprung up on the bus's ground level. Then with that idea firmly in mind, I try to sit down again. And this time, I don't pass through.

Grinning widely, I give myself a satisfied nod and settle back further in the seat. It worked. It took some clever thinking, but it worked.

About a month after dying, when the monotony really started to set in, I spent weeks entertaining myself by exploring ghost physics. I tried to figure out what I could pass through, what I couldn't, and if I had any control over the matter. Before dying, I had heard plenty of whacky ghost stories—stories of cupboard doors opening on their own, thuds from dusty attics, and a bunch of other weird scenarios that suggest ghosts could interact with the material world. So I started exploring everything.

What I learned is that I naturally don't pass through floors. I can walk upstairs and explore different levels of a building without passing through the ground beneath me. I can step onto a bus because the floor of the bus becomes a new floor to my mind. I can also walk onto a boat, step onto a playground, or pass through the ceiling of an attic and pull myself onto the roof above. Essentially, if a surface is a floor in my mind, then my spirit will treat it like a floor. I won't pass through.

But if an object is freestanding and separate from the ground, then my chances of interacting with it are nonexistent. I can't sit on a chair because it can be moved and lifted. I also can't sit on a couch, sit at a desk in school, or plop myself onto a beanbag. Those things aren't part of the ground beneath them, and I can't warp that perception, no matter how hard I try. But if I think hard enough, the edge of a counter or the lip of a tub are fair game. I can sit on things that are immovably attached to the surface they're on. But everything else is hopeless.

I don't know if, with practice, I will get better at touching things. I assume that I might, since according to some spooky stories, ghosts can open cupboard doors while I still can't. But I don't remember hearing that any items within a cupboard were ever moved or stolen. So I've just come to figure that the cupboards in question must have all been bolted to the ground, and that the ghosts in question were just really skilled at thinking the cupboard was part of the floor, hinges and all. I don't know. I really don't. But either way, I like to practice with physics any chance I get. And today, sitting on the bus is a great success.

Spreading out my legs, I lounge back and lace my fingers behind my head as I watch people. It's kind of weird—I get no physical relief from sitting because I never get tired from standing. Fatigue, it turns out, is a plague of the body and not of the spirit. But sitting down does make me feel a little less different. A little less *other*. And for the hour-long ride to the hospital, I allow myself to pretend that I'm another passenger on the bus, alive and tangible and real, just like everyone else.

ALEX

I have a really good cry fest while my mother is gone. Or at least, the best that I can. Crying impacts the pattern of my breathing and generally isn't a smart thing to do after lung surgery. It tends to hurt a lot.

But seeing as my life is now on borrowed time, I figure that even a painful cry might be warranted. So I weep to myself, quietly and for a long time, until the pain grows unbearable. Then sucking weakly for air through my cannula, I wipe off my cheeks and try to get a grip on myself. After all, the nurses are scheduled to come in shortly.

And come in they do. Thankfully, my face is clean of tears and they don't suspect a thing. They just administer my medications, check my vitals, and try to put on a cheery, bright persona for me. I mimic them, of course, trying to put on my own happy face despite the fatigue. But once they leave, I am lightheaded and thoroughly depleted. I close my eyes, focus on breathing, and slowly drift into a heavy sleep.

When I open my eyes again, I'm disoriented and have to blink back the grog. The light in my room is a much more muted gray than it was previously, indicating that time has passed and the sun is no longer as high in the sky. I glance at the clock on the wall, seeing that it is late afternoon.

And then I startle. I do a double take. I am not the only person in the room.

There, standing at the foot of my bed, his back turned to me as he stares at my whiteboard medical chart, is a boy.

I can tell he's young, though not by his size. In fact, he's got to be nearly six feet tall and there is an athletic tautness to his frame, suggesting he enjoys good health. So under normal circumstances, I probably would assume he is a doctor or something.

But this man—this boy—carries himself with too much casualness to be that old. One knee is bent, both hands are shoved into his jean pockets, and he's wearing a simple white cotton T-shirt. Nothing more. No lab coat. No stethoscope around his neck. Just blonde hair, a white shirt, and faded jeans.

"Um, excuse me?" I ask, my voice sounding weak. After all, I just woke up and I am feeling crummy.

Casually, almost as if it's more of a reflex than an actual response to my greeting, the boy glances over his shoulder. He looks at me briefly, then looks to the cracked doorway into my room. He almost seems confused not to see anyone entering. But he shrugs, then turns his attention back to my medical chart. In my estimation, he is being quite rude.

So I try again. I push myself up in the hospital bed, trying to sit higher on my pillows. I gasp at the pain that lances through my torso, but otherwise grit my teeth. Perhaps my voice just needs to be louder.

"Hey," I say again, my voice thick with more volume but still croaky. "Who are you?"

The boy glances over his shoulder again, looks at me. Then when it registers that I am looking straight at him, expecting a response, he startles. He jumps and whirls around, his hands jerking out of his pockets. His eyes flit frantically between me, my medical chart on the wall, and the door. Judging by his expression, it seems he isn't supposed to be in here. Maybe I caught him doing something he isn't supposed to? Maybe he snuck in?

Squinting through the pain and lightheadedness, I try to think straight. I don't *think* I have ever seen this boy before.

"Who are you looking for?" I ask again. "Are you in the wrong room?"

The boy's eyebrows rise sharply and his lips part in surprise. He stares at me, astonished, then looks wildly around himself. What is his problem? I start to wonder if maybe he has a mental handicap. Could he be a special-needs visitor who happened to wander away from his parents when they weren't looking? The thought makes me hesitate. I should probably be nice to him.

"I...uh," the boy stammers. His vibrant blue eyes are wide and he points at himself, at his chest, his mouth working but not able to form the right words. My hypothesis is being proven more correct by the minute. Until, that is, he continues talking, his voice deep and strong. "Me?" the boy finally says incredulously. "I'm sorry, are you talking to me?"

At this point, I can no longer hide from my expression just how crazy I think he is. "Well..." I clear my throat, then do an obvious sweep of the room with my eyes. Moving only my eyes like that keeps the pain in my chest to a minimum. "I really don't think there's anyone else I could be speaking to. Is there?"

"Uh..." The boy hesitates again. He follows the path of my eyes, stares at me in bewilderment, then glances around the room yet again. "Um...no," he acknowledges slowly. "No, I guess there isn't."

I nod. I'm feeling really exhausted despite the nap, but there's no way I'm going to let that show. There's an unknown man in my room, and I have to be on my A game.

"Ok, so...help me out. What is it, exactly, that you're doing here?"

"I'm...uh..." And the boy is *still* baffled. When he answers, it's more of a question than a statement.

"I'm...visiting?"

"Ok. Does that mean you came to visit *me*?"

"Uh, yeah. Yeah, I did. You're Alexia, right?"

"Alex," I correct immediately, grimacing. "No one but my dad calls me Alexia. You must be from the school?" I guess, thinking back to my mom's recent conversation with the principal.

"Um...yes. I guess you could say that. Yes." Only, he stops talking after that. And I don't say anything in response. I'm waiting for more of an explanation, but he doesn't give one. He just winces, and it grows silent and awkward between us. Really awkward. Finally, the boy seems to have a light bulb moment. His face brightens and he suddenly blurts out, "I'm here to tell you about a banner! I mean, I'm here to tell you that the school is bringing you a banner. Volcano Vista, you know? All the students are signing it and it's, uh, it's a gift. For you. From us. And, uh, yeah. I just wanted you to know that. I came here to, like, tell you about it so you can expect that it's coming. And, uh...yeah. Now you know."

"Oh." I nod politely, pursing my lips. "A banner, huh?" And then I find myself having to hold back a laugh, because the boy nods so earnestly at me it's almost funny.

"Yeah, it's uh..." He brings a fist to his mouth, clearing his throat. "Yeah, it's massive. Sort of. It's longer than my arm span." He holds out his arms, demonstrating for me.

"And it says *Keep fighting, Alexia! Volcano Vista High School loves you*! But...I'm guessing that comes across as kinda insincere, doesn't it?" He scrunches his nose. "You know, since it says *Keep fighting, Alexia*, not *Keep fighting, Alex*."

Unbidden, my lips twitch in a small smile. This boy is ridiculous, truly, but at least he's being insightful. "A little," I admit. "But that's ok. A gift is a gift, so...thanks? Besides, it's been two years since I was healthy enough to attend Volcano Vista. I don't expect anyone to remember I prefer Alex."

"Two years, huh? Well that, uh, that is a while." And then his smile falters a little and his hands go awkwardly back in his pockets. His gaze drops to the floor.

As he looks away, I take the opportunity to subtly look him over. And I have to admit, he is...nice-looking. He's strong, with a narrow jawline and a soft nose. His hair is a messy, dirty blonde, and there's just something about him that seems...different. And wow, those eyes, especially, are extraordinary. They are such an intense, bright blue that it's hard for me to look away. It's unlike anything I've ever seen.

"So uh, what about your dad?" he suddenly asks, looking up and catching me staring. "He still calls you Alexia? What's up with that? Especially if you don't like it."

I laugh once, very breathily, and avert my eyes. I'm blushing a little, too, which is dumb. Admiring boys is pointless for someone hooked up to a hospital bed. "No, I don't like it. But my dad does. So..." I shrug. "That's all that matters, right?" To offer more of an explanation, I add, "My dad is an immigrant from Egypt. So maybe Alexia sounds more Egyptian to him? At the very least, it sounds more exotic than Alex does."

The boy's eyebrows shoot up and his bright eyes scan up and down, taking their own turn to appraise me. Probably taking in the subtle copper tone to my skin, my brown-almost-black hair, and my intensely dark eyes. But my hair is still so short it's nearly gone, I have no makeup on, and I'm also gaunt and sickly thin. A year ago, perhaps I would have liked his attention. But now it just makes me want to bury myself in a hole. Desperate to take his mind away from my pitiful appearance, I keep talking.

"But it's ok. My dad? He only calls twice a year, so I don't have to put up with being called Alexia very often. My parents met in college, and it didn't work out—the usual, you know?"

The boy nods. His eyes finally go back to mine. "Got it. Still sorry to hear about that though. He doesn't call more than once every six months? Even now? Now that you're..." His voice trails off and he grimaces, as if he's embarrassed about how that sentence should end.

"Now that I'm dying?" I scoff. I'm getting out of breath from talking so much and everything is swirling slightly. I try my best to ignore it. "No, he doesn't. It's kind of uncomfortable to have a child you don't know who's marching to their grave without you. It's shameful to only step up at the last minute. Seems kinda...guilt-driven? Insincere? Probably best to just stick to the same old, half-hearted routine, I guess. He's a professor in New York anyway. So I don't blame him. That's a far distance."

But the boy's frown deepens. "That's not far for a phone call."

My only response is a shrug. The silence creeps up between us again so while I have the chance, I quickly change the topic. "But...you haven't told me your name," I remind him.

And that seems to catch him off guard. The boy startles. "Oh. Right. Uh, yeah. I guess I'm not used to meeting new people. Not lately, at least. My name is Lucas."

"Lucas," I repeat. The pain in my chest flares, and I can feel a cough coming, but I really don't want that to happen. Swallowing, I fight the sensation back and keep talking. "So should I look for your name on this cool banner I'm getting? Like, will it be written on there?"

"Ha, no," he snorts. But seeming to realize that came across as rude, he quickly backpedals. "I mean, my name's not on there. But if you want, you can look for my sister's name. She signed it. Her name is Brinley, and her signature is in the bottom right-hand corner, orange ink."

53

"Ah." I pause to catch my breath, then add, "Well, that was nice of her. You'll have to thank her for me."

But suddenly, as if I said something wrong, Lucas's expression falls. So severely, it's as if my attempt to be polite just punched him in the gut. His gaze drops to the floor again, and he winces. "Sure," he whispers, barely audible. "If I ever get the chance to."

"Huh?"

"I'm...I'm not a very big part of my sister's life anymore. I'm not as involved as I used to be."

"And why not?"

In answer, Lucas shakes his head and looks up. His expression is now pained, and strangely almost pleading. When he talks, his words are slow and careful. "Let's just say it's because of circumstances I can't control."

The depth of his reaction was unexpected. "Ah," I say, making it sound like I understand. Only I don't. I definitely don't.

But before I can say much more, that cough I've been holding off claws its way up my throat. Before I know it, I'm doubled over, bright spots bursting across my vision. Hacking, gasping for air, I squeeze my eyes closed.

"Hey, are you all right?" Lucas asks. His voice moves closer as if he's stepping towards me. But it's really hard for me to answer.

"Yeah, I'm...fine," I finally force out between coughs. It's

54

a lie, of course, an obvious one, but it's been so long since I've had a decent visitor outside of family, I don't want the moment to end. I don't want Lucas to think he has to leave.

"You don't look fine," he responds, missing the rude undercurrent to his words. "You're not...not dying on me, are you?" And honestly, he sounds so nervous when he says that, it's as if he kind of believes that I am.

"No," I laugh. Or at least, try to laugh. But the laugh turns into another painful cough, and I'm left gasping and wincing in pain. "No. Lung surgery. Just...just give me...a minute."

"Ok," Lucas responds dubiously.

But a minute later, when the coughing passes and I can finally open my watering eyes again, the boy is...gone. The hospital room is entirely empty. Glancing at the door, it's cracked precisely as it had been before. There's no sign of him, and it's almost as if Lucas hadn't even been here.

I shudder and rub at my forehead, troubled. Sure, I may have a lingering fever, but...could I really have imagined that whole thing?

LUCAS

Going four months without holding a single conversation has really done a number on me. My social skills are growing horrific. I shouldn't have left Alexia like I did. I shouldn't have fled when she wasn't looking, running with silent footsteps and passing through the door, only to stop and hyperventilate just outside her room.

But truth be told, I *was* scared. I was scared of watching someone die. And what better explanation was there for why Alexia—Alex—could see me?

From the moment she opened her eyes, they were bright. Like intensely, spiritually bright. It was like the brightness I can see in the flesh of spirits, only shining from her deep brown eyes and not her whole body. I don't know how death works, but perhaps that was a sign that her spirit was preparing to leave her body or something? And if that was going to happen, then I really, really couldn't have handled watching it.

Which is ridiculous. I know. A ghost who's scared of death? It's pathetic.

But the thing is, all I've ever known as a ghost has been four months of trailing my family. All I've ever done is follow my loved ones around like a lost puppy and wish desperately to be alive. So if that's all I've experienced, if that's all that I know, then how on earth could I be expected to handle a newly departed spirit like Alex, if that's what she was about to become? What if she popped out of her body and expected me to become some sort of a spirit guide for her?

So instead of sticking around, I ran. Quickly, abruptly, and recklessly. It was stupid of me, I get that. It is a rare, even unheard-of opportunity to talk to someone living. But fleeing was all I could emotionally handle. I really am a loser of a spirit.

Admitting that to myself, I turn away from Alex's room and stride off agitated down the hallway. As I walk, I run my hand anxiously through my intangible hair. And as I do, I swear to myself that if Alex *does* survive the day, no matter the level of temptation, I will never allow myself to return to her again.

Because deep down inside, I know it would be wrong of me to. It would be wrong of me to push against nature and physics and the laws of the universe to seek out a friend among the living. It would be wrong of me to hide my true identity as a ghost, and on the flipside, it would be wrong of me to admit to what I am and scare Alex—a stranger— before she dies.

I mean, I am dead. I am officially, irreversibly dead. And the world of the living can never—will never—belong to me again.

So I might as well just go home, buck up, and get used to it.

CHAPTER FOUR

ALEX

"Someone came to visit me," I croak, closing my eyes in exhaustion. I can sense the movement as my mother lifts the Styrofoam cup to my face, letting the straw bump against my lips. I wince, then force myself to sip. The water burns as it travels down my throat and into my aching chest. Swallowing is so painful.

"Oh really?" Mom sounds intrigued. "And who was that?"

"A boy," I answer. I clear my throat, then wince again. Because even that hurts terribly. The straw is still pressing at my lips, but I don't take another sip. I can't. Instead, I open my bleary eyes and force them to train on Mom. "I think he was from the school?"

"The school?" Mom's head cocks. "Meaning Volcano

Vista?"

"Yeah." My voice is breathy, my lungs on fire. "That's the one."

"Hmm." Mom's mouth forms a tight line and she bumps the straw against my lips yet again. Eyes tightening, I give her a small shake of my head. Sighing, she removes the cup.

"I didn't think they were allowing outside visitors, Alex. Your immune system isn't up for that right now."

"I know, but..." I shrug weakly. "He was here."

"Do you want me to talk to the nurses about that, Eileen?" Craig asks from across the room. He's seated on the couch, wearing his favorite flannel shirt and leaning forward as he frowns at me in concern. Craig is a kind man, tender to my mother and anxiously protective of me. His years in the military drilled a sense of duty and concern into him that he's never quite adjusted out of. Even decades later, his peppery hair is still cropped military-short, and he's so stocky that I don't doubt his ability to intimidate a negligent nurse. He even works as a security guard, contracting his services out to any company that needs him. Craig is different from my biological dad—as different from the lean, accented music professor as any person could be. And yet, he's good. So good to us that I can't help but love him too, just like my mom so obviously does.

"No, no, that's all right, honey. If they let a visitor in, I'm sure there was a reason for it. Did you enjoy the visit at least?" she asks, turning to me. Her tone is pleasant but her brow is furrowed, and I can tell that despite the words, she's worried.

"Yeah, nothing about it was bad. It was just...short. He left really suddenly."

"Hmm." She searches my face, then reaches out to swipe a strand of hair behind my ear, like she's always done my whole life. Only this time, there isn't much left. The strands are short and close to my scalp, with only a few months of wavy regrowth since the chemo. Which is odd because for most of my life, my hair has always been dead straight and even.

"Well, I'm glad to hear it was nice," she murmurs, pulling her hand back when she can't get the two-inch strand to tuck. But as she does, she looks over her shoulder and shares a glance with Craig. Judging by the look that passes between them, I know they're going to talk to the nurses after all. Once I'm asleep and when they think I won't know.

Because in Mom's eyes and Craig's eyes, my life is too precious to jeopardize with a stranger. Lucas's visit, I'm sure, will be his last.

Saddened, I sigh heavily and let my eyes close again.

BRINLEY

I hate dinner. Dinner is always horrible and quiet without Lucas around. Especially tonight. Mom made teriyaki lettuce wraps, which unfortunately, used to be Lucas's favorite. It's obvious we are all thinking about him, but no one dares acknowledge it. Instead, Mom has on her cheerful, Barbie-like smile again, just like she always does. I wonder sometimes if it isn't plastered to her face like that, glued there as a permanent side effect of her daily overdosing on endorphins.

As usual, she starts her dinner interrogations with my dad, cheerfully asking how his day went. He answers like always with a drab, jargon-filled response that I can hardly understand. His job, I suppose, may sound relatively cool to the outside world. He works as a lead scientist and engineer for Sandia Laboratories, which research and develop nuclear arms. But honestly, when it comes to dinnertime conversation, there is absolutely nothing fascinating about his career.

The good news, though, is that the longer Dad drones on, the less time Mom will have to interrogate me. So although he is dreadfully boring, I find myself praying that his speech will never end. Except that...it does. My internal pleadings are rarely, if ever, answered.

"So, Brinley," Mom says the second Dad stops speaking.

She swivels in her seat, turning the full force of her undivided, motherly attention on me. "How was your day, sweetie?"

"It was fine." I don't look at her as I answer. I just stare at the tabletop and strategically shovel another bite of food into my mouth. If Mom wants to keep me talking, she's going to have to wait while I chew.

Which she does. It's just a shame that eventually, I have to swallow. "I saw that you missed only one question on your science exam. Brinley, that's so great! Keep it up and you might follow in your father's footsteps after all."

I'm tempted to scowl at her, but I don't. I just stare at the table and take another bite. While Lucas was alive, Mom never once hinted that I could become a scientist. That was always Lucas's thing. He was always the child destined to go to college, earn a prestigious degree, and lead teams into the future of nuclear science, just like Dad. Whereas me? I was supposed to co-own Mom's female fitness center. She always wanted me to embrace sweaty armpits, fake smiles, and inspirational, estrogen-pumping catchphrases. But now? Now I'm smart after all? Now I have options? Funny how one simple death can change so much.

"So what happened at school today?" Mom prods. As she asks her question, Dad peers at me over his rectangular glasses, munching on his lettuce. "Did you see any of your friends?"

"Of course I did, Mom," I grunt, rolling my eyes. "I always do."

"And how are they doing? I haven't seen Kaitlyn in a while. Or Emily. Not even Savannah. How have they been?"

"Great," I offer. "Just great. Look, I'm done eating now. Can I be excused?"

Right on cue, Dad jumps into the conversation. Clearing his throat, he straightens taller in his chair. "You've only eaten one lettuce wrap," he points out, as if it's some grand, scientific fact he's presenting to a group of investors, and not a comment on my food.

"Yeah? Well, I'm full."

"Honey, you usually eat at least three wraps. What's wrong tonight?" Mom croons. "Are people being rude to you at school?"

"Oh my gosh. No, Mom, they aren't. Why would you even think that? I'm done here, and I'm leaving." And with that, I shove my chair roughly back from the dinner table. While both of my parents look on—my mother concerned and my father irked by my attitude—I dump my plate into the sink. I can feel their eyes bore into my back as I stalk around the corner and turn towards my room.

LUCAS

I left the hospital immediately after the fiasco with Alex. And just like I knew it would, it does take me hours to walk back home. I meander through the streets of downtown Albuquerque, dodging people on the sidewalks and speed-walking past alleys where dark-looking ghosts lounge. I try not to make eye contact with the other spirits and, like usual, they pay me no mind. I leave them alone, and they leave me alone. For that, I'm really grateful.

Eventually, I make my way out of the densest part of downtown and reach the cement barricade that runs along the freeway. I grimace at it, hating what I'm about to do. Then I lunge through. The sensation makes me gag and shudder, but at least it only lasts for a moment. Once it passes, I take my place on the shoulder of the road and start jogging. I hug as close as I can to the cement wall and flinch every time a large vehicle or semi flies by. I don't like walking on the freeway like this, and it's something I never would have done if I were alive. But the problem is, I don't know how else to get home. I can't use a phone. I can't use a GPS. So the only way I can get from downtown to the outlying suburb where my family lives is by memory. So for that reason, I take the route we always drove as a family. Back when I was alive.

I could have chosen to take the city bus if I wanted and

spared myself the discomfort. It's early enough in the evening that the bus lines are still running. But I feel so agitated, so worked up, that I don't want to. There is a higher density of spirits in downtown than the suburbs, about one to every hundred people that I see. They seem to congregate there, loitering around in small groups, and lazily pass their days by watching the bustle of a busy urban area. So if I have to choose between sitting on a bus, staring out the window and seeing the occasional ghost, or walking alone on a freeway, I am going to pick the freeway. Tonight, I crave the solitude.

Because I don't want to see another ghost right now and be reminded of what I am. I don't want to admit, yet again, to how much I don't understand. Because yeah, I may be dead, but no one explained to me the rules of the afterlife. I don't know what I'm doing here, why I still exist, or even why Alex saw me. I don't understand why there are fewer spirits than mortals, where they all go, or what I'm expected to become. After all, more people have died throughout the history of the world than those who are currently alive. So if that's the case, then what's happened to all the spirits? What's going to happen to me?

Truthfully, I am incredibly, incredibly lost. And tonight, there is nothing that I need more than to get back home and return to what I know. To return to the only remaining thing in my existence that makes sense: my family. So for the next two hours, I distract myself with thoughts of them and put one foot in front of the other.

But when I get back home, the house feels all wrong. It feels empty and quiet. It's past dinnertime and Brinley is in her bedroom. A scowl is on her face as she does her homework, earbuds securely in place. My parents, though together, don't seem to be doing well either. They are in their own bedroom, lying on the bed, propped up by pillows and watching a movie together. My dad has his arms wrapped around my mother, stroking her hair while her head rests on his chest. But the problem is, her eyes are red and bloodshot, her mascara is smeared, and I know she must be sad about my death again.

So rather than watch their suffering and rather than watch Brinley scowl her way through algebra, I go to our living room floor and lie down spread-eagle. I can't sit on the couch because I'll pass right through it. I can't turn on the TV because I don't have working hands.

I'm a spirit. Just a really dead spirit. And while the rest of my family suffers, I lie on the floor and stare straight up at the ceiling, unblinking. From its position on the couch, my cat stares at me without blinking too.

CHAPTER FIVE

LUCAS

What I hate most about death is the monotony. The isolation, the boredom, and the sadness. All combined, it's nearly enough to drive a person crazy.

For the first few days after visiting Alex, I do my best to return to my old, standard routine. I lie awake on the floor of the living room all night long. I get up when Brinley gets up. I watch her get ready for the day and I follow her onto the bus, standing in the aisle as the vehicle bumps towards the school. Then when we arrive, I get off. I trail Brinley into her classes or visit some that I used to be in myself. I try to learn as I stand in the back corner, arms crossed, watching the teachers. But to be honest, my heart isn't really in it. Not when I'm dead. Not when everything feels so pointless.

So after several days of trying, I give up. It hasn't even been a full week yet and already I can't handle it. Before I know what I'm doing, I'm passing through the front doors of the building—shuddering at the sensation—and turning towards the hospital. It's ridiculous, I know. It's not like I'll even enjoy being downtown again. But walking to the hospital takes time. And having some sort of destination, some sort of purpose, is exactly what I need to stay sane.

But for the full two hours it takes to walk there, I am stuck inside of my head, fighting with myself. Part of me seems to think that I'm going to the hospital to see Alex again. The other part of me yells that doing so would be stupid. And not just stupid but unacceptable. Irresponsible. And wrong. Deeply, morally wrong.

It's a tug-of-war inside me—one so perfectly matched that I don't know what I'm going to do by the time I reach the hospital's front doors. I just stand in front of them, craning my neck, and stare up at the massive building. Time passes, and I stand still.

Eventually a mother walks by, carrying a young child in her arms. Her presence causes the automatic front doors to slide open and, with a sigh, I trail her. I walk inside simply to capitalize on the moment, to avoid walking through the solid glass if I don't have to. And once inside, I just keep walking. I walk past the lobby desk and around a corner with no real destination in mind.

For the next several hours, I wander. Though I don't love passing through closed doors, I do. Again and again and again. I poke my head into random hospital rooms, trail nurses to listen to their gossip, and wander into surgeries where I watch doctors take scalpels to knees or place screws into bone. It's seriously gruesome but also incredibly fascinating. And for the time being, I find myself distracted and able to ignore my problems. I even successfully ignore the temptation to visit Alex.

Later in the evening, after I've watched as many surgeries as my stomach can handle, I roam towards a new, unexplored wing of the hospital. As I do, I come across a room that intrigues me. It's near the maternity ward and the plaque near the door reads *Neonatal Intensive Care Unit*. My interest piqued, I let myself in.

The room is large, tiled, and a sterile white. There are rows of clear plastic boxes hooked up to machines, each holding a tiny, delicate infant. I walk between the rows, then eventually decide to crouch and peer at each little face. The newborns look almost like aliens, because most of them are very premature. Yet, I can't help but feel drawn to them. A sharp pang of emotion rips through my chest, and I find myself hoping that each one survives. Deep down inside, I want these little bodies to make it. I want these little people to live, to grow up, to experience the life that I no longer have, and to influence the world that I'm no longer a part of.

Though I know it won't do anything, I even reach a hand through one of the incubators, fighting through the sensation, and gently hover my hand over the bare chest of one of the infants. I want to touch it, to cradle it. But I don't. I just look down at the name written on the front of the incubator, then smile sadly at him.

"Hey, Thomas. Don't give up," I whisper. "Life is worth the fight." Surprisingly, Thomas stirs, stretching his tiny, frail arms. And then he is still, settling back into his sleep. Slowly, I withdraw my hand.

I continue deeper into the room and eventually notice two people in the back. One is a young man, probably in his early twenties. He's spread out on a recliner, his feet kicked up and his hand stuck through the gloved entrance of the incubator so he can touch his child without exposing it to germs. The guy is asleep, a baseball cap pulled low over his eyes so I can't see his face. Standing behind him and staring tenderly at the infant is an older gentleman, probably in his late fifties. He has a clean-cut beard and short, wavy hair that is graying around the temples. When I walk near, the man looks up. And immediately, his eyes land on me. His eyes, like the rest of his skin, seem to emanate light. Not like an aura, exactly, but rather as if the light is a characteristic imbued within his skin. Looking down at my own hand, I recognize the similarities. Like me, he's a spirit. But unlike me, his incorporated light is a whole lot brighter than mine.

"Hello," he greets me, giving me a nod.

I look back up from my hand and nervously nod back. Though I've seen plenty of spirits since my death, I've never actually tried to talk to one. Strangers in death are kind of treated the same as strangers in life. We spirits may acknowledge each other, share a head nod or a polite smile whenever we cross paths, but that's really it. Other ghosts never seem to take an interest in me, and I'm too nervous to take an interest in them. After all, I don't know the social cues of the afterlife. I hardly even know if "hi" is an appropriate greeting. So unless a spirit approaches me first, I am not about to approach them. Spirits, even apparently good ones like this man, still give me the heebie-jeebies.

"Um, hello," I finally say back, clearing my throat. The man is still looking at me as if expecting me to say more. So I clear my throat a second time. "Hi. You're uh, you're a spirit," I state. "Just like me?"

The man cocks his head and a twinkle enters his eye as if he's amused. "Yes," he says simply. Then after an awkward pause, as if wondering why I'm still standing there, he politely adds, "And this is my granddaughter, Amelia." He gestures at the incubator and the tiny human inside. "She's named after my wife. My Amelia is still in the other room, looking after our daughter, but I expect she'll be here soon."

"Ah," I respond. And then I kind of freeze. I don't know

what else to say. When the stranger looks up again, raising his eyebrows questioningly at me, I fumble for something, anything to fill the silence. "She's beautiful. Your granddaughter, I mean."

The spirit nods once, then turns his attention back to the incubator, an expression of extreme tenderness on his face. "Yes. She is. It's a marvelous thing to watch our posterity live and grow, isn't it?"

I open my mouth to answer, then snap it shut again. Gulping, I look over at the infant in the incubator and at her father, resting his hand across her small torso as she sleeps. The dad is so young; he can't be more than three or four years older than me. And for the first time in my existence, the reality that I will never be a husband or father hits me like a battering ram.

The grandfather doesn't glance up from the infant again, and it's probably for the best. My throat is constricting and my emotions feel thin as I turn and exit the room. I know I'm going to return to the hospital again. I know there are so many interesting things here that I won't be able to stay away for long. But tonight, I can't handle anything else. In no time at all, I dash down the staircase and flee through the front doors.

BRINLEY

This isn't the first time I've done it. It's late at night, my parents are asleep, and I'm in the bathroom. The light is on, the door is locked, and I'm holding a razor in my hands.

"Come on, Brinley," I mutter to myself, my teeth gritted and my hand trembling as I grip the handle tighter. "Don't be a chicken. A pathetic, worthless chicken."

And then, with those words and that clench of my teeth, I do it. I let the blade rip across my forearm and gasp. The sting is profound...and satisfying. Yet still, it nowhere near matches the pain that I feel inside. To better express what I'm feeling, I do it again and again.

And then there's a sound. I jump. I drop the stained razor. Shaking, I leap to my feet.

"Who's there?" I croak out. My forearm is trembling, blood is dripping from the deep cuts just beneath my elbow, trailing down my wrist. I feel its warmth drip from my fingertips onto the floor.

"Hello," I quietly croak again. But no one answers. There's nothing there. And then, suddenly, I hear it again. I jump and almost scream. There's a thump. A pause. Then another thump. Followed by another and another and another.

It's my cat, pawing at the door.

"Agh, I hate you," I spit. I look down at my scarlet arm,

still trembling. I look down at the blade on the ground, glistening red. And then, with a grit of my teeth, I shake my head.

I could have sworn that I heard Lucas calling my name. But that was nothing more than a wish, a delusion. With a disgusted sigh at myself, I bend down and pick up the razor. I stare at it blankly for a moment, then run it under water and shove it deep into my pocket. Grabbing a towel, I wipe the red stains off the floor then wrap the dirty fabric around my arm, pressing hard to staunch the bleeding. It aches when I do that, and I like it.

With a rough shove, I push open the door and leave the bathroom. I don't even bother looking down at Misha as I stalk past her, her glassy feline eyes staring beyond me and eerily into the bathroom.

LUCAS

It's a fluke that I'm home tonight. A mistake. A happenstance.

I was planning to spend all night at the hospital—to go there this afternoon and just stay. Stay away from the agony in my home. Stay away from the pressing silence. And stay away from the despair I've caused.

Because my home is unraveling. All the threads that

used to keep my family close, safe, and bound to each other are deteriorating. Ever since I died, Mom has become sad, Dad has become vacant, and Brinley has become bitter.

It used to be that evenings were the best time in my home. We used to laugh a lot at dinnertime, all eating at the same table, throwing teasing jabs at each other and reporting on our days. When it was over, we would all help clean up. Then Brinley would wander into the living room where Dad would sit next to her, coaching her through math. I would wander to the piano or outside to the trampoline, practicing my flips before doing my own homework. Mom would often watch me through the window, or meander out onto the porch, cheering me on and giving me pointers on how to improve.

We never had a perfect family. Of course we didn't. But we had a happy family. One that was close. We cared about each other and were involved in each other's lives. We always knew what was going on and we always had each other's backs.

At least, we did. Until I died. I don't understand why precisely, but my death seemed to knock a pillar out from the foundation of our family, an essential column that held everything together. And now? Now everything is falling to pieces. Now I stand in the center, helpless, and watch as everything—my family—crumbles around me.

And Brinley, my sweet sister, is crumbling worst of all.

Because I saw her cut tonight. For the first time in my existence, I saw her deliberately and purposefully slide a blade across her arm.

And when she did, I screamed her name. I lunged forward, trying to grab the razor from her hand, and screamed at her to stop.

But she didn't hear me. My hand passed right through. And as I stood in front of her, sobbing, she continued to cut. She kept sliding the blade across her skin, pressing hard, digging as deep as she could and drawing up blood time and time again.

And what was worse, what was nauseatingly, sickeningly worse, was that those weren't the only cuts on her arm. The fresh ones weren't the first. There were others, baked and scabbed over as if they had been there for weeks.

I hadn't known. I had never guessed. Brinley often used the restroom at night, and I had never once thought to follow her. I never assumed she was cutting. I never once thought that something might be wrong.

Not until tonight. When I had a hunch.

And that hunch proved to be horribly, dangerously correct.

CHAPTER SIX

BRINLEY

My arm hurts, but the throbbing is welcome. I bandaged the lacerations this morning with a thin piece of gauze and some medical tape, for no other reason than to keep the blood from marking my shirt. I'm wearing a long-sleeve today, so no one is the wiser. My parents don't know about my newfound habit. And if I have any control over it, they never, ever will.

The cutting, I know, isn't healthy. I know if my parents find out, they'll flip and send me immediately to a shrink who certainly would try to convince me to stop. But the thing is, I don't want to stop. I've come to like cutting. Or rather, to *need* cutting. It's a compulsion now. It's like cutting myself, making myself physically hurt, is the only way to validate that I'm in pain. The only way to scream that

I'm suffering and truly be heard by the universe. I cut deeper and deeper because the agony it represents is building and building. And like bile that rises in the back of one's throat, the pain needs a way out. It demands a way out. And when I cut, I release it.

If that isn't enough, I deserve it too. I deserve the cutting. I deserve to suffer. After all, I was the one who killed Lucas. If it wasn't for me and my stupid friends and that stupid party, he wouldn't have been on Unser Boulevard that night. It's because of me and my selfish rebellion that he's dead. Lucas is dead because of me.

I ruminate on this, seeping in the acrid torture of my murder as I sit slumped in the back of the biology classroom. I twiddle my pencil, watching the tip of my eraser bounce erratically against the desktop, as frantic as my desire to cut right now. Behind the bouncing pencil and sitting one row in front of me is Kaitlyn. In the row in front of her is Savannah. Only, Savannah is turned around backwards in the seat, talking and laughing and smiling. At the beginning of class, Mr. Barker gave us permission to work together on the assignment. We were permitted to scour the textbook for answers in groups as large as four. Savannah had whirled around, immediately pouncing on the chance to work with Kaitlyn, just like I knew she would. But when Kaitlyn turned around, smiling and opening her mouth at me, I clenched my jaw and shook my head. Before the words even left her mouth, I told her no. I didn't want to work with them. I *couldn't* work with them.

"No thanks. I work faster alone," is all I muttered. Then I looked down at my worksheet and didn't look back up. Slowly, Kaitlyn turned back around, returning her attention to Savannah. Something passed between the two of them, I could sense it. But just like I hoped, they said nothing. As time goes on, they are saying fewer and fewer things to me. I am earning the privacy I crave.

But unfortunately, what I said turned out to be prophetic. I *did* finish faster alone. The worksheet was simple and I filled every vacant line with the correct term eons ago. Mr. Barker is sitting at his desk, grading papers, and doesn't seem interested in reining in the class anytime soon. With another glance at the sluggish clock, I sigh. Then I slump deeper in my seat. Fifteen minutes until the bell rings.

After seven more minutes of twiddling my pencil, I finally give in. Glancing around to make sure no one is watching, I reach into my binder and pull out a clean sheet of lined paper. Kaitlyn and Savannah are still working on the assignment and ignoring me, just as I hoped. So I discreetly start doodling. I first draw two straight, vertical lines. Then with a ferocity that almost breaks the tip of my pencil, I begin slashing the space between them with harsh, horizontal dashes. The doodle is cryptic; no one will understand the meaning behind it, even if they look. But...I understand. Perhaps I can't cut right now. But I sure can think about it.

Then my doodles begin to morph. The more I think of self-harm, the more I feel like cutting just isn't enough. The bile of depression rises in the back of my throat, and I start drawing more cryptic shapes, shading them dark and black. There are dark rectangles—coffins—and a large square with even semicircles on the bottom: a car. There are jagged triangles—broken glass—and uneven circles of squiggled blood. I think about that night, the night Lucas died. The night I killed my brother. And all I can think about, all I can obsess about, is the fact that I really, really should be dead too.

So taking out a new sheet of paper, I stop drawing and begin writing. I write exactly why and exactly how, all while acrid tears well up in my eyes and burn the bottom of my eyelids.

LUCAS

It's getting worse. Brinley is getting worse. Night after night ticks by and the cuts are growing deeper. Her crying grows harder and more broken. The letters are getting longer, and the things she writes are getting more morbid.

Everything about Brinley is spiraling. And it makes me sick—*sick* to my stomach—that I can't do anything about it. That nothing I do can stop her.

I clench my teeth, my hair, even harder, pacing back and forth in front of Mom's exercise bike. I will her to look at me and not at the class in front of her.

"Mom," I growl. "Listen to me. For once, just listen to me!" I whirl to a stop right in front of her. I grab the handles of her bike, or at least try to. My hands pass right through them. But nonetheless, I lean forward until my nose is just centimeters from hers. I can see each individual drop of sweat streaming into her blue eyes. She blinks once, hard. But her eyes are still focused beyond me.

"Mom, Brinley needs you. Do you hear me? She needs you! She's cutting herself at night. She's writing letters. Suicide letters! She's depressed, and she thinks she wants to kill herself! Do you hear me? Brinley is going to kill herself!" I lean forward even closer, every particle of my spirit screaming to get through to her, to get her to understand, to do something. "Brinley is going to die, Mom! And she doesn't...she doesn't get it! She thinks she wants death, she thinks she wants this, but she doesn't! She can't want this existence! Please do something to save her!"

But still, nothing. Mom doesn't respond. The energetic music is blaring over the stereo, and it suddenly switches songs. With it, Mom grins.

"All right, ladies," she calls out. "Let's see what you're made of. Out of that saddle now. Stand up and pump those legs, really pump them. Come on, now."

And with those words, Mom pulls back from me, standing up on her pedals, her body swaying back and forth with each rhythmic stroke. Her blonde ponytail whips back and forth against the bare skin of her back, revealed by her black tank top.

"Mom!" I scream. "Listen to me! Do something!"

But she doesn't listen to me. She doesn't get what's going on. She just keeps on pedaling with a charismatic grin on her face, putting on her coaching persona for all the women she's helping.

All while her daughter is slumped deep in her chair in history class. She's not paying attention; instead, she's plotting her way to die.

I know, because I read the letter she's writing. It's the sixth letter she's written this week.

CHAPTER SEVEN

ALEX

I'm getting better. Well, sort of. My infection cleared up, and although I still have that looming deadline of six—now five—months to live, they decided to release me from the hospital. Finally. My mother is coming to pick me up as soon as Craig gets off his night shift, and then we are going home. We will pack up in our family's old 1996 Buick Roadmaster and trundle down the road to my final resting place—our tan stucco rambler with a rock-and-dead-cacti lawn—where I myself am expected to die.

I am grateful though, to be honest. One can only spend so much time in a hospital before it starts feeling more like a prison than a healing facility. In fact, I'm feeling kind of contemplative, but not exactly sad, as I stare out my window and consider what it might be like to die at home. I watch as the sunrise slowly brightens, painting warm colors across the closed blinds, and I do my best to appreciate the moment. My sunrises, at this point, are extremely limited. So I watch the lightening colors, listen to the rhythm of my breathing, and knead the smooth hospital sheets between my fingertips, reveling in that simple sensation. The room is filled with an overcast gray that is just beginning to warm into a peaceful daylight. And that's when I feel the presence.

I glance over my shoulder, then startle and gasp, my whole body jerking violently. Because sure enough, someone is there: the boy. Lucas, from school. My strange visitor from nearly three weeks ago, who hasn't shown his face since.

"What the crap!" I immediately yell, making myself cough. Next to me, my heart rate monitor starts beeping, logging an increase of heart rate and alerting me to the change. "What are you doing here?" I demand, still coughing as I recover from being scared out of my wits.

"Alex," the boy says immediately. "You can see me?"

"Yes, of course I can see you," I cry, shaking my head at him, my hand over my heart. "I may be dying, but I'm not blind! How on earth did you get in here?" I look over at the door, which is still tightly closed, just like it has been all morning. I literally didn't hear him come in.

But as my own alarm increases, Lucas's seems to decrease. He sighs heavily, as if relieved, then takes a step back from my hospital bed. He was really, really close to me.

"Sorry. I didn't mean to scare you. I just...I have a favor to ask. Please?"

"A favor to ask?" I repeat back, raising one of my eyebrows and shaking my head incredulously. I'm still coughing, and I try not to grimace too much at the pain.

"Yeah, I...ugh. You know what? I'm being rude, aren't I? Sorry, I just...talking to people, I.... How are you, Alex?" Lucas asks, clenching a hand through his hair as if flustered. He is standing two feet away from me, still in his signature white T-shirt and jeans. His blonde hair is disheveled, and his bright blue eyes are as strangely piercing as ever. Almost, in a weird way, as if they are filled with light.

"How am I?" I repeat slowly, giving him another crazy look.

"Yeah. I, uh, heard you're getting released. Today." But his eyes squint when he says that, as if the idea troubles him.

"Um, yes," I say slowly. I glance over his shoulder at my whiteboard medical chart. My release date isn't written anywhere on there. "And how exactly did you hear about that?"

"I, uh," Lucas hesitates. "Look, I just know, ok? The principal—our principal—she's been in communication with your mom. Your mom called to tell her and I...I just overheard. I was in the school office when she took the call."

I stare at him, skeptical. I mean, his story checks out. Kind of. I know that Principal Meyers regularly calls my mom. I also know that they spoke yesterday. And yet, what on earth was Lucas doing in the office at that time? And how could he possibly have overheard?

"Ok," I say doubtfully, cautiously. "I'll believe you on this. But that still doesn't answer the question of why you're here. Are you here to say goodbye? Here to ask your...favor?"

With a terrifying drop of my gut, I start doubting my sanity. I look down at my hand, flexing it, then over at the clock. It reads 7:07 in the morning. A moment ago, it read 7:04. So this couldn't be a dream, right? Time doesn't stay consistent during dreams. But what about during hallucinations? Does it stay consistent then?

But either way, Lucas is answering me. And whether this is all just a figment of my imagination or not, I guess I have to go along with it.

"Yes. No. I mean, yes. I came here to say goodbye. And I...I came to ask for a favor."

"Ok. So, what favor?" It has been a long time, and I mean a *long* time, since anyone asked me to do something for them besides take another sip of water or try harder to rest. The idea of being needed is becoming intriguing, to say the least. Lucas, if nothing else, has my attention now.

"I need..." Lucas hesitates, biting his bottom lip. Then with a pleading look in his bright, desperate eyes, he blurts out the rest. "I need you to write something for me. Please." His expression is so sincere, I think he might drop to his knees. Or perhaps start crying. "It's really, *really* important."

Clearing my throat, I press my lips together then look down. If I don't look him in those stunning eyes of his, maybe it will be easier to think about this rationally. "Let me get this straight. You're asking that I *write* something for you? Like, write something with a pen and paper?"

"Yes!" he cries. "Yes!" Lucas's face is incredibly earnest and inching closer when I look up. Subconsciously, I slide away from him on the bed.

"That seems like an odd request," I point out. With a glance at my heart rate monitor, I see that my heart is still beating much faster than it should. I have to get a grip on myself or the nurses might start getting nosy. "I mean, why don't you just write it yourself?"

"Because I...I can't." When he says that, Lucas's shoulders sag, as if he's confessing to some incredible, sad weight he's been bearing. "I just can't, all right? It has to be you. And it has to be today."

"It has to be me?" I stare at him, tongue in cheek. Everything about his demeanor is haggard and begging. Whatever this favor is about, he seems to care intensely that

I do it. "Well, give me some more details then. What exactly do you want me to write for you?"

"A letter. A note. Something that might save my sister's life."

My mouth pops open in a small, surprised "O." One glance at my expression and Lucas keeps bulldozing on, both hands running through his hair in agitation. "I'm telling you this is important. I wouldn't ask, but I'm coming to you because I have no other options left. My sister, Brinley, remember her?" He jabs a finger towards the banner which, since receiving shortly after Lucas's first visit, has been strewn across my room. "She signed that, remember? Well, guess what? She's suicidal right now. She's *extremely* suicidal. She's depressed and planning to kill herself. She knows how she's going to do it. And my parents, they...they won't listen to me! Ok? Brinley won't listen to me! And I'm thinking that maybe you, Alex. Maybe you can help her. Please! You're my only chance to save her life."

Lucas rips his hands out of his hair and stares me down, his expression agonized. All I can think to do is cough. And cough again. Painfully.

"Alex," Lucas whispers, his face crumpling. But this time, his tone is tinged with what seems like concern for me, not just his sister. Quickly, I shake my head.

"I'm...fine," I rasp. "Just...ok." I clear my throat and

wince, trying to wrap my head around everything he just told me. "If you need me to, I'll help you. I don't know why on earth you think that I of all people can make a difference, but I'll try."

"I...thank you. Thank you. You won't regret this; I swear that you won't. I just, I was thinking you could write her a letter. Just tell her from...from *your* unique perspective," he says, wincing at the obvious reference to my cancer, "that she shouldn't want to die, right? Like, you get it. You get why life is valuable, probably more than most. And I want you to convince Brinley to stay. Use your experiences, your perspective, whatever you need to, to make her realize she's being an idiot if she thinks she wants to die. An absolute *idiot*," he growls.

"So, essentially, you want me, a dying girl, to tell your sister that she's stupid to want to die?" I say, not humored. "You're completely serious?"

"Yes! Yes, yes, yes! Because she'll listen to you! She's not listening to me, Alex! She hates listening to my parents! And so that means you are my only chance. You're Brinley's only chance! You need to write her a letter, take it to her, and convince Brinley to keep living. Tell her why life matters. And just...just save her. *Please*. And if she's not listening, if she still doesn't get it, you can even tell her that I sent you. Ok?" Lucas says, his voice cracking a little. "If it gets to that, tell her that I'll kick her butt so hard, so *freaking* hard, if she keeps thinking death is a better option. Convince her that it's not. Tell her what I wish with my entire being that I could say to her but can't. *Please.*"

And this time, Lucas's plea is so adamant, it looks like he is about to puke. There is a teenage boy in my room, a good-looking one with obvious athletic skills and a cool demeanor to uphold, and he's almost in tears. He's falling to pieces right in front of me. And for the first time, I believe him. I start to realize that his sister must actually be in trouble. Severe trouble. And with that realization, I gulp. "Ok, I'll do it, Lucas. I don't know if it will work. I don't know what on earth I'll say to her, and I don't know why on earth she'll listen to me over you, but I'll try."

"It has to work," he growls. "Please make sure that this works. Don't give up until it does, ok? Brinley's life is riding on you now. Do you get that?"

"Lucas, I—"

Just then the door cracks open and I am cut off. A nurse is standing in the doorway, looking over her shoulder and talking to someone in the hallway. With a quick, wide-eyed glance at her, then one final, pleading glance at me, Lucas whispers something.

"Largo Vista. Last house on the street, three-car garage." And just like that, he turns on his heel. As the nurse is pushing the door open wider, still talking over her shoulder, he ducks under her arm and right out the room.

She doesn't even notice him. She didn't even realize he was here. She just says a few last words to whoever is in the hallway, laughs, then enters my room without batting an eye.

"So, Alexia," she says in her happy, oblivious voice, "how are we feeling today?"

BRINLEY

Tonight's episode of *The Bachelorette* isn't only pathetic, it's aggravating. It's obvious that the guy she's falling for is nothing more than a fake, overzealous Romeo. Every time she looks at him, he slants his eyebrows down and puckers his lips subtly, as if he thinks the expression makes him look hot or something. But it doesn't. It really, really doesn't. And oh my freak, if he calls her "bae" one more time to her face, I am going to lose it. I am literally going to lose it.

In fact, I'm able to watch the show for approximately five more minutes before I am done. With a grit of my teeth, I snatch the remote off the arm of the couch and turn it off. All of it. The dude's over-scripted flirting, his overly large muscles, and his blonde hair and blue eyes that remind me just a little too much of Lucas. If the bachelorette knew what was good for her, she would have sent him home long ago. She would have made the Lucas impersonator leave, and I wouldn't have to scowl the entire time I watch my favorite TV show. It used to be my escape, the way I turned off my mind and forgot about Lucas. But not anymore. Not because of him.

With an angry puckering of my own face, I slam the remote back down on the arm of the couch and get roughly to my feet. Mom is at the kitchen sink doing the dishes, and I keep my head ducked as I pass by the open doorway, praying she won't intercede, praying she won't ask for the millionth time how I'm doing.

And thankfully, she doesn't. She doesn't even look up. She doesn't even seem to notice I'm walking by.

Heaving a silent sigh of relief, I straighten and take longer strides towards my bedroom, my mind on the razor in my top dresser drawer.

But I never make it. Just as I reach for the doorknob, grabbing the cool metal that will let me into my bedroom, the doorbell rings. And quick as anything, my mom calls out, "Brinley, honey, can you get the door?"

My hand clenches tighter. My teeth grit.

"It's probably just a package!" I call back.

"Well, will you go and check? Please? I'm up to my elbows in hot water here. It's not great timing for me."

"Yeah, well, it's not great timing for me either," I mutter under my breath. But rather than push back, I release the doorknob. Because if I fight with my mom, if I tell her no, all it will earn me is more of her attention. She'll come to my room, barge right in, and try to lecture me.

And if she does that, then I won't be able to cut. Not for a few more hours, at least. And I kind of want to cut—need to cut—now.

So with a huff of irritation, I turn on my heel and march back the way I came. I go to the front door, take a deep, steadying breath, then yank it open.

And there, standing on my doorstep, is the sorriest-looking girl I have ever seen in my life.

She's older than I am, maybe about Lucas's age, and is average height. Only, she's so rail-thin and bony, it makes me want to cringe. It's like her delicate skeleton got wrapped in this olive-toned skin, but nothing more. Like, there's no padding. There's no muscle where muscle should be, just straight bone. She's also got oxygen tubes stuck underneath her nose, the tubing trailing across her sharp cheeks, up and over her ears, and disappearing into a small black backpack on her back. She looks harrowed, exhausted, and her hair is so short, it's as if the person who styled it didn't quite know the difference between a pixie cut and a boy's cut. There are a few short inches of dark, wavy hair on her head, just enough to cover her ears halfway, but that's it. That's literally it. There is a stranger on my porch—who looks like a wraith, can't breathe, and has almost no hair—

and she's staring at me. Just staring at me. With big brown eyes and a look of worry, confusion, and anxiety on her face.

What's worse is she hasn't said a thing. Not one word since I opened the door.

"What?" I finally ask. I raise both eyebrows and look down at her hands. She's holding a white envelope clenched tightly in her long, bony fingers. With a flash of annoyance, I wonder if she's here to solicit for donations or something. "What?" I repeat again.

At my harshness, the girl flinches. "Um, sorry, I—" she says quickly, then cuts herself off. She clears her throat, looks down at her envelope, then looks back up with a grimace. Her expression is so worried it's almost sick. Like she's trying to hold back vomit or something. "I'm sorry, are you...are you Brinley?"

"Um, maybe. Maybe I am. Who are you?"

"I'm Alex. Alex Ahmed. I, uh, came here to drop something off for you," she says, timid and uncertain.

"Ok..." I draw out the word slowly. And then I wait. The girl is being incredibly unsure of herself, and I really don't care for it. I'm longing for the moment that she gets off my porch, leaves, and just lets me go to my room in peace.

"Um, right." Alex glances down at her hands again. Then swallowing, she holds out the envelope. I can't help but notice that her slender hand is shaking a little. "This is what I want you to have. It's a letter. I wrote it for you, and I think it's really important that you read it."

But I don't take the letter. I just stare at it doubtfully, then look back at the girl. Her face is pale and even as I watch, she discreetly leans against the stucco entrance to my home. The creeper looks like she needs to sit down or something.

"What is it?"

"I'm sorry, what?" she asks, sounding a little out of breath.

"Why did you write me a letter? I don't know you."

Alex frowns and lets her hand drop, returning the letter to her side. I look over her shoulder, peering at an old white car parked along my street. It has outdated wood panels on every door, and it's almost as shabby-looking and run-down as she is.

"Right. I get that you don't know me. I'm sorry, this must seem really strange to you." She takes a shaky breath, then her lips press tight. When she speaks again, it's with more determination. "But I'm here because I know Lucas. He asked me to write you this letter, and I'm here to fulfill a favor. For him."

Immediately, my eyes snap away from the car and back to the girl on my porch. "What did you just say?" I demand.

"I said that this was Lucas's idea. I spoke with him this morning. He told me where you live and asked me to give you this letter. He's worried about you and he...well, he wants you to know that it's important to him that you keep living. And it's important to me. So that's why I'm here." Alex locks eyes with me and her expression takes on a look of...empathy? Concern? Determination? "I wrote this letter to ask you to keep living, Brinley."

An electric current runs through my body, rooting my feet to the ground. At first I can't say anything. I can't respond. And then an unstable snapping feeling ricochets through my body. I reel and clench my fists, my long fingernails digging deeply, painfully into my palm. "What the freak?" I nearly shout. "Who are you?"

At my shout, Alex flinches. Again. So severely, it's almost like I slapped her or something. "I...I told you. My name is Alex. Well, Alexia. I guess you could say I'm a friend of Lucas's. Though, to be fully honest, I just met him a few weeks ago."

"You met him a few weeks ago?" My heart hammers even harder.

"Yes. He came to visit me in the hospital. I recently had lung surgery, and he just showed up. Is...is everything all right?"

"No!" I nearly shriek, making the girl jump. When she does, she takes a startled step backwards and almost loses her balance. Her knees give, and she has to catch herself against the wall. She's so broken, so sorry-looking...and Alexia? Where have I heard that name before? "No!

Everything is not all right. Who the crap are you, and who put you up to this? Was it Savannah? Emily?"

"I'm sorry, what?" The girl is still holding herself up with the wall. She blinks rapidly, shaking her head. "Who put me up to this? I told you it was Lucas."

"No, it wasn't!" I shout. "Because Lucas is dead! He died nearly five months ago! Now tell me the truth!"

"I'm..." The girl's jaw drops. Her face seems to grow even paler. "I'm sorry. What? What did you just say?"

"I said my brother is dead." I enunciate slowly, my voice toxic with anger yet choked with emotion. "He's dead. So whatever story you're trying to feed me, I see right through it. Now who told you to write me a letter, and who told you that I need to keep living?" I hiss those last words, consciously and abruptly dropping my voice so that my mother, who must still be in the kitchen, won't hear. She *can't* hear that last part. I can't let her. "Who put you up to this? Who knows?" I demand in an angry, spitting whisper.

"Brinley, I..." The girl is bewildered, shaking her head with wounded eyes. "I don't...I'm sorry. What are you saying?"

"Oh, forget it," I hiss again. Behind me, I hear the clanking of pots and pans. The running water shuts off. My mom must be getting curious. I only have seconds left, and tears are already blurring my vision. "You know what? This is just sick. Your lies are disgusting. And if Emily or

Savannah or Kaitlyn put you up to this, then tell them to get the freak out of my life already! And tell them to mind their own business!"

And with that, I slam the door and whirl around. My mother is standing in the kitchen doorway, holding a hand towel, looking at me in concern. Without another word, I rush past her and flee straight into my bedroom.

Once I'm inside, I slam the door as hard as I possibly can, making it clear that I need to be left alone.

LUCAS

What an absolute disaster.

I didn't expect things to go perfectly, but I sure didn't expect them to go so horribly either. After she turned off the TV, I could tell that Brinley was in a depressive spiral. I knew how bad things were about to get. So when the doorbell rang and I thought that it might be Alex, I practically leapt for joy. Knowing she would be able to see me if I followed Brinley too closely, I hid myself around the corner. I watched anxiously through a crack in our curtains as the whole conversation went down.

And just like that, it blew up in our faces.

The moment that was supposed to save Brinley detonated. And by the end of it, she locked herself in her bedroom and started cutting herself mercilessly, sobbing and leaving me helpless to stop her.

When she finally put down the razor, Brinley's thighs, not just her arms, were hamburger.

Hours later, I now sit in the corner of her darkened bedroom, hugging my knees to my chest and staring numbly at her sleeping silhouette. As I stare, I replay those moments over and over again, reliving the moments she slashed at herself. As I do, my soul fills with a black and agonized hopelessness. I despise the fact that I, her brother, am only inches away yet doing *nothing*. Brinley cuts herself to shreds, and I just stand by to watch.

It's horrifying. But what makes me even sicker and angrier is that Alex's letter was supposed to fix it all. She was supposed to make things better. Instead, she only made everything worse.

I mean, I understand that the girl is sick. I get that Alex has cancer. I know that I barged into her life and asked her to do a lot. But she promised she would help Brinley! She promised. And she failed.

My hands clenching, my spirit trembling, I know that I won't stand for this. I can't. With a burst of determination, I decide that I will not let Alex fail. No matter what it takes, I am going to drag her back here. I am going to make her fix her horrible mistake, and I am going to force her to try again. It may take hours, it may take days to find where

Alex lives, but I don't care. I'll do it. When she drove away from our house, I saw through the window what kind of car she owns. It is a beat-up, old Buick wagon. A white one from the 1990s with wood paneling. Not many cars have wood paneling anymore. So if I find her vehicle again—if I find that unique Buick—then I find Alex. It will be hard, but it won't be impossible.

And then, when I find her, I am dragging Alex back here. Whether Alexia Ahmed wants to or not, I will force her to save Brinley's life.

Because if she doesn't, if she says no, then my little sister may very well die.

And I will not—cannot—let her die.

CHAPTER EIGHT

LUCAS

I wasn't wrong. It does take me hours to find Alex. I spend all night and all day jogging through neighborhoods within the boundaries of Volcano Vista High, looking for Alex's car. I check for vehicles in driveways and stick my head through every closed garage door I find. Which, as simple as it sounds, actually turns out to be an awful experience. Letting any object pass through my spirit is a nasty sensation regardless. But letting something pass through my *head*, such as a metal garage door, is absolutely wretched. It's like I can feel the atoms of each door slide between my brain cells, entering spaces that shouldn't be entered. It creates a pressure, a tingling, and a sensation of vertigo that leaves me gasping every time. The experience is kind of like dunking my head into a bucket of ice-cold water over and over again, just so I can find a stupid vehicle. So after hours of jogging up every street and sticking my head repeatedly through metal, the dark anger and wild determination I felt earlier cools. My jogging slows, and I'm left feeling not physically exhausted but rather emotionally, mentally, and spiritually wrung out.

But despite that, I force myself to press on. I take breaks when I need it, sitting on the curb with my head between my knees, but I don't let myself stay there. Each time, I get up. And many hours later, I do find her car. It's sitting in an open carport in the poorest part of Western Albuquerque.

When I see it, sitting out in the open air like that, all I can do is groan. I run my hand down my immaterial face and slump to a crouched position on the sidewalk. Finally, I bury my face in my hands and groan again.

"So much for all the doors," I mutter. Grimacing, I lift my head and squint at the car. Then I take a deep, bracing breath. When my lungs are filled to capacity, I hold it. Like, literally, I stop breathing. It feels uncomfortable, just like any interruption of an ingrained habit might feel, but otherwise I'm fine. After all, I'm a ghost. I am dead. Alex's car was in her driveway this whole time, and I didn't need to stick my face through hundreds of garage doors. All of that agony was entirely pointless.

In an aggravated gust, I let out the breath in a scoffing, humorless laugh. I look down at my slightly luminescent hands, flipping them forward and backward, then I look up at the sunset. I left my home during the dark, early hours of morning and now the sun is setting. If I have to guess, it's probably nearing eight o'clock. Which, what? Means that Alex is still awake? That she is sleeping? I just spent seventeen hours searching for her, yet I didn't spend nearly enough of that time planning what I would do once I got here. After all, it's not like I can just march through the walls of her home, stand in front of her with hands on hips, and accuse her of failing. That wouldn't go over very well. She would scream. But also, I can't exactly ring her doorbell either.

Frustrated, I sigh again. I slump down until I'm sitting cross-legged on her sidewalk. Then I put my chin on my fists and stare morosely at Alex's vehicle. Behind her house, the sunset is surprisingly impressive. Splashes of deep red and vibrant orange are splattered across the clouds, glowing like an ember above the spiny desert landscape. It's one of those stunning sunsets that New Mexico is so good at offering. So, while I have no clue what to do next, I decide I might as well enjoy it.

And I do. For approximately two minutes. But around minute three, Alex's front door creaks open. To my complete astonishment, Alex timidly pokes her head out.

"Lucas?" she calls out nervously, very confused.

I gasp. I scramble to my feet and brush at my jeans,

trying to knock off the dust that I know, logically, can't actually be clinging to me. Alex bites her bottom lip and watches, her oxygen tube under her nose and her short hair mussed up.

Not knowing what else to do, I give up and force myself to straighten. Then, feeling very unsure of myself, I just kind of smile awkwardly and wave. "Uh, hey, Alex."

"Lucas, what are you doing here?" she asks, bewildered. Then suddenly, realization seems to hit. Alex looks down at herself and her expression changes into one of horror. She's wearing a very grubby, overly-large T-shirt and her sweatpants are ratty, old, and fraying. Blushing furiously, Alex runs a hand through her thin, struggling hair and doesn't look back up at me. Her eyes flicker in my direction once or twice, but that's it. Apparently, she's too humiliated to meet my gaze. With a sudden tidal wave of pity, I find myself hating that. I hate that she thinks I'm the kind of guy who would care if she wore sweats in front of me. Who would care more about what she looks like than who she actually is.

So almost before I realize it, I'm speaking again. "Hey," I call loudly from the sidewalk, wanting her to look at me. She does, briefly, then immediately blushes and looks down again.

"Hey, you want to know why I'm here? I'm here to thank you!" I say, spreading my arms out wide to either side. The words that are tumbling out of my mouth aren't planned. They're nothing like the accusation I thought I had come here to make. But Alex is so self-conscious right now, I can't help it. I'm melting in pity, and I feel this sudden protective urge to make her embarrassment go away. "Look, I know that things didn't go over very well yesterday. I know that Brinley can be kind of difficult sometimes. Or at least, lately she can be. But, uh, you tried, and I...I just came here to say thank you for that. Thanks for even giving it a shot. I actually really appreciate it."

The whole time I spoke, Alex was looking down and to the side, grimacing. But when I finish, she meekly steals a glance at me. And when she does, my spirit lurches. I force my smile bigger yet and, encouraged, I try even harder to come across as friendly. "Like, really. You hardly even know me, yet you're trying to help my family. That's pretty cool. So, uh, what do you think? Would you like to come out here and watch the sunset with me? We should have a few minutes left, and it's pretty amazing. I think you'll like it."

And with a lopsided grin, I lift my arm and beckon Alex out.

ALEX

What the crap is Lucas doing here? When I first saw

him, I was lying on the couch, trying to convince myself to take another bite of the tuna fish sandwich that Craig made me. My couch is strategically angled so I can see out the front window, even when lying down. We positioned it that way purposefully, so that on days when I'm too sick to get up, I can still look outside and enjoy what's happening in my sliver of the world. So when Lucas walked by and stopped in front of my house, I saw him. When he stared at my driveway and squatted into a crouch, I saw that too. And when he plopped down cross-legged and showed no indication of leaving, I definitely, definitely saw that. It was bizarre. And unexpected. And also, really weird.

In fact, I almost didn't come outside. I was tempted to just gawk at him and let him sit on the sidewalk, doing whatever it was that he was doing. But then I realized something. With a clench of my gut, I realized that this was Lucas sitting in front of my house. *Lucas.* I had consigned myself to the fact that I might never see the strange boy again before I die. Yet here he was, staring at my driveway. If I let this moment pass, I knew I might never, ever get the chance to see him again. So almost before I realized I was doing it, I leapt to my feet and ran, stumbling, to the front door. It all happened literally before I realized I was in my pajamas, I still hadn't bathed since the hospital, and my breath smelled like tuna fish.

So naturally, when Lucas calls for me to join him, I feel

more than a little hesitant.

"Come on, Alex, the sunset is amazing!" Lucas cajoles again, grinning and pointing at the fiery clouds in the sky. "I bet you didn't get views like this when you were in the hospital, did you? Didn't your window face east, away from where the sun sets?"

I scrunch my nose, impressed by how smart his observation is. Truth be told, I *had* only seen sunrises, not sunsets. But...still. I hesitate. I look down again at my sweats and run my tongue over my gritty, unbrushed teeth. I'm terribly grungy right now, and I really don't want to do this.

Yet at the same time, I'm burning with curiosity. I have questions that I want answered. Brinley told me that Lucas was dead. Yet here he is, obviously not dead. So what on earth is his game?

"Come on, Alex. We've got minutes left. Come sit with me on the curb?"

"On the curb?" I finally call back, looking up and cringing. "I'm in my pajamas, Lucas. And we have neighbors."

"Yeah, so?" Lucas waves a hand in front of his face as if it's nothing. "Anyone who sees you will just be jealous. Seriously. Half the world would rather be in their pajamas than jeans any day. Besides, you look great!" And with one final grin, he turns his back and walks to the curb, plopping down to wait for me.

Panicking, I look over my shoulder. Mom is working on an accounting project in her office, the door closed. Craig is fast asleep on the couch, his mouth lax, his feet propped up, his fishing show still running. Honestly, they won't miss me if I leave, not if I'm gone just a moment or two. So with another grimace at my sweats, I finally leave the doorway, my wheeled oxygen tank in tow.

Lucas doesn't look behind him while I walk up barefooted. He just keeps waiting patiently, keeping his eyes riveted on the horizon as I gingerly, achingly, seat myself next to him on the curb and settle my oxygen tank next to us. He seems to sense that it would've embarrassed me further had he watched while I approached. After all, I certainly move like a grandma these days.

But once I'm settled, he grins mischievously and peeks at me out of the corner of those brilliant blue eyes. "Hey there," he says, nodding towards the sunset just over my shoulder. "Thanks for joining."

I nod slightly back, then wrap my arms around my abdomen, leaning into them. Taking a deep, slow breath to steel my nerves, I angle myself towards the sunset to see it better. Lucas does likewise. "Sure. Thanks for the invitation. The sunset is nice," I comment.

"Isn't it?" He stares at it with me, smiling and putting on an air of pleasant contentment. Yet as I look at him more closely, I can't help but notice that something seems...off. The corners of his piercing eyes are tight and his smile is just ever so slightly too wide. Lucas, I realize with a start, is acting. He *has* to be acting. Because though his words say otherwise, his body language screams that something is bothering him.

Uncomfortable, I clear my throat. "Hey, Lucas," I begin.

"Hmm?" he asks. He turns to fully face me, his expression open and innocent.

"Besides a thank you, what is it, exactly, that brings you to my house on this sunset, Monday night?" I ask. Then realizing just how stupid I sound, I cringe and look down at my bare feet. Craig is always telling me that I need more practice talking to people my age, and judging by how awkward I just sounded, maybe he's right.

But to his credit, Lucas keeps rolling with the punches. "Oh, you know," he answers nonchalantly, shrugging. "Sunsets are always better from this part of town. I thought I might come check it out, see the sky from your perspective."

"Ah," I answer lightly, nodding. Then, "Ok, but no, really. What are you doing here?"

Lucas chuckles, taken aback by my sudden bluntness. But slowly, the good humor drains away. I watch him gradually deflate until he gets so depleted, his head dips and he leans back on his hands, his palms resting behind him on the rough, cold sidewalk.

"You really want to know?" he asks, lifting his head to squint at the sunset. "Like, really want to know? To be honest, Alex, Brinley cut again last night. Pretty badly. There was a lot of blood."

"She what?" I lean forward, not sure if I heard right. "Wait. Did you just say she *cut*?"

"Yeah. *Cut*. As in, with a razor. On her arms, on her thighs. She's been doing it for, oh, how long now? At least since I first met you. Probably longer. It's...it's hard to say for sure. I only recently noticed."

"Oh," I respond lamely. Then my face crumples and I stare down at the asphalt road. "Lucas, I'm so sorry," I say, my voice sincere. It's husky not with the usual cancer this time, but rather with emotion.

"Yeah," he sighs heavily. "Me too. Me too."

It grows quiet between us for a while. I'm not sure what Lucas might be thinking, but I for one am replaying last night's fiasco in my head over and over again, desperate to figure out where I went wrong. Trying to dissect at which point I blundered and made Brinley suddenly get so hostile towards me, towards herself. After a moment of intense thought, I think I pinpoint it, and I look up abruptly.

"So you..." I say quickly, my voice hoarse. Then I clear my raspy throat and try again. "So you know? You know that I went over to your house last night to drop off the letter?"

"Yeah, I know."

"And you know that she didn't accept it? That she thought her friends put me up to it or something?"

"Yup. I know that too," Lucas says. But he seems to be growing uncomfortable and his frown deepens.

"So do you...do you know why? Because, Lucas, I have to admit, I am *so* confused right now. Brinley said something to me last night, something that didn't make sense. Can you explain it to me? Please?"

"I dunno," Lucas answers slowly, stiffening and growing cautious. He glances at me from the corner of his eye. "Depends on—"

But he never gets the opportunity to finish. Just at that moment, a car whips around the corner and onto my quiet neighborhood street. Lucas startles and jumps, then immediately clamps his mouth shut. He straightens, watching the car with narrowed eyes as it nears us. I watch too. Then, realizing that the driver is my neighbor, I wave at her. Lucas seems bothered by her presence, and I want to show him that it's no big deal. Only, instead of just waving back, Jenny starts slowing the car and approaches the curb.

"Hey there, Alex." Jenny grins, rolling down the window as she comes to a stop right in front of us. "It's good to see you back already! When did you get home from the hospital?"

She's enthusiastic, positively beaming at me, so I smile back. "Just yesterday." Then remembering what I look like, I glance down at my clothes and nervously run a hand through the top of my hair. I hate, hate, *hate* how short it still feels up there. "You know, if you can't tell by what I'm wearing," I offer, laughing at myself in self-deprecation. "Apparently, I can't remember what the rest of you healthy people wear on a typical day. You know hospitals." I roll my eyes. "They do that to you."

Jenny laughs too, though it's only out of courtesy. "Hey, there's nothing wrong with being comfortable. Anyways, how are you feeling, girl? How did the surgery go?" she adds anxiously.

I just shrug and look sideways at Lucas. For some reason, his lips are pursed and he's holding very, very still, looking down at the ground with a clenched jaw. "It went...well enough. You probably heard about the infection? That's why it took so long to come home."

"Right, I heard about that at church." Jenny's look is sympathetic. "How about the cancer though? Are you in remission now?"

I hesitate, then just shrug, trying my best to smile. I really hate, too, how there's this sudden, unwelcome sensation of tears pricking my eyes. Forcefully, I shove the feeling down and focus on the conversation at hand. "Nah. It's still there," I tell her, still smiling. "Didn't beat it this time."

"Oh, Alex, I'm so sorry to hear that." And Jenny's expression positively melts. She's a young, fun mom, barely in her thirties, and has three rambunctious children at home that I used to babysit when I was healthy. If anything in this world has the power to tug at the woman's heartstrings, it's the idea that someone she cares about could suffer. Let alone, could die.

"Yeah, it's ok though," I say quickly, trying to cut her off before she can say anything more in front of Lucas. He's still staring at the ground, brow furrowed and lips pressed tight. I'm worried that hearing about my problems might make him clamp up and stop telling me about his. That's one of my least favorite side effects of cancer: people have stopped sharing their full lives with me. Apparently, they assume I have too much on my plate to want to hear about their own hardships. I don't want Jenny's comments to spoil this rare opportunity I have to listen to someone else. "There's no need to be sad about it. We'll just keep praying for better days ahead, won't we?"

"Oh, of course we will," Jenny responds fervently. "And you know what? Tell your mother that I'll bring dinner by tomorrow night. Your poor family has been through enough this week. The last thing she needs to worry about right now is meals."

"Oh, that's so sweet of you. But you really don't have—"

"No, no, no," Jenny cuts me off. "None of that. I'll be stopping by tomorrow, sometime after five. I'll text your mom to let her know the exact time."

I grimace and am about to protest further. But at the last minute, I kick myself mentally and remember my manners. Instead, I force a tight smile and hesitantly nod. "Ok, that would be wonderful actually. Thank you."

"You're welcome. Now don't be sitting out here by yourself for too long. It's getting dark out. No saying what someone might do if they see a cute girl like you sitting all alone." She gives me a wink, smiles, then finally waves goodbye. "See you tomorrow at dinnertime!" And with that, Jenny rolls up the window and drives off.

I wave back, watching as the car disappears around the next corner, then glance anxiously over at Lucas. I clear my throat, watching his hardened expression closely. "Sorry about that. Jenny is, uh, she's a family friend from church. I don't know why she didn't acknowledge you. That was really weird and really unlike her."

Lucas shrugs, still glaring at the asphalt. "No worries. I don't mind." But as he speaks, his jaw clenches.

"Lucas, I—"

"Are you still going to ask me your question?" He cuts me off, his expression getting even harder to match his tone. "The one you were bringing up before she came?"

I hesitate, not quite sure what set him off. Like Brinley,

Lucas seems capable of getting agitated very quickly.

"Well, not if you don't want me to," I confess.

"Go ahead, ask it." His words are a challenge: blunt and hard.

"Um, I just..." I take a deep breath, then shake my head to clear it, trying not to be bothered by his intense, hard stare. "I just, well, I was just going to ask you—when I was talking with Brinley last night, she said that you were...dead? That you had died five months ago? I mean, I'm talking to you now, so obviously you aren't. But...why would she say that? I mean, mentioning your name seemed to really upset her, and I don't understand what she meant. What did she mean when she said you were dead?"

Lucas doesn't answer. At least, not right away. He just keeps staring at me, his expression unreadable. Then he leans back on his palms again and squints straight up at the sky. It's obvious that he's waging some kind of war inside himself.

"Tell me. What are your thoughts?" he finally asks, his words deliberate as he still looks upward, eyes tight. "I want to hear your explanations."

"My explanations?" I repeat, surprised.

"Yeah. I mean, my sister claimed that I was dead. How are you explaining that to yourself?"

"Lucas, I'm not," I say back, shaking my head. "I just told you that I was confused by it. That's why I'm asking."

"No, don't lie about that," Lucas says mildly, dismissively. "You have ideas. Explanations. Tell them to me." And finally he looks over, his eyebrows raised in waiting.

Admittedly, it's annoying that Lucas is commanding me to obey, and I purse my lips at him. But his expression doesn't falter. So, feeling flustered, I huff a sigh and give in, throwing my hands in the air. "Fine. Maybe you're right. Maybe I do have thoughts. I don't know. I was just...I don't know. I was thinking back to that first day when you visited, when you told me that you're no longer a big part of your sister's life, and that it's due to circumstances you can't control. So I don't know. Was there a custody battle or something? Your parents split up, you chose to stay with your dad, Brinley chose to stay with your mom, and now she's mad at you for it? You chose to leave, and now you're 'dead' to her because of it?"

Lucas snorts, but not necessarily out of amusement. It seems more like he's impressed with my creativity. "That would make for a good story."

"Yeah, well, I can see now that it's wrong. So what really happened?"

And this time, instead of deflecting my question, Lucas seems to ponder it. He leans back even deeper on his palms and some of his hardness melts away. As I watch, anxiety takes its place. He starts glancing at me nervously out of the corner of his eye, almost as if he's not certain he wants to tell me. So I stay quiet, letting him think. And finally, I'm rewarded.

"So you go to church, right?" he starts out slowly, speaking carefully.

"Yeah, I do."

"All right. So you believe in an afterlife then?"

"Of course," I answer immediately, laughing a little at how obvious it should be. "I have cancer, Lucas. How else could I face down death without believing that there's at least *something* more after we die?"

"Right. Makes sense." He nods to himself, chewing on his lip thoughtfully. "That's good. I didn't always believe in an afterlife myself, you know. Though I definitely do now. So uh, Alex, what is it that you believe about the afterlife exactly? I mean, are we reincarnated? Dissolved into energy? Merged with some higher, holier power?"

I think for just a moment, then frown and shake my head. "No. Nothing like that. In my religion, we as people are made up of two parts: our body and the spirit inside. When we die, our spirit leaves. It vacates the body, but it lives on outside of it. It's as simple as that."

"Ok, cool. And...if you were to, say, meet a spirit, what would a spirit look like?"

I open my mouth to answer. But then, as the significance of my response catches up to me, I close it with a snap. As I stare at him, comprehending where this might be going, my heart speeds and my palms start sweating. Subconsciously, I wipe them against my sweats. Lucas watches me very, very closely. And at my reaction, he starts looking like he might puke.

"Hey, Lucas," I say, half-laughing but definitely not out of humor. More so out of an edging hysteria. "Don't. Don't go there, ok? I am dying. Like, legitimately dying. And it's really not funny to joke about this kind of stuff with me. So please. Stop playing around, and just tell me what happened."

But Lucas doesn't say anything. He just gazes at me long and hard, his expression unreadable, his blue eyes bright and penetrating. And when I say bright, I mean *extremely* bright. I don't know why I never questioned it before, but Lucas's eyes are so full of light, it's almost unnatural. Otherworldly. Inhuman.

My breath catches.

"A spirit looks just like its body, doesn't it, Alex?" he finally whispers, searching my face. "That's what you believe. The spirit and the body are identical, aren't they? So if you were to meet a spirit, the spirit would look just like a person to you."

"Lucas," I say warningly, my tone getting breathy with desperation. My chest feels tighter, and it's hard to get a full gasp in. Despite the oxygen tube looped over my ears and

118

beneath my nose, my fingertips start going numb. "Please," I plead in a whisper. "This isn't funny." But Lucas only maintains our eye contact, his brow furrowing. He keeps gazing at me, his eyes *so* incredibly bright. I bite my lip, and as I start to believe him, tears pool in my eyes.

"Alex, I..." As he watches me, Lucas's face falls. For a split moment, he lifts a hand as if he wants to comfort me. As if he wants to lay his palm against my face, or use his thumb to wipe away the tears that are now spilling down my cheeks. But before he does, just inches before he touches me, he freezes. His fingers slowly clench, his teeth grit, and with a sharp intake of breath, he drops his hand and looks away.

"I'm sorry," he whispers, his voice husky with pain as he stares at the asphalt. "That's all I'm going to say. I shouldn't have come here. I'm sorry." And with those words, he pushes himself up to stand. Lucas is about to turn and leave, to leave me sitting on the curb alone. But at the last minute, he stiffens. He whirls around so suddenly that I jump.

"You want to know something?" he asks abruptly, his voice pained and desperate. "Something important? My last name? It's Prowley, Alex. Lucas P-R-O-W-L-E-Y. Prowley. You can Google what happened to me if you want. But if you do, be warned." He winces. "It's graphic."

And with those parting words, Lucas stalks off,

abandoning me on the side of the street with my oxygen tank. I tremble as I watch him leave, one hand shoved deep into his pants pocket and the other running anxiously through his hair. He's still wearing the same, unblemished white T-shirt and the faded-out jeans as every other time I've seen him.

But as he passes by a car parked on the side of the road, he does something odd. He yanks his hand out of his pocket and sticks it through the car. And when I say through, I mean *through*. Right through the passenger-side door. It stays there, his hand and forearm completely gone, everything swallowed up to the crook of his elbow as he walks the length of the vehicle.

I blink.

And then he's past the car. His arm comes back, and dejected, he lets it drop to his side. Slowly, he puts that hand back into his pocket.

With one final, doleful look back at me, Lucas rounds the corner and is gone.

Leaving me alone on the cement curb, shaking, terrified, and numb.

CHAPTER NINE

ALEX

I am going to die. Soon. I know that as certainly as I know that my head throbs, my body aches, and my lungs can never get enough air. As I lie on my bed in the dark, staring at my phone and the crisp image of Lucas Prowley smiling above his obituary, I just know. I absolutely know that I am going to die.

Because healthy people don't see spirits. They don't talk to ghosts and mistake them for reality. They don't think that dead people visit them, or have conversations with them, or even hope they might want to become friends. No! Those kinds of experiences are lived by the elderly, the dementia-riddled, by people placed on hospice who are knocking on death's very door. Spirits appear to the imminently dying, not to a seventeen-year-old girl like me. A girl who should have decades left to live, who still has a rich chance at life.

Except that I have...five months. Five agonizingly short months. That is the timeline I've been given. Not years. Not decades. Not a lifetime. Just five months.

And now I'm seeing dead people.

It's a fact. And with it comes the suffocating weight of my approaching death. Never before have I felt the aches of my cancer so sharply, and never before have I been so scared. I can't stop the sobs as I lie on my bed in the darkness, tethered to my oxygen machine, biting my fist and staring at the car crash illuminated on my screen. Because there, in a four-and-a-half-month-old news article, is a picture of a crumpled car. The front hood is completely decimated, surrounded by shards of glass and debris, smashed beyond all recognition. Lucas, it says, was sitting in the front seat. Lucas, it says, didn't make it.

With another sob, I bite my fist harder. And as I stare, I know. Lucas Prowley is dead. He is dead. And soon, I will be too.

BRINLEY

I know I did the right thing by turning that Alex girl away. After all, she was trying to play me for a fool. She was trying to play some sick, perverted joke on me. She told me, outright told me to my face, that she'd talked to Lucas that very morning. That she'd met him recently. That he'd asked her to show up on my porch, to beg me to keep living, and to write me a mysterious letter. And why? Because he knew what was happening? Because he was *concerned* about me?

And that, of course, was Alex's sickest joke of them all. Her joke that Lucas, my brother, could still possibly know me. That even when dead, he could understand my pain and want to help me and want to save me. Alex had played on my deepest desires when she implied that. She had laughed at my secret, foolish hope that Lucas could still somehow be continuing on. She illustrated for me just how ludicrous that actually sounded, then mocked me as she rubbed his death even harder in my face.

Because though I wish that it were true, though I wish it desperately, I know that Alex couldn't have been telling the truth. Lucas can't be aware of me still. He can't know that I am hurting or that I want to take my life. He can't, because he is dead.

Right after the car crash happened, one of the ambulance medics who arrived on scene was an old friend of my parents. He recognized Lucas. And breaking protocol, he called my parents immediately. They, in turn, blew up my phone with calls and texts, panicked to find that in the middle of the night, both of their children were missing. When I told them where I was, they sped over to Savannah's party, picked me up, and we all arrived on the scene together, as rapidly as possible. So rapidly, in fact, that they hadn't yet removed Lucas's corpse. I saw his silhouette in the body bag. I saw the broken glass and all the dark, wet bloodstains. And I know for a fact how dead he was.

So, no. Lucas cannot still care about me. He cannot have talked to Alex.

So considering the fact that Alex is a liar, I know I did the right thing by slamming the door in her face.

Yet...there remains this part of me, this agonizingly tiny part of me, that thinks I may have made a mistake. Possibly. Because the next morning, after waking up and stumbling to the bathroom to brush my teeth, I remembered.

Alexia Ahmed. The girl with cancer.

Once I realized who she was, once I connected the dots and realized what I had done, it began to haunt me. I couldn't stop thinking about the way that I'd treated someone so sick, the way that I had been so internally rude about her looks. The girl is dying. She is *dying*. She couldn't help that she looked like a wraith or was so unsure of herself, wasting my time. She couldn't help that she was pitiful. And yet, there I was, slamming a door in a dying girl's face.

But then, after that initial wave of guilt washed over me, it was quickly pushed back by anger. I mean, just because someone has cancer doesn't mean they automatically qualify as a good person. It doesn't mean they can traipse around, playing me for a fool, mocking me, laughing at me, and do it all without retribution. No. Alexia may be dying, but that doesn't mean she deserves my tolerance or forgiveness. After all, I don't get any. I don't ask for special treatment or mercy just because of what I've been through. So why on earth should she?

I think all these things, remembering, warring with myself, and tumbling through the tumult, as I sit on my bed and stare. There are rough scars forming up and down my forearms now—raw, corded flesh that peeks through all my scabs. I stare at them and acknowledge bitterly that perhaps I'm no better than Alexia Ahmed after all. Just like her, I lie sometimes. And just like her, I am bound to die soon. It's inevitable. Because just like cutting, suicide has violently inserted itself as my next focal point, the next obsession of my wounded brain. Over the past few weeks, I have devised at least three separate ways I am going to die. The first is the easiest and what I'm banking on. All it involves are some little pills left in the back of the cupboard. The next two are contingencies, in case something goes wrong with that plan.

I look up and, chest tight, let my eyes roam around my room. Just like always, it is pristine. But unlike always, it is growing empty. For the past month, I have been removing all excess clutter from my room and either donating it or throwing it away. Because after Lucas died, cleaning his room just about undid my mother. She wailed at his belongings. She cried with every item she threw away. And the least I can do before I die is spare her a handful of sobs.

Because, in time, my death is going to hurt her. Oh, I know it will hurt her. But I also know that, in time, she'll be better off because I'm gone. After all, Lucas's death has turned me into nothing more than a demented, monstrous shadow of my former self. When he left, I morphed into a burden. A trial. A dark and crying and ungrateful child who only ever hurts her friends and who only ever hurts her parents. For the past month, sure, I've been cleaning my room. But for the past month, I've also been sobbing and yelling and plaguing my parents with worry. They don't deserve to suffer anymore because of me. They don't deserve a daughter who is such a problem as I've become. I'm a mess. A broken disaster. A thorn in everyone's side. And although removing a thorn initially hurts, it's also for the best.

So, yes. I should die. I am going to die.

In fact, I am ready to end it all. Right here. Right now.

Except for one teeny, festering problem: Alexia Ahmed offered me a letter and I didn't take it.

A letter, she said, that was prompted by Lucas.

He was real, she had told me, and he still cared, she had said.

And though I know that can't be true, though I slammed the door fiercely in her face because of it, I'm also growing to regret that decision.

Because yes, Alexia is a liar. She's a liar. But also, she has a letter. For me.

And I want to—*need* to—know what is in that letter.

LUCAS

I am a mess. An absolute and complete mess for two straight days. I hardly even go home at all during that time. I just wander through the hallways of Volcano Vista High School day and night, pacing like a tiger and trying to come to terms with the horrifying thing I just did.

Telling Alex that I am a spirit wasn't even part of my gameplan when I showed up. In my desperate fervor to convince her not to give up on Brinley, I got distracted. I conveniently overlooked the fact that Brinley told Alex, to her face, that I am dead. I just didn't think much of it. Instead, I was sidetracked by the fact that Alex failed, and I was consumed with plotting how we were going to rebound. I showed up at Alex's house simply to enlist her help, not to terrify her and give her a very valid reason to never want to speak to me again.

But what happened, the event that threw a wrench into

absolutely everything, was that stupid neighbor of hers, Jenny. I mean, she isn't stupid. She's actually super nice. But she showed up at exactly the wrong time! When she was sitting in that car, chatting with Alex, I knew perfectly well that she couldn't see me. I knew why she didn't comment about me or say hi or even "acknowledge me," as Alex put it. I just sat there holding my breath, suddenly and horribly realizing just how bad things could get if Alex *did* try to draw attention to me.

I mean, it would have made her seem crazy. Psychotic. As if she needed to be taken right back to that hospital, evaluated, and put on the highest dose of crazy medications. If I didn't tell her the truth, and she started telling people about me, then I had the potential to seriously mess up the last few months of her life. Because eventually, she *was* going to say something. And eventually, she would wind up in a straitjacket, haunted by the idea that she was not only losing her life, but losing her mind as well.

So my options were either tell her myself before things got really messy, or let her find out on her own and potentially ruin a lot of important things.

Because if I never told her, why would Alex ever have reason to trust me again? She wouldn't. She would stop talking to me, actually believe that I am a hallucination, and then I would permanently lose her.

And I do not want to lose her.

So out of complete desperation, and also this slim sense of moral obligation, I decided to do the right thing. Right there on that stupid cement curb while Jenny was talking, I decided to tell Alex the truth about me. I figured that if she reacted poorly, I would take it as a sign that I should just pick up and leave her life forever. And...she did. She was terrified when I told her I was a ghost. She cried when she learned the truth. And now that I took the jump, now that I horrified Alex, there is absolutely no going back.

Or at least, there *shouldn't* be a going back. I should just disappear now, leave her forever, and go back to watching Brinley cut herself to shreds as I sit on the edge of the bathtub. I can throw in the towel and silently plead that someone else like Alex will swoop in to change Brinley's trajectory. I could. I really could.

Or I could not. I could avoid the potentially fatal risk in that and instead go immediately back to Alex. I could plead with her to be forgiving, to give me, and also Brinley, a second chance. I could plead with her to not hate me, to not fear me, and to continue offering her selfless, courageous, and miraculous help to my sister.

I mean, I get that it's not fair. I get that I have nothing to offer her in return if I do that. I'm dead, and I can give her absolutely, pathetically nothing. But...Alex is a nice person. A church-going person. And maybe, just maybe, if I frame this right, maybe I don't have to lose her forever.

Maybe I can hold on just a little bit longer to Alex. And maybe I can keep my only friend and my only hope after all.

CHAPTER TEN

LUCAS

It takes me a full two days to work up my courage. The bell rings on Wednesday, releasing all students to their homes. As is my custom, I follow Brinley as she leaves the science classroom, wanting to make sure she gets on the bus ok. Throughout the entire period, she sat hunched at her desk and doodled dark images on her folder. One was a daisy, wilting where it stuck out of the ground. The other was a bottle of pills. The third was a pile of dirt and a deep, gaping hole. I really, really hate to imagine what all of it meant.

So, worried out of my mind, I trail her. I watch closely as she picks her way through the crowds, head down, earbuds in place, and looking utterly miserable. When she reaches the bus, I'm tempted to clamber onto it with her. I'm so nervous for Brinley that I don't want to leave her unsupervised. Besides, it's part of my daily routine to catch a ride home on the bus with her. But, grimacing, I know I can't do that. Not today. Instead of getting on, I morosely watch as the bus pulls away from the curb. Then I sigh and trudge off in the opposite direction.

It takes nearly an hour of walking, but eventually, I make it to Alex's neighborhood. The street is quiet, the road is void of passing vehicles, and everything feels kind of empty. I didn't die wearing a watch, so I don't have access to a clock or anything. But if I had to guess, I would suppose it's around 4:00. Too early for dinner, too early for commuting professionals to arrive home.

Realizing I have time to kill, I stick my hands in my pockets and slowly meander down the sidewalk towards Alex's house. The Buick wagon is sitting in the carport, so I know that her family must be home, which complicates things. With her parents there, I have no idea how I should approach her. I could stand outside her window again and hope she'll see me and come out to talk. Though I doubt that will happen. Alex was terrified and emotional when she realized I'm a ghost, so there's no way she'll come outside to meet me again. No matter how desperately I wish she would.

So that means my only option is to walk *into* her house. I could do it, of course. I am completely capable of passing through her front door. And yet, that feels invasive. Besides, won't Alex scream if she sees me unexpectedly appear in her home? And wouldn't that get her stuck in a straitjacket anyways?

Looking down, I sigh and kick absently at a pebble. It doesn't skeeter away when I do. It doesn't budge. It just lays limply on the sidewalk, looking up at me. I kick again, and it stares back.

"Well," I say. "What's there to lose, right? Think I should at least check that she's home?"

The pebble doesn't respond, so I try to kick it again.

"It's not like I'm going inside," I tell it. "I'm just going to look. One quick glance through a window, and that's all. I'm not a peeping Tom or anything. This is perfectly fine, perfectly honorable."

But still, the pebble doesn't speak. I kick at it a fourth time, and again it doesn't budge.

So I get desperate. Without thinking, I adopt a weird falsetto voice and pretend that the rock is actually talking back. "Yeah, it's not so bad, Lucas," it tells me. "Just go do it. Go do it now."

And that is when I realize what an absolute fool I'm being. Disgusted with myself, I step away from the stupid, silent rock and roll my eyes. "Great. Just great," I mutter. "Two days without her and already you're talking to rocks. That's wonderful, Lucas. Real wonderful."

And with that, I sigh heavily and run a hand down my

nonexistent face. I shouldn't do this. Logically, I know that I shouldn't. But against my best judgment, I start to trudge across Alex's rock lawn anyway. I've come this far and the loneliness is obviously driving me mad, so I might as well do what I came here to do.

But when I walk to her front window and peer into the living room, no one is inside. In the corner of the room is a rickety, upright piano, next to it is a TV, and there is also an old, fabric couch. A quilt lies on the couch, bunched up in one corner as if someone was recently using it. Looking closely, I can see that an unused nasal cannula is lying on the blanket, its tube trailing across the floor and connected to a large oxygen machine stationed against the wall. If I crane my neck just right, I can also peek down the hallway, but all three doors leading from it are closed.

Stepping back, I frown. Then with a small shrug, I start rounding the house. On the perpendicular side, the windows are too high for me to see anything. So holding my breath, I pass through the cinder block wall surrounding the backyard. Only, when I do, *I'm* the one who nearly screams. Not Alex. Because the last thing I expect to see when I pass through that wall is both Alex and her mother sitting on the cement patio, rocking back and forth slowly on a wooden porch swing.

When she sees me appear through the solid wall, Alex gasps and jerks violently in fright. Her mother, whose arm is draped behind her shoulders, jumps too. Not because she's seen me, but because Alex is absolutely terrified.

"Honey, what's wrong?" she asks, alarmed.

At the same time, I also startle. I throw my hands in front of my face and backpedal, losing my balance, then trip backwards through the wall again. I land roughly on my rear on the other side, catching my fall by throwing my hands behind me. Looking down, I realize that the calf, ankle, and foot of one of my legs is still sticking through the cinder blocks. Cringing, I yank it back out. On the other side, I hear Alex gasp again.

"Honey, what is it?" Eileen demands again, her voice urgent. "Alex?"

"I—it's...it's...it's nothing. Sorry, Mom, it's nothing."

"That most definitely was not nothing! Honey, what happened? Did you see something?"

"No, I—" Alex is fumbling for words. I squeeze my eyes shut, listening hard and cursing my stupidity. "No, I didn't. Sorry, I...I just got this really sharp pain along my ribs. Must have twisted wrong or something. Pulled at the sutures. But it's fine now."

"Oh, honey," Eileen croons. "Do you think they removed the staples too soon? Do you think you reopened the scar?"

"No, no," Alex assures her quickly. "Nothing like that. Really, I must have just moved wrong. It's fine now."

Eileen hesitates. Then, "You're sure?"

"Yes. Very sure."

It's quiet for a long moment, and I'm just easing myself to my feet again, trying to be stealthy so I can leave without causing more trouble. But right as I do, Alex speaks again. "Um, Mom, can I ask for a favor?"

"Of course. What is it, sweetie?"

"I'm feeling kind of tired, but it's really nice out here. Do you mind going inside and bringing me a pillow? I think I want to lie down on the swing for a while."

"Oh, sure. I would be happy to."

"Awesome, thanks. And honestly, I'll probably end up falling asleep. You're welcome to go back inside and work some more. I'll be fine."

Again, it's silent for a moment. "Are you sure, honey? I don't mind. I can bring my laptop out here."

Alex's answer is fast and immediate. "No, no. That's fine. You'll work faster with the two screens in your office. Besides, you need to get that account done before Craig wakes up. He'll want to spend time with you when he does, so I'm ok. Really."

"Hmm. Well, if you're sure. If you're still sleeping by the time I'm done, I'll come out to get you for dinner."

"That sounds great. Thanks, Mom. And, uh, how long do you think that will be? Dinner won't be done for a couple of hours, right?"

"Yes. About that."

"Ok, great."

There's the sound of a deep creak as, I assume, Eileen stands from the cushioned porch swing. Then there's the sound of steps. The sliding glass door opens and closes. Moments later, it opens again, and Eileen comes back presumably with a pillow. She and Alex exchange a few words, then the sliding glass door opens and closes one last time. After that, it's silent. I freeze in place, holding my breath.

"Lucas?" Alex whispers loudly, her voice strained and hoarse. "Lucas, are you still there?"

I jump but otherwise stay in place, gritting my teeth. I don't know what to do.

"Lucas, really, are you there? Please don't tell me I imagined that. Oh please, please don't tell me I'm losing it."

And at that, I cringe. Hating that I made Alex doubt her sanity, I take a slow step forward. Then another. Then another. Before I can stop myself, I pass through the cinder block wall again, shuddering as the atoms slide through my spirit. When I appear, Alex gasps dramatically again. And then, she starts coughing. Doubling over, she slams her eyes shut and wraps her arms tightly around her rib cage. A moment later, she opens her eyes and stares at me dizzily.

I grimace. Then wave awkwardly. "Hey there."

"Lucas?" she asks, eyes wide as she coughs.

"Yeah, it's me. I'm sorry. Like, really sorry. I didn't

know you were back here. There's no way I would have come if I knew—"

But Alex's expression cuts me off. Her face is paler than before, and she leans back in the swing, gritting her teeth in pain. With a quiet groan, the tendons in her neck grow tight.

"Hey, are you ok?" I take a step towards her. "Alex?"

But Alex just shakes her head. Taking a slow, shaky breath, she closes her eyes. "So how long do I have?" she croaks. In her lap, her hands are fisted and shaking.

"Huh?"

"How long do I have?" she repeats, gritting her teeth again, her eyes still closed. "How long until I die? Because that's why you're here, isn't it? That's always why spirits show up. So, what? I'm assuming I have less than five months? Do I even have a week?"

"Alex—" I shake my head in confusion. "What? What are you talking about?"

She opens her eyes, staring at me. The look she gives me is strangely resigned, yet determined.

"You're dead, Lucas. I saw your obituary. I saw the picture of the crash. And I just saw you walk through that wall."

My mouth opens. When no words come out, I close it. And swallow.

"So why are you here? Why can I see you?"

"I don't know," I confess, my voice small.

She raises her eyebrows at me.

"I don't know, Alex," I say more adamantly. "I mean, I'm not here on some sort of special mission if that's what you're thinking. I'm not, like, a spirit guide or something. I'm just here to ask for your help. Again. And actually, to really, really beg for it."

Alex's wary demeanor begins to slip, and she grows uncertain. Judging by her expression, I'm worried I might never get this opportunity again. So while I still have the chance, I plow on.

"I'm serious, Alex." I take a step closer, my voice growing desperate. "I'm just as confused about this as you are. Because four months ago—I guess almost five now—I didn't even know that spirits were real. I didn't even know that life after death was possible. All that happened was one night, I was driving through Albuquerque and going a little too fast. Next thing I knew, a car in the oncoming lane swerved. I saw their headlights, I felt a lot of pain, and the very next moment, I was standing next to my body. Like this!" I gesture at my ghostly torso. "And ever since then, I've been wandering around lost and confused and...and dead. You're the first person who has ever been able to see me. The first person who can hear me. And yeah, it freaks me out! I don't know what's going on here, or why you can see me. All I know is that you can. And because you can, I need your help. Desperately, I need you."

I cringe but keep my eye contact with her, yearning with all my might for Alex to see how sincere I am. Watching me, her brow furrows. She's confused and her expression is cautious. When she speaks, her words are slow and hesitant. "Are you here because of Brinley?"

"Yes. I am."

"Is she ok?" Alex immediately asks, leaning forward in concern. As she does, she winces in pain.

"Yes. No. I don't know," I admit, shrugging helplessly. "For now she is. But I came here today because I'm really, really worried about her. Not to be too graphic or anything, but her arms and legs are so sliced up, they're like hamburger at this point. She's getting more and more isolated, and today she kept doodling about death. There's so many warning signs, even more than just the cutting. She's withdrawing from everyone she knows, she's giving away her things, she's writing those suicide letters, and she can't stop crying when she goes to bed at night. And to make matters worse, my parents have no idea," I say, hating how dangerous those words sound out loud. "They don't have a clue. No one but me—and now you—know about her letters and cutting. If nothing changes, I'm worried that Brinley is going to kill herself. In fact, I'm certain of it. I've read what she's written, and I know exactly what she has planned."

As I admit that, my voice chokes off. It's growing thick with ghostly emotion and what should be tears. Gritting my teeth, I look away but force myself to continue. "Brinley is going to kill herself because of me. She thinks my death is her fault, and I can't do anything to stop her. She can't hear me, she can't see me, she doesn't know I'm here. And she doesn't know how badly she doesn't want this. She *can't* want this existence. Do you understand?"

I look back up and Alex is on the edge of her seat, eyes riveted on me in absolute concern. Her wavy hair is as short as ever, she's barefoot in jeans with a worn-out jacket, and her face is pale and terribly gaunt. But I swear, I have never seen such a profound look of compassion on another human face before—nothing as deep, as kind, or as determined as Alex's is now.

"Lucas, I'll tell your parents," she says earnestly, once she has my eye contact. "I'm not going to let anything happen to Brinley. I promise. I won't."

But I shake my head, already knowing how disastrous that would be. "No," I answer, my voice still thick. "No. That won't work. I know Brinley. I know how she's playing this game. If my parents find out, she'll only kill herself faster. Remember how she reacted to your letter? If my parents try to intervene, it will be even worse. She'll shove them away, pretend that she's fine, then end it all when they aren't looking."

Alex's face scrunches. "Are you—"

"Yes, I'm sure," I interrupt sharply, swallowing another lump in my throat. "Trust me when I say that I'm sure. I know how Brinley works. That's why I asked you to give the letter to her, not to my parents. She has to decide for herself that she wants to keep living. If anyone tries to force her into that, she'll only move faster and with more determination. There's nothing that Brinley hates more than trying to be fixed."

Alex nods, biting her lip. "Ok. I'll...I'll go back then. I still have the letter. I'll try again."

"And what if it doesn't work?" At the thought, I groan audibly. Not able to take it anymore, I whirl around and run a hand through my disheveled hair, knotting it in my fingers. I'm tempted to yank it out, just like I've seen Rory do at times. But I can't. Physically, I can't. So instead I groan again and think harder.

After a moment, I finally admit to myself that there are no perfect solutions, nothing guaranteed to work without risk. Distraught, I throw my hands into the air and whirl around to speak again. As I do, my eyes land on Alex—and my mouth clamps shut.

She is sitting on the swing, watching me, with her skeletal arms wrapped around her torso. She looks frail sitting like that, really frail. Her pale copper face is gaunt, her expression tight with agony, and for the first time yet, I let myself see the deep fatigue swimming in her eyes. Alex is sick. Like, really sick. And as I realize that, a tidal wave of shame slams into me. I lose all steam and my arms fall to my side.

"Look, I'm sorry," I mutter, turning my face away and hating myself. "I shouldn't have come here. You have cancer, and I never should have bothered you with this. I'm sorry."

I'm about to turn away, to leave her backyard and leave her forever, but a growl stops me short. "Stop that," Alex says, her voice so fierce it's almost a snarl. Turning, I find that her chocolate eyes are blazing. "Stop that," she repeats again. "I'm sick of hearing that. I'm sick of it! I may have cancer, Lucas, but that doesn't mean I need to be babied or coddled. I have five months left to live, not five months left to die. And so help me, if I can help even one more person before I leave this world, then I am going to do it. I won't walk away from your sister, and I won't let you stand there and tell me that I should. I may be sick, but I am still capable, thank you. And I'm not"—she glares at me, her eyes ferocious—"not," she repeats, "going to give up on Brinley. Not if I can help it."

Her expression, her words, her sheer compassion and adamance, all of it is too much. I swallow, my emotion too great to speak. Slowly I nod, and she nods back.

"Good. I'm glad we got that straight," she says, pursing

her lips and leaning gingerly back in the swing. "Now, if you say that Brinley has to decide for herself whether she wants to live or die, then fine. We can work with that. I think I have an idea forming."

"You do?" I ask. My voice is still thick, but for the first time in months, it's tinged with hope.

"I do. Now Lucas, please sit. I need to lie down so if my mom looks out the window, she doesn't get suspicious. But otherwise, let's talk. If this plan is going to work—and I think it just might—then we don't have a second to lose."

CHAPTER ELEVEN

ALEX

"So you're telling me that you can't sit on a porch swing, but you can sit inside of a car? What's up with that?"

It's been exactly one week since Lucas and I discussed our plan to save Brinley. Since then, we've spent nearly every evening together in my backyard, booking hotels and thinking through even the most minute of details. In fact, I've spent so much time around Lucas that I've actually grown accustomed to the fact that he's a spirit. Well, sort of. If nothing else, I can at least anticipate his quirks now. Like the way he never sits on furniture, only on the ground. Or the way he gasps and shudders anytime he passes through an object. Lucas still isn't normal to me, not by any means, but at least I'm growing used to him. At this point, it's almost amusing to watch Lucas stand outside the passenger door, staring at my family's Buick in deep concentration.

"Yeah, it's...it's hard to explain. But a car is different from furniture. It has a floor, and I can step onto floors. So just give me a second. This takes a lot of concentration."

I nod but, honoring his request, remain quiet. Mutely, I watch as he leans forward, brow furrowed, and sticks a leg right through the passenger door. He plants his ghostly foot on the floor of the car and jiggles it slightly, as if testing that it's secure. Then he grins at me through the window. The rest of Lucas's body passes through the door and next thing I know, he's sitting next to me in the vehicle, positioned perfectly in the passenger seat and grinning like a madman.

This time, it's not him that shudders. It's me. "That's freaky, Lucas," I mutter, biting my bottom lip. Trying to collect my wits, I look away and fumble with the keys, stabbing them into the ignition. "Like, really freaky."

He shrugs. "Sorry? I know it must be weird for you. Ghost physics were bizarre to me too at first. Even now, passing through solid stuff feels really...gross. There's just something about it that isn't right. Like, there's this instinctual part of me that hates it, you know?"

I pull out of the driveway and nod obligingly, filing his comment away for future consideration. In an effort to be polite, I haven't questioned Lucas much about what it's like to be dead. I figure my time will come soon enough to learn for myself, and I'm surprisingly reluctant to broach the topic. But little comments like that? I pay attention to them.

"So anyways, thanks for bringing me with you tonight," he continues. "I'm glad you feel well enough to drive, and honestly this is kinda fun. Like, it almost feels normal." His face scrunches when he says that and, despite his words, I can tell that Lucas feels just as awkward about this shopping trip together as I do. I bite my bottom lip again but force myself to nod and keep my cool.

"Yeah, no problem, Lucas. I've always wanted to go shopping with a ghost. It was a major item on my bucket list, so I'm pretty pumped that I get to check it off before I die."

Blanching, Lucas looks over at me, his face shocked. I try to hold my expression steady, but the longer he gawks, the more I can't take it. Finally, my composure bursts, and I start laughing. Next to me, Lucas catches on and slowly he starts to grin.

"I'm kidding! Gosh, Lucas, ever heard of sarcasm before?"

"No," Lucas drawls. "That was sarcasm? It couldn't be."

I laugh again, rolling my eyes. "You're impossible. I can't believe I actually had you going there for a second." I look over at him and smile. "But, I guess to tell the truth, I am sort of happy to have you along. Like, it's freaky. Of course it's really freaky. But at the same time, I've never gone shopping with a friend before. So, this is good for me,"

I add, shrugging.

Lucas seems reluctant to believe that. He eyes me critically, as if trying to decide whether I'm being sarcastic again. "Wait, are you serious? You've never gone shopping with a friend before?"

I shake my head. "No. Seriously, I haven't. I was homeschooled most of my life, so it's not like I have many friends. Granted, I went to public school for sophomore year, but that was just for a few months. I decided I wanted to experience life to its fullest after I beat cancer that first time. I wanted to see what public school was like. But then I relapsed and I got too sick to keep going. And, whelp, two years later and here we are. If you think about it, four months in high school isn't exactly long enough to find your social niche."

"Oh," Lucas says. He stares at me for a moment then frowns and looks out the window. Just outside, rocky suburban lawns, cacti, and nearly identical adobe houses fly by. We're still in the neighborhoods and have yet to turn onto the main road that will take us to Walmart. "That surprises me, Alex."

"Oh yeah?" I ask. "Why's that?"

"Well, it's just that the more I get to know you, the more I realize how cool you are. I would have thought that four months in high school would have been plenty of time for someone as great as you to make friends. I'm just shocked that no one gave you more of a chance. They should have."

I open my mouth to speak, but the words get stuck. Awkwardly, I clear my throat and tighten my grip on the steering wheel. If I'm not mistaken, Lucas may have just given me a compliment. A really kind and sincere compliment. "Um, thank you. That's, uh, kind of you to say. And kind of you to think about me." I clear my voice again, still feeling awkward. "But to be fair," I quickly add, my words getting fast with embarrassment, "it's not like people didn't want to give me a chance. It's just by that point in life, everyone has their friend group already established, you know? People were kind to me. They really were. They just weren't exactly looking for a best friend. You know what I mean?"

Lucas nods, his brow still furrowed. He looks out the window some more then suddenly turns to stare at me, those extraordinary eyes of his bright and penetrating.

"I'm sorry," he says, his voice surprisingly sincere.

"What?" I'm taken aback.

"I'm sorry. You and I must have been sophomores at the same time. Maybe we even had classes together or passed each other in the hallway sometimes. I dunno. All I know is that I should have talked to you. If I hadn't been so focused on myself—my cheerleading, my friends, what was going on in my personal life—maybe I would have. It's kind of funny, you know?" Lucas says, shaking his head and scoffing at himself. "Hindsight really is 20/20. Now that I'm dead, I can see how self-centered I sometimes was, and I regret that. Since becoming a spirit, I've become lonely. And now that I'm lonely, I see other lonely people *everywhere*, all around us, all the time. I just wish I had recognized that while I was alive. I wish I had talked to more people when I had the chance to."

Unable to respond, I glance over at Lucas, my brow furrowed. There is genuine sadness in his eyes as he stares at his hands, flipping them forward and backward in his lap. The mood is somber in the car, and I really want to say something to comfort him. Anything. But I don't have any clue what.

Finally, so abruptly that it makes me jump, Lucas looks up and forces a cheery smile. "Whelp, no use worrying about it now! Can't help the fact that I'm dead now, can I?"

"Um, maybe not?" I cringe, realizing that's probably not what he wants to hear.

"Exactly. I mean, what does that weird monkey dude on *The Lion King* say to Simba all the time? 'Just get over it'?"

"Um, that depends. Are you talking about Rafiki?"

"Yeah, probably."

I laugh a little, trying not to, but I can't help it. Lucas's expression is just so funny right now. "Well then, yes. That's essentially what he says. Something like 'Learn from the past, don't dwell on it.'"

"See! Wise monkey, isn't he? So that's what we gotta do here, Alex. We should forget the past and move on to happier topics. Like, I dunno, music? Do you have any good playlists?"

I raise my eyebrows, feeling whiplashed by the sudden change in conversation. "Music, huh? That's what you want to talk about?"

"Yeah. Like, on your phone. I really miss being able to pick out my own music. All I can listen to these days is whatever other people pick, especially Brinley. And all her stuff is so angsty, it's insane. It drives me crazy and gets really old after a while. So what do you have?"

"Oh." I look down at my phone in the cupholder, grimacing. "I guess I didn't think about missing music after death. Um, I can play whatever you want. Most of my playlists are classical, but we aren't limited to just that."

"Wait, you listen to classical?"

"Yeah. Mostly classical piano. I play the piano myself, so it's fun to listen to people who are better than me. But that's beside the point. What do you like?"

But Lucas is definitely not over this new revelation. His own eyebrows raise as he appraises me, looking me over. "You play classical piano?" he asks slowly.

"Yeah, but it's really no big deal. Piano practice was always a main part of my homeschool routine. I've been playing several hours a day for as long as I can remember. I started lessons when I was like four, maybe three."

Lucas lets out a low whistle. "Dang. So that means you're good then?"

I blush. "Well, not necessarily. I mean, my plan was always to go to college on a music scholarship and major in piano, and then teach lessons for the rest of my life. If I got ambitious, maybe I would have wanted to become a professor and teach piano at the university level, just like my dad does. But with that said, I've never actually played in any concerts or at a dream location like Abravenal Hall, if that's what you mean."

Lucas's eyebrows climb higher. "Not exactly, no. I was actually wondering if, like, you know how to play 'Mary Had a Little Lamb' with both hands or something? That's more my standard of excellence."

"Ah. Gotcha. Then yeah, I can do that."

"Huh." Lucas chews on the inside of his lip, looking at me thoughtfully out of the corner of his eye. "I get the sense that you're being modest right now."

"Not exactly."

"I think you are. What's the hardest song you can play?"

"I...well, I enjoy playing Chopin's *Fantaisie-Impromptu* in C♯ minor. I've been working on perfecting it for a long time now, but cancer treatments keep getting in the way of practice." I grimace as I remember all the times I puked over a toilet, then lay bedridden on the couch, staring at the piano while too sick to play. "It's a fast piece, really fast, and I kind of love that."

"Show it to me."

"What?"

"Play it for me on your phone. I want to hear this song before we get to Walmart. Please?"

"Lucas," I say, incredulous. "This is classical piano we're talking about. You'll be bored."

"Will not! Give me a little credit here. I may have been a jock in high school, but I also played some piano during my lifetime. Nothing classical, of course, but at least I knew my way around a keyboard. I want to hear how good you are."

I open my mouth, about to argue further. But the look Lucas gives me changes my mind. So, feeling flustered, I sigh and adjust the cannula beneath my nose. Talking so much is making me light-headed, and that's not a great thing when driving. "You're serious, aren't you?"

"I am. I'll never get classical from Brinley. I really want to hear this."

Sighing one last time, I look over at Lucas, at his pleading face and gorgeous blue eyes. Then I give in. Picking up my phone, I activate the voice recognition and speak into it hesitantly. "Play Frédéric Chopin's *Fantaisie-Impromptu* in C♯ minor."

I set the phone down. Then deliberately avoiding Lucas's eyes and judgment, I stare straight ahead out the windshield.

"Keep in mind, it took me *years* to get this fast," I tell him quietly, even as the rapid scales and arpeggios cascade from the stereo. "But, yeah. Welcome to my world, Lucas. Before cancer, classical piano was my life. And, well," I shrug, "it was supposed to be my future too."

"Holy crap," Lucas whispers, his eyes growing wide. Then he looks over at me, his mouth gaping. "Holy crap, Alex. You've been holding out on me!"

Embarrassed, I laugh and shake my head, feeling really self-conscious. "Have not! I've never lied to you about this. You just never asked."

LUCAS

I don't feel quite the same around Alex after she plays Chopin's "Fantastic Impromptu" for me, or whatever the heck it's called. I mean, here is this seventeen-year-old girl with no fat or muscle, desperately short hair, and who lugs around a black backpack with a portable oxygen tank inside. And this whole time, she's been a prodigy! Or at least, she's been severely gifted. Or determined. Or something along those lines. That classical piano piece she played for me was absolutely no joke. And to top it off, I've seen the upright piano in her living room. It is a dingy little thing that has to be a million and a half years old. The fact that she can play a piece like *that* on *that* thing, without it entirely falling to splinters, really means she's impressive. No, miraculous.

And the more time I spend around Alex, the more I begin to feel like she, not just as a pianist but also as a person, is miraculous. After all, she can see me. She can hear me. She cares about my problems. And even though Brinley was so rude to her, she hasn't given up on my sister.

As we walk through the store, I keep stealing glances at Alex out of the corner of my eye, thinking how I've never met anyone else like her. Because here we are, wandering in Walmart, two total misfits. I'm a spirit, and she's a teenage girl driving one of those old-people carts. Before coming into the store, Alex explained to me that she only has forty percent lung capacity left and has really bad anemia. Basically, her body sucks at first getting oxygen into her bloodstream, and then second, transporting that little bit of oxygen throughout her body. The perks, she said, of having bone marrow cancer and really low red blood cell counts. So without the cart, she told me she would tire and get lightheaded really quickly.

But I don't care. Or at least, it doesn't change my perception of Alex, except to make me think more highly of her. Since I am technically invisible to the general public, Alex can't really look at me or talk to me while we wander around the store. But I can look at her, and look at her I do.

I can also talk to her, and talk to her I do. In normal volume, I direct her where to go in the store. I tell her what aisles to go down, what duffle bag to pick for Brinley, what sizes of clothing she wears and what her style is like, and finally what hygiene items she typically uses.

After nearly an hour, we end the trip by going down the food aisles, picking easy-to-prepare microwave meals, sandwich stuff, and plenty of snacks. Alex still hasn't told her mom or Craig about our crazy plan, and she is tiring fast. So realizing that her energy clock is ticking, we check out, hop into the car, and head back to her house.

I stand by her side, unseen and unheard, as Alex sits down with her mother at their dining room table and informs her that she is leaving for the weekend. Eileen is stunned and, as anticipated, demands to know why. Alex carefully explains that while her health is still good enough, she wants to go on one last road trip. Alone. She doesn't want her mom or Craig to come because she wants time to think about her death and process things on her own.

Eileen, of course, insists that she can't. She's worried there could be a medical emergency. She barters with her daughter, taking different angles, and pleads with her in every way possible. But Alex is completely adamant. While being kind yet firm, she reminds her mother that she is almost an adult and that this personal trip is one of her dying wishes. Besides, it will just be for one weekend, just a few days, and it's for her mental health. And though she doesn't say it, it's actually for Brinley's mental health. She never tells her mom that Brinley is the true reason for this trip, and she never mentions that she's going to be bringing a stranger.

Finally, after enough rebuttals, Eileen has no solid arguments left. She seems stressed and concerned but reluctantly agrees. She promises Alex she'll help her pack in the morning and, in a sharp tone, tells her to go to bed. After all, though it's only eight o'clock on a Thursday night, Alex is absolutely wilting. Shopping took a toll on her.

Eileen grabs her daughter's elbows, keeping her steady as she helps Alex stand then walk to her bedroom. I follow close behind, anxious for Alex and wrestling with a pang of jealousy. The feeling is unexpected, but for a moment, I intensely wish that I could replace Eileen. I wish I could be the one supporting Alex. Touching her elbow. Holding her up. Strengthening her and helping her stand.

Because Alex has done *so* much for me. And all I want to do is something kind in return. Just to be real and tangible and there for her, just this once.

But it's a pointless longing. I can't. And after Alex collapses on the bed, I watch her mother continue to help. She turns on her oxygen machine and places a large mask over Alex's mouth and nose. Alex's eyes keep flickering to mine, and I can sense that my presence embarrasses her.

She doesn't want to be seen like this. She doesn't want me watching. So with a small wave from my hip, I give her a sad smile.

"I'll see you tomorrow," I say softly. "Thank you for everything today. Really." Eileen doesn't hear, but Alex does. Above her mask she blinks once, hard, in acknowledgement. And perhaps, beneath her mask, she gives me a weak smile? Then her eyes close in exhaustion, and she turns her head away to sleep.

I steal out of her room, walking through her far wall and into the crisp, Albuquerque night air. I take a deep, false breath, then angle myself towards home. Shoving my hands deep into my pockets, I prepare myself for another long night of watching Brinley cut.

Only hopefully, if all goes well tomorrow, this could be her final time doing it.

CHAPTER TWELVE

BRINLEY

It is Friday, a full week and a half after the fiasco with Alexia Ahmed, and I still can't get her out of my mind. Or more precisely, I still can't get her stupid letter out of my mind. The letter that Lucas supposedly told her to write. The letter that I've been ruminating about all day, doodling about it in the side margins of my homework, and pressing my palm against my bloody forearm in punishment for. It hurts whenever I do, whenever I add pressure against my sleeve and the gauze bandaging underneath, but I want it to. I want it to hurt. I want it to ache and sting and throb every time I think about that letter, and I want to physically hurt myself for not taking it.

Because it was stupid that I didn't. That idiotic blunder made me curious. Painfully, stupidly curious. If I had just taken that letter, if I had just snatched it from Alex's hands then walked inside and slammed the door with it in my possession, then I could have been dead by now. I could have carried through with my plan even yesterday if I had wanted to, and everything could have been done and finished and over with. I could have been free from this pain. From my guilt.

But no. Instead, I am alive. Instead, I sit here, doodling about a really stupid, aggravating letter. And the pill bottle I have in my backpack is still left unopened, untried, and unused. It's a really stupid thing.

I keep doodling even harder as I think through this, pressing my free hand against my burning arm as I draw, stoking the pain until the bell rings. When it does, I don't wait. I stand up abruptly and immediately. I shove my things into my backpack, moving as quickly as I can, then I fling it over my shoulders and move to leave the room. But just as I do, Savannah stands up. She sits next to the door, and she waves to catch my attention.

"Brinley—" she starts to say. But I don't need to think about how to react. It's a habit. It's ingrained in me. And just like I've been doing for months, I deliberately choose to ignore her. As if I didn't hear, I storm past Savannah and push my way out of the room, the first one to leave for the day.

Because after all, I'm not the only reason that Lucas is

dead. Savannah's party is the whole reason he was out on Unser Boulevard that night. He caught me sneaking out of the house that Friday, and instead of turning me in to our parents, he decided to drive me to her house himself. He wanted to save me from breaking the law because I don't have a full license yet. He wanted to save me from my parents and their wrath if they found out. He wanted me to attend that party and have fun and be wild and be popular. So Savannah, and all my friends, really, are as much to blame for his death as I am. They are the reason he died after dropping me off.

At least, that's the lie I tell myself. That cyclical, repeating lie is my sad, sorry attempt to alleviate some pain. Because if Savannah is to blame, then I'm not the only monster here. I'm not the only killer in this school. She would be too. And Kaitlyn. And Emily. And I would no longer be the only hideous murderer.

But in my sad and gruesome reality, I know that isn't true. I'm too smart to believe my own lie. I know they didn't kill Lucas. They didn't pull him onto the road at one o'clock in the morning like I did. They didn't let him drive them to a party. They didn't sit there as he laughed and joked about dumb boys, then made me solemnly swear to text him if I needed a ride home. He told me that if anything went wrong, he would have my back. He would always have my back.

Because Lucas loved me. He loved me. And I killed him.

Tears are pooling in my eyes as I think of this, as I push the school doors open wide in front of me. The classroom I left is one of the closest to the exit, and I'm fleeing so fast that I'm one of the first students to leave the school for the day. Not many people are milling about in the courtyard yet, and that's a relief. Because honestly, I am breaking down. Gritting my teeth, I hold back the tears and walk even faster towards my bus, trying to beat the crowds. I look down, fumbling in my pocket. My earbuds are in there, and I can't wait a moment longer to put them in and drown everything else out.

But as I look down to grab them, something happens. Someone calls my name. I ignore it. Then moments later, someone steps in front of me. I see their feet, simply because I'm looking at the sidewalk, but I don't see much else. I yelp, shocked. But I don't have time to react. Even as I throw on the brakes, locking my knees, I collide right into Alexia Ahmed, and both of us go sprawling to the ground, smacking the sidewalk hard.

Alex hits first, landing on her side and cushioning my fall. Beneath me, she gasps. She groans.

"Alex?" I cry out, shocked. She is pinned beneath me on the cement, and she's so rail-thin and emaciated that landing on her felt like landing on a pile of sticks.

Beneath me, Alex groans again, coughing. I stare at her,

still in shock, not understanding what happened. Then as the doors fly open behind me and more students come milling out, I scramble to my feet. Not wanting them to think that I tackled the girl or something—although I kind of did—I reach down and yank Alex to her feet. She stumbles as I do, doubling over. And as she stands, she sways.

"Ahg," she gasps between her teeth, pressing a hand to her side. I'm afraid that if I let her go, she will topple over. So instead, I grab her by the elbow and start dragging her to the side of the school, out of the way of the stampeding students. Stumbling, she follows behind. Once we are around the corner and out of sight, I whirl on her.

"Alex?" I say incredulously, releasing my grip on her elbow. When I do, Alex slumps heavily against the bricks of the school building, her hands pressed tightly to her ribs. She is wearing her backpack and oxygen tank, though the cannula is now knocked out of place. Gasping, she lifts a shaky hand and gets the tubing back under her nose. "Alex?" I repeat again, still not believing my eyes.

"Yes." Her answer is incredibly out of breath. She is still buckled over and cringes as she leans into the wall. "It's me."

"What are you doing here?" I demand, my voice getting louder and angrier, even though I don't mean it to. After all, isn't Alex *exactly* the person I've been wanting to see all day? Isn't this what I want? Isn't she precisely what I asked the universe for? "What the crap are you doing at my school? I mean at...our school?"

"I'm here—" Alex wheezes. She stops, breathes shallowly through her mouth a few times, then tries to straighten to a full stand. She is still leaning against the wall and still can't take her hands off her torso. But at least she's looking me in the eyes now. "I'm here to...talk...to you."

"To talk to me?" I cry, hardly believing my ears. I've been thinking about this girl so often, so repeatedly, so incessantly for the past two weeks, that it's unnerving to see her suddenly appear in front of me. She is a figment of my imagination come to life, come to haunt.

Only, with a sinking feeling in my gut, I realize that this can't be a coincidence. It's just too perfect to be a coincidence. Does the universe really, really want me to die so badly, then? Did it really just send me the final piece of my puzzle, the very thing that I've needed to feel confident in my death?

Am I really going through with this?

"You're here to talk to me?" I repeat, processing it. And then my mind whirls ahead. If Alex gives me that letter, I can read it on the bus. The pills are in my backpack. My parents won't be home. I could read it, know her farce, then do it. By night's end, I could do it.

At the thought, my heart slams hard against my chest,

trying to escape. It knows its fate. It knows what's coming.

"Yes," Alex whispers, gritting her teeth. Her eyes are pained, her expression contorted. "You didn't let me...finish...last time. You closed...the door on me. But I still have...more to say. We need...to talk."

"To talk? About what? That letter?" I bark out, my voice sounding really acidic. The fear, apparently, is making it toxic and mean.

Alex shakes her head, still grimacing and kind of gasping, yet trying to rein it in. "No. Not exactly. I...gave you a chance to read that letter...but you didn't... take it. So now, rather than have you...read...what it said, I'm going to...show you...what it said."

"Huh?" My mind is spinning. The pills in my backpack are feeling heavier, heavy like lead. "What are you saying?" I demand.

"Brinley, I want to show you why life is worth living," Alex pleads, her chocolate eyes growing wide as her knees buckle slightly. "But I'm not..." Alex's knees buckle even further and she groans. Gritting her teeth, she forces herself to straighten against the wall again, crying out in pain. "Just, please. I...I know things. I know about your cutting. I know about Lucas. I know about...about your plans. And please, Brinley, I just..." She stops, gasping in agony as she presses her hands harder against her ribs. She bites her bottom lip and for a second, it looks like she's about to slide down the wall and collapse to the ground. But she doesn't. She just moans, brokenly, and looks up at me with tears swimming in her eyes. "My car, please?" she begs quietly. "I have to sit."

"Are you...are you hurt?" I ask, suddenly feeling unsure.

"No, I just..." Alex cringes again, gasping. "I'll be...fine. Just...follow me."

And with that, she shoves herself off the wall and starts dragging her body to the parking lot. She's still hunched over, cradling her side, and it looks like she's about to collapse.

I hesitate, watching her. And then she stumbles and I leap forward. When I catch her elbow, Alex throws me a grateful glance. There are deep bruises under her brown eyes and I know she's hurting.

I tell myself that the reason I keep that grip on her arm and help her towards the parking lot is because I'm kind. This girl may be a weirdo, but she's sick and she needs my help. It's the nice thing to do.

But even though I tell myself that, I know it's not true. Not entirely. As I walk slowly beside Alex, steadying her as we head to her car together, I know that I'm not doing it because I am kind.

I'm doing it because I am curious. Lethally curious. And all I'm actually doing right now is helping Alex help me towards my goal.

ALEX

"Alex, Alex? What's wrong? Alex, you're hurt. Oh crap, please don't tell me you're hurt."

Lucas is standing beside me, keeping pace with Brinley and me. He's so worried, he is practically pulling out his hair as he scans me up and down. Though I can't say anything in front of Brinley, I yearn to answer him. I want to tell him that I'm fine, that he shouldn't worry about me. I want his attention to be on Brinley, and I want him to make sure that despite this little hiccup, our plan still moves forward.

But the thing is, deep down inside, I know I'm not actually fine. I can feel it. I can feel it in my ribs; I can feel it in my bones; I can feel it in the fiery, breathtaking pain lancing up my side and into my collarbone and neck. Because the thing about my cancer is, it started in my bone marrow. The soft center of my skeleton has been scarring over for years, affecting my blood production and hardening my bones into dry twigs. In these final months, I've developed osteosclerosis so severe, every part of me aches incessantly. And because my bones are brittle, the tumble I took with Brinley wasn't just a simple fall. The fire in my side is so great, I know I've fractured ribs. At least one.

Probably two. Likely even more. The pain is so debilitating that I can hardly breathe, can hardly think. And that just makes me even dizzier.

"Alex, come on. Give me something here. A head nod, a thumbs up. Anything."

Breathless, still being held up by Brinley as we stumble across the parking lot, I look at him. I raise both eyebrows, slightly nod, and Lucas raises his back. But he doesn't nod like I did. He still looks incredibly anxious.

"Brinley," I croak immediately after, hoping she didn't see our little exchange, "my car is that white one."

Brinley nods and slightly changes directions. Thankfully, I parked close to the school. I don't know if I could have made it much farther.

"Alex, we don't have to go forward with this," Lucas intones seriously. "Let's get you home. Just take Brinley back to my house, and let's get you to your parents. They'll know what to do."

But nauseous and dizzy with the agony, I only grimace. And almost imperceptibly, I shake my head. I know what will happen if I go to my mom. She'll take me to the hospital. I'll be cooped up there for hours, days, as they run test after test to make sure I'm ok. But in the end, all they will find is that I'm dying and that I have some broken ribs. There's nothing they can do for broken ribs. There's nothing they can do to stop me from dying. They'll just send me home and I'll be stuck in a bed forever, hovered over by my overprotective parents. I'll never get this chance again. Once my parents know that my bones are cracking—that this dreaded step of my death has begun—they will never let me out of their sight. They will never stop waiting on me hand and foot, trying to help. Because my cancer-stricken bones *aren't* going to heal. These ribs *aren't* going to fix themselves. Not at this stage in the cancer game. It's not like I can just wait for them to get better, then try to save Brinley's life later.

No. Despite what Lucas says, I can't take Brinley home. Time is ticking and this is my only remaining chance. *Our* only chance, before I become too bedridden, broken, and sick to try.

My painful, torturous death is inevitable. But Brinley's doesn't have to be.

Brinley's doesn't have to be.

BRINLEY

"Thank you," Alex gasps, collapsing against the car when I lead her to the driver's side. Trembling, she leans against the frame and, with the hand not pressed to her ribs, she grasps the door handle and yanks. But she is weak and it doesn't open. What's more, the simple movement has her crying out in pain and clutching at her side again. It looks like she is about to cry, about to faint. So I reach around her and pull the door open. Again telling myself that I'm doing it because I am kind.

Of course I'm doing it because I am kind.

"Thank you," Alex whispers again. Gritting her teeth, she delicately removes the backpack from off her shoulders. She leaves the tubing looped around her ears and the cannula beneath her nose, but she sets the backpack gingerly on the floor of the car. Then she follows suit, lowering herself into the driver's seat.

Still unsure of myself, I stand awkwardly just outside Alex's door. Looking over at me, panting, she jerks her head at the passenger seat.

"Get in," she says.

And mechanically, numbly, I obey. Not because I'm curious, but because I'm concerned about her. I need to make sure this sick girl makes it home, I tell myself. I'm not doing it because of the letter.

I climb in. Close the door. Then looking over at her pale, sweaty face, I ask, "Are you ok?"

"Yes, I'm...I'm fine."

"You don't look fine. I don't think you should be driving."

Leaning her head back against the seat, Alex winces. "Do you have your license?"

"No. Just my learner's permit."

She grimaces deeply, and her eyes grow tight. "I thought so. But it's fine. I'll just drive then."

"So, what? You're taking me back home?"

"Not exactly."

I freeze. "What do you mean not exactly?"

"I have different plans."

"And those plans are...?"

Alex opens her mouth to answer, then closes it again, jaw tight. But it's not because she can't think of what to say, but because another wave of pain has hit her. The fingers of one hand tighten like talons on the steering wheel. The other she fists and puts in her mouth, biting down.

"Oh gosh," she says, her words sounding like a sob as they come out muffled around her fist. "This wasn't supposed to happen."

And now I'm getting scared. I'm realizing more and more that this girl is injured. Like seriously, this girl is injured. Images of Lucas's body and the crumpled car flash through my mind. Panic floods my veins.

Whoever this girl is, I did this to her. Just like Lucas, I did this to her.

Groaning, Alex removes her hand from her mouth and takes a deep breath. She coughs, the breath interrupted, then tries again. And again. Finally, she succeeds in getting an unbroken gasp of air. She looks over at me. And through whatever she's feeling, I see a flash of determination light her eyes.

"I know your brother," she tells me suddenly, almost growling.

At her words, the panic floods through my veins faster, but I don't let it show. I can't. Carefully, I keep my voice deadpan as I answer.

"My brother is dead."

"I know that. But I've seen him. Stay put and hear me out. Ok, Brinley? Like I told you before, I have cancer. The doctors told me I have five months left to live, but I suspect it might be less than that. I feel so terrible, it has to be less than that. And for whatever reason—*whatever reason*—I've seen things. Ask me a question about your brother."

"What?" I balk, incredulous.

"Ask me a question about your brother," she growls again through clenched teeth.

I look at her, shocked. Then, "No," I say. "No. I don't know what kind of sick game you're trying to play right now, but I am not playing along."

"Fine then," Alex spits. She stops, clenching the steering wheel tightly again, then continues. "I'll tell you about him. He died in a car accident five months ago. He was hit head-on by a drunk driver. He was wearing a white T-shirt and a pair of faded blue jeans that night. He was a cheerleader for your school, and his best friend was Rory Campbell."

"No duh! Everyone knows that!"

"Oh yeah? Well I know more. I know he misses you. He misses your family. Sometimes when you go home after school and watch *The Bachelorette*, he sits on the ground next to you and watches it with you. He hates seeing you get ready for the day because he knows how often you cry when you look in the mirror. He knows you fought with your mom last night and told her that you hate her. But afterwards, he also saw you go into your room and cry really, really hard about it. You wrote her a letter. You told her that you don't really hate her, and that you hope she doesn't remember you said that after you die. But you didn't give her the letter. You never give her those letters. You keep them in a box under your bed, one with a lock on it. You keep the key to the lock under your pillow. Your plan is that after you die, your parents will find the key and read them. You want them to read all the letters you've ever written, so they'll know how deeply you wanted to die. You think that will comfort them. Only it won't, Brinley. It won't!" Alex's voice swells with emotion, her expression more pained, more pleading. "Don't you get that? Because Lucas? He hates those letters! He hates them, Brinley! He sobs because of them. He sobs because he loves you and he doesn't want you to die. He feels like he *can't* let you die. Nothing agonizes him more than the thought that you actually believe you should kill yourself. And that's why he came to me. He showed up in my hospital room as a spirit after my lung surgery, and he asked that I help you out. Because apparently, I am dying and no one else can see him. For the past several weeks, he has been *begging* me to help you. And he's sitting here in the car with us, right here, right now, anxious for your answer. He needs to know that you'll keep on living. He needs you to promise him that you will! Your brother loves you, Brinley. Lucas loves you. And he desperately wants you to live."

CHAPTER THIRTEEN

BRINLEY

It was the wrong idea to listen to Alex. If I had known what was good for me, I would have gone running headlong towards the bus the moment I bumped into her. I mean, I had thought Alex was a creeper the first time I met her, and turns out, I was right. My intuition was spot-on. Alexia Ahmed *is* a creeper. But also, she is an incredibly, horrifyingly correct creeper.

And for that reason, I start crying. And I can't stop crying.

"Brinley?" Alex eventually asks, out of breath and coughing ever so slightly. "Brinley, come on. Are you ok?"

But I just howl and yank on the door handle, trying to get out. When it doesn't work, I bury my face in my hands, my shoulders heaving. I've never before had an emotional breakdown quite as severe as this one, and I'm an absolute wreck. It's like my emotions are a pack of stallions that have finally gotten loose, and under no circumstance do they want to be reined back in.

"Look, Brinley, I'm...I'm going to start driving now, ok? Lucas is here and we are taking you on a road trip. A two-day road trip to Utah, just for the weekend. All right? I wrote that letter to tell you why it's important to keep living, but I'm not going to give it to you. Instead, I'm going to show it to you. I'm going to show you why life is so worthwhile. And...and Lucas is going to show you too. He's sitting in the back seat right now, listening to everything we say."

Again, I howl. My face in my hands, I can hardly function.

"Brinley, is that ok? I don't want this to be a kidnapping, so I would really prefer if you agree to this first. It's what Lucas wants, I promise. And I think it's really important."

My throat constricted, my face buried and ugly with tears, I croak out a harsh, shrill, "Just go!"

I don't see her; I can't see anything past my hands and tears. But I can feel Alex hesitate. "Brinley, I—"

"Just go!" I shriek again.

And this time, Alex listens. I feel as she reaches down, shifting the car into reverse, and backs out of the parking stall. I feel as the car then glides forward smoothly over the new pavement and comes to a stop at the exit of the parking lot. I also feel as she angles her wheels to the left and turns on the blinker. Lifting my tear-streaked face from my hands, I shriek at her again.

"No! Not that way!"

Alex jumps and looks over at me in bewilderment.

"That's the way to my house! No! Go the other way!"

"Does that mean you do want to go on the road trip with us?"

I sob, and I don't answer. Instead, I bury my face into the crook of my elbow and throw myself against the frame of the door, my shoulders heaving with sobs. After another long hesitation, Alex finally seems to get a clue, and she cranks the wheels the other way. I hear her flip the turn signal.

"Ok. I'm going to go the other direction," she tells me. "I'm going to drive us out of Albuquerque and I'm just going to keep driving. Tell me now if you want to go home, or we aren't stopping."

I don't answer her. And Alex doesn't stop. True to her word, she pulls out of the parking lot and drives the two of us—perhaps three of us if she can be believed—out of the town where I was born and raised.

LUCAS

Brinley is a mess. Alex is a mess. I am a mess. But perhaps Brinley is the biggest mess out of us all. Because the thing is, she doesn't stop crying. Ever. The minutes tick by. Then an hour. Then an hour and a half. And nothing. She still has her face pressed against the crook of her elbow, buried against the passenger-side door, and her shoulders don't stop heaving. Alex drives us nervously through Albuquerque and towards Grants. Then she drives us through Grants. Two hours pass, and still, she's driving and Brinley is crying. And although Brinley's problems are the most obvious, I can tell that Alex is really suffering too.

"Alex," I murmur. It's the first time I've spoken since we left the school. Alex startles slightly and looks at me in the rearview mirror. But she doesn't say anything. Talking to me would only creep out Brinley more.

"You're not doing ok," I say, my voice tight with worry, my volume low. I don't need to be quiet, since Brinley can't hear me, but it's a habit.

Alex's eyes tighten and her grip gets harder on the steering wheel. But otherwise, she shakes her head. She's trying to convince me that she's fine, but I'm not buying it. Her shoulders have been hunched in pain for the last hour, and though her eyes always remain riveted on the road, her head keeps dipping lower and lower, centimeter by centimeter, on her neck. She's hurting, and she's tired. She was exhausted before we even left.

"You need to pull over," I tell her.

Again, she shakes her head. And rather than keep looking at me, she stubbornly returns her gaze to the road.

"I'm not kidding about this, Alex," I say, my voice getting louder and more adamant. Next to us, Brinley is continuing to sob. It has us both on edge. "I'm not going to let you hurt yourself like this, not for me and not for my sister. Brinley is fine. She's coming along. It's not like she can back out now. Let's just find a motel in Gallup and get you some rest as soon as possible. You're scaring me."

"I'm fine," she whispers, so quietly I doubt Brinley can hear it over her tears.

"No, don't say that. I can see it in your eyes that you're not. Besides, my guess is you have a migraine on top of whatever is wrong with your side, and it's not safe to drive with a migraine. Pull over in Gallup. Please."

"But what about Orderville?" she whispers. Only this time, Brinley certainly hears. Her sobs hitch, and her head lifts a miniscule amount off her arm, as if she's listening. Alex grits her teeth, cursing herself. I lean back in the seat, quiet now.

A moment passes and then, "Hey, Brinley," Alex says. Her voice at full volume really is haggard and exhausted-sounding. Brinley doesn't reply.

"I hate to say this, but I'm feeling really awful. I was hoping to make it to Utah tonight, but we've gotta pull over. Mind if we get a motel in Gallup for the night? I'll call my mom to check in with her, and maybe you can call yours? It's probably not good if we let her worry. Your parents don't know where you are."

Brinley's body stiffens, but she doesn't respond. Knowing her, she's probably worried out of her mind about my parents and their reaction.

"You can tell them the truth. Tell them I'm taking you on a weekend road trip. You can even give them my number or my mom's number. We'll talk to them if needed. But uh, I really do have to stop. Soon. And Gallup is just fifteen minutes away. Is that ok?"

Brinley is quiet for a long moment. Then there is a quiet, almost inaudible whisper. "Ok."

Thankfully, Alex hears it. She nods and returns her gaze back to the road, her expression anxious and pained. I watch, worried, and don't take my eyes off her as she speeds through the empty desert and drives us into Gallup.

BRINLEY

I finally lift my head when we get into the city, somewhat surprised to see how far we've come. We really are in Gallup, a rural desert community on the edge of the Navajo Nation. Looking at the clock, it reads 5:34 at night. We've been driving for over two hours, and Alex is right. I haven't touched base with my parents. They're probably home from work by now and will be wondering where I am, so I take out my phone and text them.

Hey, I'm not coming home tonight. I'm fine though. I'll call you in the morning.

And then I darken the screen and turn off my phone. Completely.

"I texted them," I say quietly, my voice husky from the tears.

"Huh?" Alex glances over at me.

"I texted my parents. I'll call them in the morning." And then I turn away from her and stare out the window, wiping the tears off my cheeks. Thankfully, Alex doesn't press me. She stays quiet.

I keep my gaze focused out the window as we weave our way through Gallup, eyes roaming the dry landscape and the historic tourist shops that line Main Street. It seems that almost every storefront we pass is advertising the same thing: Native American rugs, turquoise jewelry, and pottery. Known as the "Heart of Indian Country," most people from New Mexico have passed through Gallup at least once on a road trip. The city borders Arizona, is situated on Route 66, and is an important place to stop for gas. I've driven through here a couple times with Lucas and my parents, but we've never stopped except to use the restroom. It's strange to be back and, this time, to know I'll be spending the night.

Alex soon drives us through the main part of town and turns into the parking lot of an old, two-story Motel 6. The building's exterior is made of white stucco that's yellowing with age, and the blue metal doors to each room are so sun-bleached and weatherworn, it's a wonder they haven't fallen off their hinges. I grow uneasy as Alex pulls up to the main office where a large, shredded welcome banner is strewn out front. She parks the car, but she doesn't get out. Instead, she leans her head back against the seat and her eyes flutter closed above her cannula. I watch her for a moment, getting even more nervous when her eyes don't open again. They are deeply bruised underneath, and it's almost as if she has two black eyes.

"Brinley?" she finally says, her voice weak.

"Yes?"

"If I give you my card, can you get us a room?"

"I...I've never done that before."

"It's easy." This time her eyes do open. Grimacing, she gingerly leans forward and fishes a small, cute leather wallet out of the backpack at her feet. With trembling fingers, she opens it and pulls out a debit card. "Just go in there and tell them you want a room with two queen beds. Lucas passes through furniture anyways, so he doesn't need one for himself. Besides, he doesn't sleep."

I look at her, my eyes bulging, but she doesn't seem to notice. Alex's words are slurring slightly, and the moment she's done talking, she leans her head back again. Hesitantly, I take the card from her.

"Thank you," she whispers hoarsely, her large, brown eyes tortured. "I wish I felt well enough to do it myself."

And with that, she turns away from me and closes her eyes yet again, holding a hand against her ribs.

LUCAS

Brinley has to help Alex. At first, it doesn't seem like Alex is going to let her. Stubbornly, she yanks herself out of the front seat and supports herself against the frame of the car. Her face is pale and her whole body is trembling. She seems to have a hard time keeping her eyes open, as if just standing is enough to make her pass out. Brinley stands anxiously to the side, looking very worried. Like me, she's never really been around sick people before. Or at least, not people sick like this.

"Hey, if I pass out..." Alex says to Brinley, her words thick as she leans heavily against the car, "don't worry, yeah?" Her eyes are closed and her head is starting to dip towards the ground as if pulled by an invisible magnet.

But her words only freak out Brinley more. Her own face grows pale. "Um. Wh-what do you mean?"

"I just...sometimes...I can't get enough air. But it...usually passes. Can you..." Alex pauses, taking a shallow breath through her cannula. "Can you...grab the...duffle bags? They're in the trunk. Lucas and I...packed you one. He told me what...sizes you wear...what...clothes you would need."

Brinley's eyes grow huge and she looks down at her feet, incredibly uncomfortable. But Alex is so far gone she doesn't notice. She just leans further against the car, eyes closed, trying to breathe.

"We also have...food. We went...shopping. I'm not hungry. But if you are...help...yourself."

And with that, Alex grits her teeth, and by sheer force of will, pulls her eyes open. She takes several deep breaths, head bowed, then pushes herself off the car. But as she does, she stumbles. Thank goodness Brinley is close enough to catch her, because even though I jumped forward in panic, I would have been useless. Totally and utterly useless.

"Good job, Brinley," I murmur, hands half outstretched as I watch her steady Alex. "You're doing great. Take care of her for me."

Alex hears my comment and looks down at the asphalt, blushing furiously. "Sorry," she croaks, agonized. Whether to Brinley or to me, I'm not sure. "I haven't been this bad...in a while. It's been a...long day."

"It's ok," Brinley offers timidly. "I'll help you get inside."

My brotherly heart swells with pride as I watch Brinley loop an arm around Alex and help her hobble towards their room. Thankfully it's on the bottom level, and Brinley gets the door unlocked and Alex to a bed in no time. She gingerly lowers Alex to sit on the edge of the mattress, then asks if she's ok, brow furrowed. Like I knew she would, Alex nods. She forces a smile and insists that she's fine. Then, seeming embarrassed that she can't help, she politely asks Brinley to bring in their luggage. Brinley agrees eagerly, desperate for something to do.

I watch and, like Alex, feel bad that I can't help Brinley unload the car. Though this trip is intended to last just a weekend, there is a lot to carry in. Alex packed a cooler, a case of water bottles, large oxygen tanks for the nighttime, and multiple duffle bags. Brinley, as slight as she is, struggles under the weight. But eventually, she gets everything in. By the time she does, Alex has laid herself back on the pillows, pressing a hand against her side and staring with exhausted, pained eyes at the ceiling. She weakly asks Brinley to bring her a box of meds from one of the duffle bags and promptly takes them. Then with a sigh and a pained, hacking cough, she lets her eyes slide closed. Within minutes, she's asleep—shoes on, fully dressed, and lying on the covers.

At this point, Brinley gets intensely worried. I can tell she doesn't know what to do with herself. She gnaws on her lower lip as she looks at Alex, then looks around the room, then looks at Alex again. Eventually, she wanders to the window and peeps between the curtains, eyes searching the gathering dusk. I stand close by her side, as close as I dare, and watch her with an aching longing. I yearn to reach out and speak with my sister, to assure her that I'm near, to hug her and tell her that everything will be all right. She's scared, terrified, and I don't want her to be. With all the sincerity I can muster, I close my eyes and imagine hugging her, trying to radiate my love for her. It doesn't work. Of course, it doesn't. She can't feel it and nothing about Brinley's demeanor changes. But at least my efforts allow me to feel like I'm trying.

As time passes, Brinley steps away from the window and settles in. She heads for the cooler that Alex packed and, after searching through the contents, pulls out a microwavable meal. She heats it up, filling the room with a growing scent of lasagna, then plops herself on her bed. Grabbing the remote from the nightstand, she flips on the TV and, unfortunately, settles for a sappy show with loads of drama. And for the rest of the night, she stays there, staring numbly at the screen. Every so often, she looks over at Alex. And every so often, she searches the room with troubled eyes. Each time she does, I know she's thinking of me.

And yet, despite the discomfort evident on her face, Brinley doesn't cry again and she doesn't go to her backpack either. She doesn't pull out the razor that I know is nestled in the small, front pocket. And she doesn't lock herself in the bathroom to cut.

I mean, Alex is asleep. I can't be seen. And yet Brinley doesn't self-harm.

So no matter how imperfectly this day may have turned out, no matter how semi-disastrous it was, at least we had this little win.

Despite all odds, sweet Alex is pulling off a miracle.

CHAPTER FOURTEEN

ALEX

It's pitch dark when I gasp awake, wheezing and choking on the fire. My chest is being squeezed, my lungs are screaming in agony, and my head is absolutely splitting. The pain is sickening, dizzying, whirling, and violent as it burns. In a panic, I fumble for my cannula, desperate to take a breath. Like always, the tubing is underneath my nose. But unlike always, the steady stream of air that I've come to rely on isn't there. The tank, the small travel-sized tank that I brought in from the car in my backpack, is empty. It's been on for hours. It doesn't have hours of oxygen to give.

Gasping and near crying, I roll and slide off the bed to my knees. The vertigo is fanatical, cackling at me like flames, and I nearly puke. I nearly collapse too. I'm on my knees, clinging to the bedding, knotting my hands in the comforter and trying with desperate terror to keep myself upright. Bright spots burst across my vision like explosions, and next thing I know, the whole world spins. My cheek is pressed against carpet.

"Alex?" A voice reverberates in the heated darkness, a boy's voice. "Alex, are you ok?" It's getting nearer to me, and I want to plead with it to stop. The volume of its words is splitting my head open, crushing my skull like an iron vice. I cry out in pain, a strangled, choking sound, and suddenly lose all bearings.

Moments later, I hear the voice again, calling me back to the fire, the smoke, back to the pain. "Alex?" It sounds distant, so very distant. Everything is erupting. Everything is numb. Everything is spinning. "Alex, stay with me! What's happening? What's wrong? Tell me what to do!"

But I can't, I don't. I can't breathe, let alone speak. Mustering all my ebbing strength, I reach out a hand and claw at the ground. It hurts, I want to shriek, it sends fire lancing up my side. But despite the agony I inch forward, crawling and dragging my carcass across the floor. If I remember correctly, Brinley brought in the oxygen tanks. She placed one at the foot of my bed. If I can just get to it. If I can just reconnect my oxygen tube.

The rest, what happens next, is a violent blur. I can hardly remember, can hardly understand. The splitting in my skull, the spinning vertigo, the fire coursing through my lungs. There's a voice calling to me through the darkness, yelling at me where to place my hands, what to do, how to continue. I follow the commands. At least, I think I do. Several times I must pass out, but the voice keeps screaming at me, reminding me what I'm doing. Reminding me that I'm here.

Finally, after an interminable amount of time, my body coated in slick sweat and every muscle trembling, I get a tube connected. The voice cheers. A blessed stream of air returns to my nostrils and I lie on my back on the carpet, gasping for life like a fish out of water.

Slowly, gradually, the fire recedes. The vertigo steadies. And though my head continues to pound and my muscles continue to cramp and scream, I can make sense of things again.

"Alex. Alex? Are you all right? Please, *please*, tell me you're all right." The voice is Lucas's. His silhouette is crouched near me, his voice strangled with unshed tears.

"Luc...as?" I wheeze, my whole body numb, my head still pitching and heaving.

"Yes, yes! It's me. Alex, it's me. Are you all right? Can you breathe? Is it working?"

"Lucas," I moan dizzily again.

"Yes, yes. I'm here. I swear to you, I'm here."

"Lucas, I'm dying."

"What? No! No! You're not! Alex, you're alive! Do you

hear me? You're alive. You're not dying. You're not dying!" His own voice grows choked, desperate with emotion. "You can't be!"

I open my mouth, wanting to speak, but it's difficult. My eyes roll with the vertigo and my teeth clench in pain. The oxygen may be flowing, but my brain is still under attack. My body and thoughts are still racked with inexpressible pressure, ravaged with a lack of air and limited by cancer-torn lungs. They struggle to breathe, even when air is offered.

But what is it that I would say to him anyway? That death is inevitable? That if it doesn't visit me in this moment, it will visit me in the next? My fate is to run from a monster destined to catch me, to be consumed by a flame already licking at my heels.

I told Lucas that I am dying. And though he said I wasn't, we both knew it was a lie.

The carpet, pressed against my sweaty and trembling palms, is a testament that he was lying.

*****

"You were talking to Lucas in your sleep," Brinley tells me the moment I open my eyes. At first, I'm incredibly disoriented. I'm on the ground, and I'm not in my room. I'm wearing shoes, and I'm still in the same T-shirt and jeans I put on yesterday. It takes me a while but blinking, I eventually realize I'm in Gallup.

"What?" I groan blearily, rubbing at my eyes.

"I said you were talking to Lucas in your sleep."

"Oh." I rub my eyes harder, then stop, looking around the room. For some weird reason, Lucas is nowhere to be seen. And there is a dull, aching throb emanating from the back of my head and radiating to the front. With breathtaking fervor, there is also a blazing pain along the left side of my rib cage. In strange, jilting images, splashes of memory flood back to me. Splashes of falling off the bed, not being able to breathe, and a brain-splitting, fiery migraine. Shocked, I look down at my oxygen tube, then over at the new, larger oxygen tank it's hooked up to. If all of that happened, then I truly am lucky to be alive.

"So really, I don't believe you anymore."

"Huh?" I'm having a hard time distinguishing the trail of thoughts in my own brain from the trail of thoughts flowing from Brinley's mouth. Everything is blurring together. As I stare at her, my stomach growls weakly.

"I don't believe you about Lucas's spirit. Because obviously, you're crazy. You're just a deluded lunatic who dreams about things and gets dreams mixed up with reality. You're on pain meds, you're delusional, and I don't believe you. I want to go back to Albuquerque. Now."

My brain is slow but at least it's powering back on.

Catching up to Brinley's meaning, I grunt. "Yeah? Well, I can hardly believe it myself. And...ugh...I hate that I'm on the floor," I say, disgusted with myself. Trying not to moan, I stiffly push myself up, being gentle with my agonizing ribs. Gingerly, I seat myself on the edge of my disheveled bed, across from Brinley's perfectly made one. She's sitting on her mattress, facing me, arms and legs both crossed.

"What time is it anyway?" I ask, rubbing my forehead.

"9:10. You slept in."

I grunt. "So it seems. What time were you up?"

"It doesn't matter. I want to go home."

"Oh yeah? And do what? What are you going to do once you get home?"

Brinley doesn't answer me. Her jaw just clenches tight. Irked, I snort at her. "Uh-huh, I thought so. Look, I'm not in a very good mood right now. I actually almost died last night, and here I am, having to wake up and talk to a girl who wants to purposely off herself. You just don't get it, do you? You don't get what I would trade, what agony I would put myself through, if it just meant that I could swap places with you. If it just meant that I could have a little more time—the life you live, the health you take for granted."

"Oh really? You think you want this? You think you want my life?" Brinley scoffs, shaking her head incredulously. "Then fine, take it! I would swap with you any day," she says, her voice building towards a shout.

"Because I don't want it anymore!" To emphasize her point, she throws her hands out to her sides. She's wearing a short-sleeved shirt, one of the cotton ones Lucas and I bought for her to sleep in, and I can see every cut and line and scab she's created on her skin.

Sickened, I glare at her. And she glares back.

"No, that's not true," I say quietly, narrowing my eyes and shaking my head. "You do want to live. Desperately. Deep down inside, you do want your life. But the problem is you hate yourself. You're hurting, and you don't know how to stop the pain."

In response, Brinley doesn't say anything. Her jaw just clenches tighter. Slowly and deliberately, she folds her arms, hiding her scars, and keeps glaring.

"Look," I say, trying my best to stay calm. Trying my best to think through the headache and get through to her. "I know this might sound crazy to you, but I get it. I do. Probably better than you realize. Your pain is emotional and my pain is physical. But despite that difference, there are still moments—like last night—when my life hurts so badly that I wish I was dead too. Ok? At times, when the pain is at its worst, I *long* to be dead," I say truthfully. "But that doesn't mean that I stop living. And that doesn't mean that I stop trying. Because there are people out there who love me, Brinley, who would be devastated if I simply gave up and gave in. And there are people who would be devastated if you gave up too. So even though every moment hurts, and every breath hurts, and every day hurts, I keep living through my cancer. Day in and day out, as long as I possibly can. And I've made it my mission to teach you to do that too. No matter what it costs me, I'm going to teach you to live through pain. And I am not—*not*—going to take you home."

"But you're a liar," Brinley spits.

"About what? About Lucas? No, I'm not. I didn't lie to you about him. He's here in Gallup with us. But if you don't believe me, then fine." I throw up my hands, wincing when it tugs at my side. "I won't mention your brother again. Not if you don't want me to. But either way, I *am* completing this trip with you, and I *am* going to show you what you'll miss out on if you die. Because this trip, Brinley? It's my final one," I admit, my throat tightening with emotion. "I've been planning this trip for myself for *weeks*. I thought about it, dreamed about it, planned it, to get me through long, terrible nights in the hospital after surgery. I was going to invite my parents to come with me. They would have *loved* to come. *I* would have loved them to come. But I didn't. I left them at home and chose to invite you, a stranger, instead. *Why*? Because regardless of what you think, your life matters, Brinley. It matters to me, it matters to Lucas, and it matters to this ridiculous, pain-filled world."

But at my words, Brinley's face twists in anger. She shakes her head vehemently, denying and denying and denying. "No. No! That's not true! None of that is true! You're lying to me!"

"Am I? Am I really?" I cry, my ribs aching, the burn in my lungs flaring. "I *am* dying, Brinley! I am! In less than six months, I will be in a coffin. My body will be decaying. But the crazy thing is, though I don't have a choice in my death, you do. You can choose to live. You can choose to keep your life. And if you can't see what a privilege that is, if you can't understand how lucky you are to even have that choice, then I don't know how to help you," I say, my eyes welling up with tears. "I just don't, ok? I'm trying, but obviously it's not helping. So whatever. Call me a liar. Call me whatever you want. But would a liar really bring you on their final road trip? Would I really leave my family behind and pay for our motel, and pay for gas, and pay for food, and honestly try *so* hard? No! I wouldn't! Not if I were lying. I'm telling you the truth about everything," I say through my tears. "And whether you believe me or not is entirely up to you."

And with that, I shove myself off the mattress and painfully stand up. Still shaking from the ordeal of last night and the emotion of my monologue, I rip the cannula out of my nose. I throw it on the hotel bed and, clutching my side, I stumble for the door. I try to hold my head high as I yank it open and leave. I really try. But even as I do, I limp with pain, and I can't help the tears that fill my vision and pour down my cheeks.

CHAPTER FIFTEEN

LUCAS

Alex finds me outside by the motel pool, sitting on the edge and swinging my immaterial legs back and forth through the glassy, blue water. The liquid isn't so dense, so disconcerting as solids are, and I don't mind the slight tingling sensation it creates throughout my lower calves and feet. In fact, even though I don't make any ripples, I almost appreciate the false sensation. It's the closest thing to touch that I've felt in a long, long while.

Tearing my gaze away from the water, I look up as Alex approaches, terribly ashamed of myself. I'm about to open my mouth and beg for her forgiveness, to plead with her to forgive me for dragging her on this wretched trip. I prioritized Brinley's needs above hers, and I nearly got her killed. But as I'm about to speak, Alex's narrow face crumples. Before I can say a word, she drops to the ground in a squat, tightly hugs her shins to her chest, and buries her face in her knees, gasping. Both in pain and in tears.

"Alex?" I ask, immediately scrambling to my feet. "Alex, what's wrong? What happened?"

Running to her, I drop to my knees and reach out a hand, wanting to rub her back to comfort her. In fact, I kind of do. But my fingers pass through Alex's skin and the sensation is so repulsive, I can't take it. I yank my hand back, gasping, and Alex's shoulders only shake harder with tears.

"Lucas?" she whimpers, her voice small, broken, and muffled as she speaks into her knees.

"Yes, yes, what is it? Are you ok?"

"Lucas, this is hard. Everything about this is *so* hard."

I don't say anything for a moment. I can't, really. I've never seen Alex like this before. She's always been so strong since I've known her, so tough even in the worst of pain. It scares me to see her so shaken up.

Finally, I hang my head, crushed by the weight of what I've done and the agony I've caused her. "I'm sorry," I whisper. I bite the inside of my cheeks, and if I really could cry real tears, I'm pretty sure I would have started crying with her. I feel horrible, wretched, for my role in what Alex is feeling. And I know, deep in my bones, that I did something wrong and selfish by involving her in my life. Or rather, my lack of a life.

"Was Brinley rude to you?" I finally ask, forcing out the anguished words.

But Alex just shakes her head, still curled up in her tight ball, her feet flat on the ground. "No, she...she wasn't rude. She's fine. I just...Lucas, I'm scared," Alex blurts, lifting her tearstained face to look at me. The anguish on her face is almost palpable. "I'm *so* scared. I don't think I have five months left to live. I *can't*. I don't feel good enough to have five months left. And what if...what if I really had died last night? What if I really had stopped breathing? What would that have done to Brinley? What would that have done to my *parents?* I can't...I can't die, Lucas. I don't want to die yet! Please don't let me die!"

"Alex," I murmur, my heart absolutely breaking for her. I search her pained, pleading eyes, scrambling to find something, anything to say that could help. "It's not...it's...it's all right. Yesterday was a bad day, I know that. But don't let it get to you. You've gotta have hope, yeah? Things are going to be ok. You're going—"

And just then Brinley's voice rings out across the pool deck, making both of us jump. "Talking to Lucas?" she says bitterly, her tone sour.

Alex whirls to her feet, turning towards the voice. Brinley is standing by the open gate to the pool, her arms crossed, her brow furrowed into a scowl.

Alex doesn't answer her. Instead, she grits her teeth and stares at the ground, hurriedly wiping her eyes with the heel of her hand. Brinley watches, and then sighs deeply. Unfolding her arms, she slowly steps forward.

"Look, I'm sorry. Ok? I didn't come here to get mad at you. I actually came here to apologize."

Alex's head snaps up, surprised. Then biting her bottom lip and still trying to rein in her emotions, she shakes her head. "No, you don't need to apologize," she says thickly. "You've done nothing wrong."

At that, Brinley snorts. "Ha, that's nice of you. But no. We both know that's not true." She comes to a stop in front of Alex, then gestures to the pool chairs. "How about we sit? To be honest, I don't like it when you stand. It makes me worry you're going to fall over."

I wince, knowing how deeply those words must bother Alex, especially when she's already panicked about her deteriorating health. But to her credit, Alex doesn't react negatively. She just nods and follows behind Brinley. They each take a seat in the hard, white plastic chairs, angling them towards each other. Alex sits stiffly, holding a hand to her side, and Brinley is the first to break the silence.

"Really though, were you talking to Lucas just now?" she asks, her brow furrowing again.

Alex takes a breath, and for a moment it looks like she's going to say yes. Then she stops herself and just shrugs.

"Maybe. I dunno. I thought that I was. But perhaps you're right. Maybe I really am just crazy."

There's real pain in the answer, making me cringe. Brinley purses her lips, looking Alex up and down. "Yeah, well...you knew about my cutting, didn't you?"

Alex shrugs.

"And my *Bachelorette*-watching habits."

Alex shrugs again.

"And my letters. So if you're crazy, then how did you know all that?"

Alex grimaces, staring at her fingers as she clenches and unclenches a hand. It's trembling subtly. "Beats me. Crazy good luck, maybe?"

Brinley scoffs. "Yeah, I would say so." She looks out at the pool, her brow furrowing. "You know, Alex, I actually want to believe you. I really do. It's just, you have to understand. You're wanting me to believe some *really* ridiculous stuff. Things that I almost want *too* much to believe, you know? And that's scary. I don't mean to be rude. I'm just kind of...guarded, is all."

"Well, yeah. That's understandable. If our roles were reversed, I would have a hard time believing all this too."

Brinley nods in acknowledgement, still looking out over the water. "Thanks. Thanks for saying that. I'm not super proud of how I've treated you. Of course I'm not. But I just...I want to know. Can you offer me any more proof?"

"Proof?" Alex raises her eyebrows. "What kind of proof do you want?"

Brinley hesitates, then bites her bottom lip hard. Tears are pooling in her own eyes, but she fights them back. "He's here? Lucas is here with us now?"

At such direct mention of me, I startle. And if I had a heart, I'm sure it would have started hammering. My palms, likely, would have started sweating too.

Alex nods. "Yeah, he is. He's right there." She points to where I'm standing a few feet away, precisely dead center at my chest. "He's watching you. He's really worried about you. He's gone to some pretty crazy lengths to make sure you're ok."

Brinley nods, trying to look at me but not quite succeeding. It's more like she's looking past me. "Ok..." she says slowly, still glancing in my general direction. "And, like, can he speak?"

"Definitely."

"Is he speaking now?"

"Not now, but...Lucas?" Alex asks, her voice changing slightly as she addresses me. "Do you want to say anything to Brinley?"

My heart, my nonexistent heart, nearly rips out of my chest. I open my mouth and close it a few times, not taking my eyes off Brinley. How long, how many weeks and months, have I been aching to speak to my sister? How desperately I've wanted this! And yet, when given the opportunity, I'm frozen. I'm almost paralyzed.

Alex is patient, seeming to understand what an emotional moment this is for me. And finally, I nod.

"Yeah. Yeah, I do," I say, speaking slowly with a husky voice. "Tell her I like her shoes. The new ones she was wearing yesterday. They look good on her."

Alex cocks her head, surprised. Then she turns back to Brinley. "He said he likes your shoes. The new ones you wore yesterday. He says they look good on you."

Brinley startles. She looks down at her feet, but she's barefoot and in pajamas right now. She looks back up. "My shoes? I guess that makes sense. Lucas always had a thing for high-top Converse. I bought them because they reminded me of him."

"Tell her I noticed."

"Lucas said he noticed. And also, he's touched. He's too manly to admit it, but I can see it written all over his face. He appreciates it," Alex adds, winking.

Brinley laughs a little, looking at Alex with wider and less guarded eyes. "Oh yeah?"

"Yup. Definitely. Lucas, is there anything else you want to say?"

"Uh, yeah. There is, actually." I clear my throat. "I want to redeem my reputation that you just slaughtered. Please explain to Brinley that even though I'm touched—which I am—that I'm still being very manly over here. Just because I like her shoes and all does not mean that I'm being an emotional baby wipe. Tell her that word for word, she'll like that."

Alex laughs but otherwise does as I ask, relaying what I say precisely as I said it, inflections and all. Brinley's eyes widen, and her mouth starts gaping open. Her eyes start darting frantically between Alex and the empty space just a little too far left, where she thinks I am. My words were strategic because "emotional baby wipe" used to be one of my favorite, weird phrases I used often in life. It was a Lucas quirk. Something that only I would say. And no one knows that better than Brinley.

"Anything else, Lucas?" Alex prods.

"Yeah, tell her to ask me stuff. Like, quiz me. Let's convince her I'm real once and for all. And tell her to make the questions hard. Really, really hard."

Alex, like the good friend she is, relays the message. In response, Brinley's brow furrows. But she also seems to be getting excited. She thinks for a while, pondering just the right question, then throws it like a spear at Alex.

"What's his favorite food?"

I answer, and Alex relays the information only half a second after I do. "Teriyaki lettuce wraps."

"What's his favorite color?"

"A pale shade of lime green? But um, he says that

favorite colors are lame. And to quit asking him kindergarten questions—he said to make them hard."

Brinley laughs. "A kindergarten question? Well, yeah, that sounds like him," she admits. "Ok, um, how about his favorite sport?"

"Oh, I can answer that one," Alex says immediately, not even bothering to wait for my response. "He was on the cheerleading team. I agree, you need to make these tougher."

"Ok, ok...um, how about this then? What did he get me for my twelfth birthday?"

I answer, and Alex looks at me, raising her eyebrows. Then she shakes her head and chuckles. "Apparently, he can't remember. That was the year your family went to Hawaii for your birthday, he said, so he's guessing he probably just picked up a crab and stuck it in your face or something. Does that sound accurate?"

"Uh, yeah. Yeah, it does. And where did we stay when we were in Hawaii?"

"At a bungalow? He says it looked really nice on the outside, but totally smelled like weed on the inside. Your mom was really upset about that and made you all sleep outside in hammocks that first night. Only, it rained on you guys, in the middle of the night." Alex laughs. "Seriously? Did that really happen? That's hilarious."

Brinley, grinning a little, bites her bottom lip and nods.

Her eyes are getting bright with excitement, and I can tell she's starting to believe us. "Yeah, that happened. Me and my mom went back inside, but Lucas convinced my dad to stay out in the rain with him. That lunatic," she mutters, rolling her eyes.

Alex grins wider, then encourages Brinley to ask another question.

And the game goes on, just like that, for the next fifteen minutes. I try to make my answers funny and throw in as much personality as I can. By the end of it, not only is Brinley laughing, but Alex kind of is too, the best that she can with injured ribs. And seeing her smile again after being so emotional makes me feel downright proud.

"Ok, ok," I finally say, rolling my eyes as the two girls continue to giggle at my most recent comment, which made fun of my dad's balding head and his obsession with regency dramas. "That's enough now. Tell Brinley this has been fun and all, but it's my turn to ask a question."

Alex, smiling even as she clutches her side with pained eyes, nods and turns to Brinley. "K, Brinley. Lucas just said that it's been fun and all, but that it's his turn to ask a question now. You ready for it?"

Getting somber, Brinley nods. "Yeah, I guess that's fair. Tell him that's fine."

"I don't need to. He can hear you. Lucas, you ready to ask?"

"Yup, I'm ready. Will you ask Brinley if she believes me or not already? And tell her that if she doesn't, I'm first going to kick her puny butt, and second, I'm going to start haunting Jonathan Michaels and scare him out of his wits. She's had a crush on the guy since first grade, and it's about time she fesses up to it."

Nearly word for word, Alex copies what I say. Brinley's eyes grow huge and wide, and she looks over at my empty spot again. Then her face blushes scarlet red. "I do not have a crush on Jonathan Michaels!"

"He says you do too."

"Do not!" And with that, Brinley jumps to her feet, her hands on her hips. "Alex, will you please tell Lucas that one, he's an idiot. And two, I don't believe him. At all! And no matter what he says, I never will!" Then Brinley turns on her heel and stomps away from the pool deck, her hands fisted on her hips and her face cherry red. I laugh as I watch her go and shake my head at her with the biggest, goofiest smile on my face.

"Oh, she believes me all right," I chuckle.

Alex, not able to help her own grin, shakes her head indulgently at me. "You really know how to push her buttons, don't you?"

"Sure do," I say proudly. "After all, I'm her brother. What do you expect?"

CHAPTER SIXTEEN

BRINLEY

Oh my freak. Oh my freak, oh my freak, oh my freak.

Lucas is alive. He's dead, but he's alive.

He's a spirit. Apparently, according to Alex, he is a spirit. Yet he can still remember things. And he can talk. And he can see me. And he has been floating around somewhere, following me and observing my life. And apparently, despite all that I did to him, he still loves me. And doesn't hate my guts.

Feeling absolutely stunned, I lean heavily against the motel wall and slowly slide down it until I'm crouching, my hand pressed to my forehead. I'm in the room alone. Alex is still at the pool, and I am having a total mental breakdown.

Because it doesn't make sense. This shouldn't be happening. Lucas is dead and death is final. There's nothing after. There's never been any proof, any evidence, any believable research that suggests that an afterlife isn't anything more than a bunch of fairy tales. When I killed my brother, that was final. He was dead. He *is* dead.

And yet...he's here. In Gallup. With me. Because apparently, he's seen me cut. And apparently, he wants me to knock it off.

Tears well up in my eyes and I bite my fist, slowly rocking back and forth. This can't be happening. I truly can't believe this is happening.

And yet, there is a wild, little part of me that does believe it. A rebellious sliver that realizes the odds of Alex knowing so much about me, the odds of her answering every single one of my random questions correctly, is next to nil. I realize that either she's been stalking me obsessively for years, or she's actually talking to Lucas. So a part of me believes her. A radically hopeful part of me does.

But then, there's also the other part of me that doesn't. Because when I went out on that pool deck, there was no one there. It was just Alex, crouched on the ground, hugging her knees, and crying as she talked to herself. She stood up and moved to the chairs with me. She sat down. She kept looking at the same spot of air each time she referred to Lucas. But nothing was there in that spot of air. Nothing changed. It was just me and just her. Sitting in Gallup by a pool with no one, absolutely no one else.

There's no way that Lucas can be real.

And just as I think that, just as I decide I'm crazy for believing her, the door swings open and I leap to my feet.

It's Alex, standing in the doorway, grinning as she looks at me.

"Lucas says he isn't sorry for teasing you about Jonathan. I told him he should apologize, but—" she shrugs. "He says apologies are beneath him."

I freeze. My reality splinters again. Those words, that attitude, it's all familiar. It's Lucas's. And yet, I'm staring at Alex. Only at Alex.

"Oh yeah?" I finally force myself to say. "So what? Does that mean that death hasn't humbled him at all? My brother can literally die and still be as arrogant as ever?"

Alex laughs slightly, that hand still on her ribs, and looks over her shoulder. I follow her eyes, staring where she's staring. But there is nothing, absolutely nothing. Just Alex and an empty doorway.

"Nah. He says it will take something much more life-altering than death to teach him humility. He says that apologies will always stay beneath him."

"Ah."

"But on a more serious note, he also says he's very, very happy you believe us now."

"But I never said that I believe you." I gulp, my mind whirling. What am I even saying? What *do* I even believe?

"Didn't you hear me on the pool deck? I actually said that I don't."

But Alex just smiles and shrugs. "Yeah. I heard you. *I* got the message. But Lucas over here seems to think you're convinced. I'll leave it up to you to talk him out of it."

And with that, Alex finally enters the room fully. She waits a moment, tracking something with her eyes that drifts in after her, then she softly closes the door. As I stare, heart pounding, she turns and looks at me.

"Well, I hate to say this. But checkout is at 10:30 and it's nearly 10:15. Do you think we can pack the car in time? If we can, I would love to avoid an extra fee."

"Oh." Her words startle me. In all my edging hysteria, I didn't even consider what time it might be. I didn't even remember that checkout was a thing. And ever since Alex reminded me that she's paying for this entire trip herself, I've been feeling kind of guilty about it. If we've got to go, then we've got to go. "Right. Um, yeah. No, yeah. Let's, uh, let's get the car packed. Where do you want me to start?"

"Can you grab the oxygen tanks, food, and, um, water bottles? We still need to change out of our pajamas, so leave the duffle bags here. In fact, mind if I take mine and change in the bathroom right now? That is, unless you want to change before me?"

"Oh. Um, no. Go ahead. I'll pack while you get dressed." And just like she asked me to, I walk over and pick up the heavy case of water. But just as I bend down, I hear a gasp. A terribly pained gasp. I straighten and whirl around.

"Hey, you all right?"

Alex is leaning against the wall, positioned as if she, too, was in the process of bending over to grab her duffle bag. But halfway down, she must have stopped. Because now she's leaning against the wall, her hand clutched to that side of hers.

"Yeah." Alex nods, but she's gritting her teeth and out of breath. "Yeah, sorry, I just..." She blinks hard, almost as if seeing stars, and shakes her head to clear them. She doesn't have her cannula back on, so she's not receiving oxygen. In fact, she hasn't been wearing it since we had our fight. "I'm just...wow. I've got to sit down."

And she does. Hobbling gingerly with that hand on her torso, she heads for her bed and sits heavily on the edge, wincing.

"Alex, are you..." I hesitate, not wanting to hear the answer. "Are you hurt?"

Though I asked, I didn't need to. I know that she's hurt. Ever since yesterday I've known that. But assuming she's injured and hearing it confirmed straight from her own mouth are two very different things. I'm scared of what she'll say.

But Alex, being Alex, shakes her head. "No. I'm fine. I'm just a little sore is all."

"Like, sore from our fall? From when I bumped into you at the school?"

Alex nods. "Yeah. But it's nothing to worry about. Really." She looks down at herself and carefully lifts the corner of her shirt, as if checking the damage underneath. What I see makes me gasp.

Her skin, which is usually such a soft, subtle copper, is bruised horrifically. Starting one hand's width above her waist, her whole left side is a hideous, dark purple, the edges bright red as if inflamed. Alex cringes, as if seeing the injury for the first time herself, and quickly drops the hem of her shirt. She looks up at me, the worry evident on her face.

Yet, she's not worried about herself. She seems to be worried about *me*, and the horrified expression that must be etched across my face.

"Really, Brinley, it's nothing," she insists. "It's not as bad as it looks."

But it's too late. The tears are already welling up in my eyes.

"Alex, I broke your ribs," I whisper, my voice growing choked.

"No, no! We don't know that! Not for sure anyways. Besides, even if they are broken, it's not your fault. I was the one who stepped in front of you. You were walking so fast and I was trying to stop you. I wasn't thinking, and I didn't want you to get on the bus before you saw me. It was my fault. So don't blame this on yourself, please. I'm so sorry."

But I can't handle this. I can't handle another horrible mistake. Another reason to hate myself. I just shake my head, biting my bottom lip. The tears are welling deeper.

"Brinley," Alex murmurs, her face scrunched with concern.

Then like a dam breaking, everything bursts out. "Why do I always do this?" I cry. "Why do I always hurt the people I love? First I kill Lucas and now...now I've hurt you!" And with that, I whirl towards the door, sobbing as I yank it open and race blindly out the room.

LUCAS

Immediately after Brinley leaves, Alex and I have an argument. Well, not exactly an argument. We kind of respect each other too much to be toxic. So it's more like...a conversation. One in which neither of us agree and we both grow increasingly exasperated with the other.

Because the thing is, I knew Alex was hurt. Of course I did. It was obvious. But I had no idea just how badly. The moment she lifted her shirt wasn't just a horror to Brinley; it was a horror to me. And I am sick, sick to my stomach, at what I saw. And I'm also sick to my stomach imagining how

Brinley must be feeling right now. The guilt that must be drowning her.

With wide eyes, Alex turns her attention from the slammed door to me.

"Lucas, I'm so sorry," she whispers, shocked. "I didn't mean...I didn't know..."

"Didn't know she would respond like that?" I fill in for her, grimacing. I run my hands through my hair then shove them deep into my pockets, sighing heavily. "Yeah, well, there's no way you could have. Brinley's just been like that. Ever since I died. She's grappling with more guilt than any fifteen-year-old should ever have to deal with, and because of that, she's fragile." Confused, Alex cocks her head at me. She still looks worried, so taking another deep breath, I keep talking.

"Look, I probably should have explained this to you a lot earlier. But Brinley thinks it was all her fault that I was killed. Which it wasn't. Of course it wasn't. But that's kind of the crux of the problem here. It's why she's struggling so much with my death. It's why she's so bothered that she may have broken your ribs. Brinley blames herself for my death, and now she's also blaming herself for your injury."

"Wait, Brinley thinks your death was her fault?" Alex asks. She shakes her head, trying to wrap her mind around that. "I know you mentioned that back in Albuquerque, but I thought—didn't your obituary say you were hit by a drunk driver? How on earth could that be her fault?"

"Exactly. Just like I said, it's not her fault," I reiterate. "She didn't make the decision to drink that night. She didn't swerve out of her lane and hit me. But she is, technically, the reason I was out driving that night. It was a Friday and I caught her sneaking out of the house to go to her friend's party. She doesn't have a full license yet, only her learner's permit, and, well, I didn't want her driving." I shrug, grimacing at the memory. "You know, because it was illegal. And if she got caught, she could lose her license for good. And that would have *seriously* ruined high school for her. So, like the 'cool older brother' that I am, I offered to drive her myself rather than turn her in to our parents. It was past midnight and I wanted her to have some fun. I trusted Savannah to have a clean party. But..." I wince. "You know how it ends. After dropping Brinley off, I went to the gas station to get myself an energy drink. On my way home, a car swerved on a two-lane road and hit me head-on. Now, here I am. A spirit. And my sister can't forgive herself for it."

"Oh." Alex sits very still on the bed, but I notice her grip tighten on her knees. "Oh," she says again.

"Yeah. Sad story, huh? To put it in perspective, Brinley was always a good kid. Sneaking out of the house was really out of character for her. Goes to show just how badly she wanted to go to that party, right? It's just..." I heave another sigh, looking at my feet. "We didn't know. No one could have known how it would end. So it makes sense now why she's cutting so much, doesn't it? It's because she's punishing herself, Alex. Each time she cuts, she's punishing herself for my death. For all the mistakes she thinks she's made."

"Lucas, that's...that's terrible," Alex whispers, aghast.

"I know, right? Try watching that every night, helpless, knowing you're the reason for it. But look," I say, shaking my head, trying to pull myself back to the present. "We gotta stop talking about that. We need to focus on something different, something more positive. Brinley didn't cut last night and she knows I'm here. She's doing better already. So now...now let's deal with the problem at hand. Let's get you back home."

"Excuse me?"

"Your ribs, Alex. I'm talking about your ribs. I don't care what you said to Brinley. That bruising is so bad, your ribs have got to be broken. So let's get you home and get you help."

But unfortunately, those words were entirely the wrong thing to say. And I should have known beforehand that they would be. I spent every day this past week by Alex's side, planning this trip with her. I came to understand her and her personality. So I should have anticipated that she wouldn't like being told what to do. I should have known that trying to "baby" her would only make her mad.

Sure enough—"Lucas, are you kidding?" Alex cries. Her mouth falls open in shock. "Did you honestly just say that?"

"Say what? Say I want us to go back home? That I want you to get help? Yeah. For the record, I did."

But Alex just scoffs, shaking her head with her tongue in her cheek. "Wow. Just wow. So you want us to go home, huh? You want us to give up, turn around, and go back to Albuquerque? Didn't you hear a word you just said?" She leans towards me, her voice getting more adamant. "Your sister is suffering. She's *suffering!* At this very moment, she is outside, bawling her eyes out. Brinley is nowhere near better, and she still needs help! Don't you care about that?"

"Oh, of course I do, Alex!" I say back, my own voice starting to rise, just like hers had. "Of course I do! And of course she's crying right now. She's crying because your ribs are *broken!* And broken ribs need medical attention. So we've got to get you home and get you help!"

Alex only snorts, leaning back again and folding her arms. "Oh yeah? What kind of help? An official diagnosis? A prescription for bed rest over the next three weeks? For all we know, three weeks could be more than half the time I have left to live! So, no. I'm not going back," she says, her jaw tightening. "I told Brinley that I'm fine, and I meant it. We planned a trip to Zion National Park, and I am seeing it through."

"No, we aren't!" I hiss, my own teeth clenching. "We're heading back to Albuquerque. Now!"

"No! Brinley needs help!"

"No. *You* need help! You do!" I suddenly burst out, my voice getting so abruptly loud it makes Alex jump. "Don't you understand? Rrrg," I groan, whirling on my heel and pacing, running my fingers through my hair. "Don't you get that *you're* the one who's dying here, Alex! You told me so yourself, last night, when you couldn't breathe! And I don't know about you, but that scared me out of my wits! Because in that moment, when you were on the ground, I believed you. I actually did. I thought...I..." My voice strangles, growing thick with the memory, with the relived terror.

"I honestly thought I was going to lose you, ok? And by lose you, I mean watch you die and have to enter this same kind of living hell—this same torture and endless purgatory—that I experience daily now. I just...I've come to care about you, Alex, all right? I really, *really* have. And the thought of something happening to you, the thought of you suffering or dying because of something I did, something I dragged you into—I can't...I can't bear it!" I yell. "I want you to be ok. I want you to be taken care of. I want you to know that it's not just Brinley who I love and want to save anymore. It's you too! And I just can't see you hurt like this! Not now and not because of me! So like it or not, we're taking you home!" I bellow, taking a threatening step towards her and clenching my fists. "I mean it, Alex. And we're doing it now!"

And if I wasn't filled with shame for the way I've treated Alex before, this moment would have sealed the deal. Because yeah, maybe I just told Alex that I care for her. But I also, in the same breath, just yelled at her. Very, very loudly. I refused to listen, and I told her to her face that she doesn't understand her own death. Her own cancer. Her own situation. I shouted in anger, my voice reverberating in the small motel room, and she has every right to shout and yell at me back.

But rather than do that, rather than get mad like I deserve, Alex's face crumples. She looks at the ground, bites her bottom lip, then looks back up at me. Tears are welling in her eyes. And in burning shame, I look away.

"Lucas," she says softly, her voice choking. "Lucas, I'm sorry. I don't...I don't want you to blame yourself for what's happened. Like Brinley, I don't want you to think that this is your fault," she says, her voice low, broken, and emotional. "It isn't. I have cancer. *Cancer*," she whispers through the tears. "And it's eating away at my bones, making them weak. So if my ribs didn't break when Brinley bumped into me, they would have broken at a different time, under different circumstances, on a different day. It's inevitable. My body is dying. And no matter how much I want to stop that—or *you* want to stop that—we can't. Ok? And trust me when I say this: it's better to just accept my death now than to keep fighting against it. Denial only makes the pain worse. Trust me, because I know."

Gritting my teeth, I look away from her, sitting on the bed with her short hair, skeletal frame, and broken expression. Tears aren't brimming in my dead eyes, but it sure feels like they are. "No," I choke, shaking my head. "No, I won't accept it. I don't want to!"

"I know," Alex whispers, grimacing. "But you need to." She hesitates, taking a shaky breath. Then she clenches her hands on her thighs and briefly closes her eyes. "My death isn't something we can stop. Ok?" She opens her eyes, staring straight into mine. "It's guaranteed. My death is going to happen and my bones are going to break. I can't choose otherwise. I can't decide to stop that. But you know what I can decide? What I do have control over? I can choose where I am and what I'm doing when those breaks happen. And hear me out: I would much, *much* rather crack my ribs helping Brinley than crack my ribs sitting at home on the couch, coughing and alone. So yes. I got hurt. And I know I'll probably continue to get hurt on this trip. But if I'm going to break bones and die, no matter what, then I want to break bones and die doing what's important. So please," she whispers, her sad, chocolate eyes begging, "don't tell me to go home, Lucas. Don't tell me I can't do this. Not yet. Brinley is crying, she has her own choices she needs to make, and there's more for us to do."

CHAPTER SEVENTEEN

ALEX

Oh gosh, I hurt. I definitely hurt. As I drive, I clench and unclench the steering wheel with white knuckles, trying not to think about how disastrous this could turn out. After all, I have cancer. My ribs are actually broken. And every breath I take feels like a dagger twisting in my side. Despite the brave words I said to Lucas, I am in pain, and pain can grow overwhelming. I try to keep every breath even and shallow to avoid inflating my lungs any more than necessary. But still, they burn wretchedly. And we still have five more hours to go before we reach Zion National Park. At this rate, with all the stops we're taking, we won't get there until after 6pm. Which means I will have to keep myself together, both mentally and physically, until after dinnertime.

Five more hours. Maybe six. Maybe even seven if we

don't pick up our pace.

Glancing over, I see Brinley is bent over a textbook and a lined sheet of paper in the passenger seat, doing math homework. In the back seat, Lucas is staring out the window, brow furrowed, watching as sagebrush after sagebrush zips by, tracking them with his eyes. He hasn't said much since I convinced him to keep going. And he didn't participate much when I went back to the pool deck and coaxed Brinley out of her tears, promising her repeatedly I was fine. But...I kind of lied. To everyone. The torturous pain in my side is debilitating. And there is nothing to distract me from it. Having done the best I could to offer Brinley silence, I finally have to break it.

"Hey, Brinley," I say, tentatively clearing my throat. My voice is hoarse and raspy from lack of use. We've already been driving for two hours.

"Yes?" She looks up.

"I'm sorry to interrupt, but have you called your mom yet?" I bring up the topic, yes, to district myself. But also because it's been on my mind for a while now.

"Oh."

I wait. Brinley doesn't say anything further. Lucas has perked up in the back seat and is now watching us, interested.

"I think that maybe you should call her."

Brinley is quiet, not saying anything. When she finally

speaks, her voice is unsure and worried. "I don't know what to say."

"Well, what if you tell her the truth? Or at least, most of it. Tell her there's this weird girl from school who is really sick with cancer and really kinda bald, and she asked you to go on an impromptu road trip with her. You can even pass the phone to me. I'll talk to her if I need to. Or I can give her my mom's number, and she can call her to verify the story. I'm sure that will help."

"Alex, your mom doesn't know that Brinley is with us," Lucas says from the back seat, quietly reminding me.

Now, my brow furrows. Brinley, watching me intently, must have noticed the way my eyes flickered to the rearview mirror.

"What did he say?" she asks immediately, urgently. Since deciding to believe us, Brinley has clung to Lucas's every word as if they are worth more than gold. Which, to her, they probably are.

"Oh, nothing. He just reminded me that I never told my mom I was bringing you along."

"Oh."

"But it's fine," I add quickly, only slightly worried. "Tell you what. How about I call my mom first, then you call yours. Do you mind grabbing my phone and calling her for me? She's in my contacts."

Brinley nods and does as I ask. Once the phone is

ringing, I grab it from her and press it against my ear, my heart hammering. When Mom answers, it leaps into my throat.

"Hey, honey, I was wondering when you would call. How's the trip going?" Mom asks, her words fast and her tone concerned.

"Hey, yeah, sorry about that. I got tired after driving last night. Forgot to call. Everything is going great though."

"Oh good. Where are you at then? Did you get to Utah last night?"

"Um, not quite. Made a stop in Gallup. Was feeling kind of tired. Decided not to risk it."

There's silence on the other end of the line. I grit my teeth, painfully aware of what she must be thinking.

"Honey, are you all right?" she finally asks.

"Yeah, yeah, totally fine." But it's kind of my lying tone. I'm terrible at lying, and I know that she can tell. "But never mind that. Hey, I was calling because...well, I forgot to tell you something. I'm actually doing this road trip with a friend."

"A friend?" Mom repeats, stunned.

"Yeah, Brinley. Brinley Prowley. She's, um...she's a friend from school. Really nice, really cool. But hey, she, uh...she didn't tell her parents she was going to do this trip with me. It was kind of my idea. I talked her into it last minute and, uh, her mom might call you later today. If she does, can you just, like, tell her that I'm an ok person? Like, verify that everything is all right? That I'm not a serial killer or anything?"

"Alex!" my mom cries.

"What? I'm not! Look, I would explain more, but I'm driving. And it's really not safe to talk and drive at the same time so...yeah. I love you. Everything's cool, I'm fine, cancer is doing great. We'll be in Zion National Park by tonight."

Mom starts saying something more, but panicked, I don't let her finish. I hang up, my heart pounding. My hand is trembling, and both Brinley and Lucas are staring at me.

"Well, that's the most rebellious thing I've ever done," I tell them, still kind of shocked at what I just did.

In the back seat, Lucas snorts. "Seriously? It's about time then. Welcome to the thrill of a rebellious life."

Scoffing, I roll my eyes. "You're one to speak."

Lucas grins, and next to me, Brinley cocks her head. But I don't explain. Instead, I just jerk my head at Brinley's phone. "Your turn now."

Hesitantly, slowly, she picks it up. But she doesn't dial.

"Come on," I coax her. "You've got this. If I can do it, you can do it."

"Um...what does Lucas think I should tell her?" she asks, still hesitating.

Raising my eyebrows, I look at him in the rearview mirror. He shrugs. "I dunno. Tell her you're going on a road trip with a dying stranger, loads of junk food, and the ghost of her dead son. That will crack her up."

I repeat his answer to Brinley, and she balks. Over her shoulder, she looks at the back seat. The back seat that must look totally empty to her. Except, of course, for our mountain of food wrappers back there.

"Crack her up? Uh, yeah. Crack her up mentally! No way in heck am I telling her that!"

Lucas simply shrugs again. "You could always try it." I repeat the words for Brinley. She rolls her eyes.

"Sheesh. You're no help," she mutters under her breath. Then frowning deeply, she scrolls through her contacts, going slowly, and finally holds the phone to her ear. Seconds pass. I hear the phone ringing.

"Hey, Mom," she says, wincing into the receiver.

Immediately, there is a long, unintelligible string of shouting from the other end. Wincing, Brinley holds the phone away from her ear. A moment passes, then two. Lucas and I exchange glances. Finally, like a tornado blowing itself out, the shouting dies down. Brinley gingerly returns the phone to her ear.

"Are you finished?" she asks, her tone flat and unamused. There's silence. Her mom isn't saying anything back.

"Good. Look, I just wanted to check in and tell you where I am. I went on an impromptu road trip with a friend.

We stayed the night in Gallup and are on our way to Zion National Park in Utah. We might be back on Monday, maybe Tuesday. I dunno. But I'm fine, and I'll see you and Dad when I get back home. All right?"

Her mother erupts again and Brinley scowls.

"No! I am not with a boy! What the crap, Mom, get a grip! I'm with Alexia Ahmed, ok? That girl from Volcano Vista who's dying of cancer? Yeah, I'm with her. So if you want to yell at me some more, go ahead. But it's not going to bring me home any sooner, and it's not going to make me like you very much either. So just get a grip on yourself and chill. I'm doing nothing wrong, and I'll see you when I see you."

Then with that, Brinley hangs up. Huffing, she folds her arms and looks out the window.

I wait for a second. Then two. But finally, I can't take it any longer. "Um, Brinley?"

"What?" she retorts, curt and annoyed.

"I think you should send her my mom's number."

"No. She doesn't need it."

"I think she might. She sounded pretty upset. It will give her peace of mind, don't you think?"

"No."

I hesitate, searching for a new angle I can take. "Please? For me? It would make me feel better. I mean, I already feel like a kidnapper as is."

"I said no!"

Scrunching my nose, I get desperate. "Lucas?" I finally try, looking in the mirror. "Back me up here? Please?"

Lucas hesitates. Then begrudgingly, he sighs. "Fine. Brinley, you heard her. Just do as Alex asks."

"He said that you should do as I ask."

"No, he did not!" Brinley balks, throwing me an incredulous, offended look.

"Did too. I swear it. Cross my heart and hope to die."

"No!"

"Yes, he really did."

"No!" Brinley nearly yells, making me jump with the sudden volume and vehemence. Her face twists like a snarl. "He didn't! The Lucas I know would never say that! He's a rebel. He wouldn't tell me to check in with my mom like that. He didn't tell me to check in with her the night that he died! You're lying to me!"

"Brinley!" She's shooting daggers, looking at me with such a look of betrayal that I can't help but believe she's serious. She truly must think she caught me in a lie. That I'm putting words in her brother's mouth. That I'm using him as a puppet for my own personal agenda. "I swear to you, that's what he said! I would never, ever lie to you about him. It's a privilege to speak for Lucas, and I would never change what he says! Your brother is my friend. *You* are my friend. And I swear on my short, cancer-stricken life that

I'm being honest! I'm honest about everything Lucas does."

"She is, Brinley. She really is," Lucas adds earnestly, leaning forward from the back seat. I throw him a grateful look in the rearview mirror, then we both grimace as we realize how futile that was. Though I appreciate Lucas is willing to back me up, Brinley can't hear him. There's nothing he can do to help convince her.

And sure enough, Brinley is not having it. She's pursed her lips, which at least means she's not contradicting me anymore, but I can tell that I still have a long way to go before I earn her trust. Before she believes me completely.

Sighing, I lean my head back against the headrest and stare straight ahead out the windshield. Brinley folds her arms and, scowling, does likewise. Minutes pass in silence and I think.

Finally, with another sigh, I lift my head and look over at Brinley.

"Hey," I say, the exhaustion seeping into my voice.

Brinley's eyes flicker towards me, lips still pursed. She might not admit it, but I think she's worried about how sick I just sounded. Which is fine. If concern is what it takes to bring her walls down, then so be it.

"Can I tell you something about me?"

"What?" she asks curtly, impatient.

"I'm a musician. I say that because I realize that I'm still a stranger to you. I took you on this trip without much of an introduction to myself, and I'm sorry about that. But right now, I want you to understand that I am a musician."

"Okay…" I can see her mind whirling, trying to jump ahead, trying to see where this is going.

"And because I'm a musician, I know a little something about language. I play the piano—I'm classically trained—and I've learned over the years that sometimes, when words are hard, I can say things better through my fingers and a keyboard than I can through my mouth. Now Lucas, he told me that he played the piano a little bit during his lifetime. But he doesn't have a piano right now, and even if he did, he couldn't play it. Not as a spirit. But you know what? I think he can still speak through music."

Now I've seriously reeled her in. Brinley's brow furrows, and she turns in her seat, looking at me hard. She sizes me up with a cautious, guarded expression. "What do you mean?"

"I mean that I know all of this must be hard and unfair for you. I can see Lucas. You can't. I can hear him. You can't. And it must be really annoying to have to use me as a translator. Admit it. It's awful. So how about we do something different, huh? For the next little while, I'm going to be quiet. I won't say a word. And Lucas, in the back seat, is going to pick out some songs for you. I'll play each one on my phone as we drive, and you just listen to him. Not to me. Listen to what he's trying to say through the music, through the lyrics, through the feelings. Does that make sense? Do you think you can do that?"

I didn't run this idea by Lucas before voicing it, and in the back seat, his mouth falls open in surprise. I glance in the mirror and give him a small, encouraging nod. Nervously, he nods back.

"Ok, Lucas agrees. He's in. Now how about you? Are you willing to let Lucas speak to you through music?"

"Um...he actually wants to do this?"

"Yes, he actually wants to do this."

"And you're sure?"

I look in the mirror. Again, Lucas nods. "Yes, I'm very sure."

"Ok. Um, if Lucas wants to...then I'll listen."

"Great! In that case, I'm going to stop talking. Lucas, take a moment to think, then tell me when you're ready with the first song. Once it's over, you'll give me the next song. And the next, and so on. Deal?"

"Deal."

Reaching down, I grab my phone from the cupholder and insert it into the case I keep on my dashboard, making it so I can see the road and the phone at the same time. Eyes flickering from asphalt to screen, I pull up my music list. When I'm ready, I give a quiet thumbs-up. Lucas gives one back.

"Ok," he says slowly, thinking hard. "What if you start

off with 'Running After You' by Matthew Mole? Brinley knows I love that song. She'll recognize it's from me, and I want her to know that I'm chasing after her. You know, metaphorically." He gives me a wan smile, probably thinking he's clever or something. "After that, try playing 'Saturn' by Sleeping At Last. It's an emotional song with a long instrumental beginning. It might make her cry. But"— he sighs deeply, looking at Brinley with a sad, longing expression—"I think it's important that she hears it. Actually, really important. There's just something about that song, and it captures pretty well how I've felt since I've died. How I feel about life, about death. It's powerful, and I just...I just want her to hear what it has to say."

BRINLEY

Lucas is ruthless. Absolutely ruthless. I've never felt as emotionally attacked as I do over these two hours, listening to Lucas pour himself into me through music.

He tells me things. He tells me how he feels about me, about how devastated he is to be dead, and about how much he longs for me to live and enjoy my life. Though, truthfully, I didn't expect that last part. I didn't expect him, over time, to start picking more upbeat songs like "Hey Brother" by Avicii, or "I Lived" by OneRepublic, or "It's OK" by

Nightbirde, but even those songs make me cry. They all make me cry. And Alex—they even make her cry too.

And after a while, I begin to realize something. Through his song choices, Lucas is trying to convey something. He is trying to convey to me that life is beautiful. That it matters to him I stay put and that I will miss out on amazing experiences if I die. He picks songs like "7 Years" by Lukas Graham that catalog the ups and downs and beginnings and endings of life. He talks about family, about dreams, about pressing on and pressing up, about love and failures, heartbreaks and victories. He paints a picture for me of the life I could still yet have.

But as he paints a picture for me, he also, inadvertently, paints a picture for Alex too. While Lucas tells me all the things I have yet to enjoy, he tells Alex all the things she is about to lose. All the things he has lost himself.

And so we cry. Alex and I both cry. We cry shamelessly and prolonged, each of our hearts breaking for different reasons. Mine because I hear Lucas and I miss him. And Alex because she hears Lucas and will soon be joining him. She, too, will soon be singing songs of loss and longing, of doors closed and family left behind.

And together, we shed our unique tears. But as we do, I realize something.

My tears are not more sacred than hers, or hers more sacred than mine. And through this experience, we bond.

Because towards the end, as we near our next destination, I'm not just crying for Lucas anymore and I'm not just crying for myself. I'm crying for my sick and dying friend, Alex, too.

CHAPTER EIGHTEEN

LUCAS

I deeply appreciated Alex's recommendation to speak through music. Unlike her, I'm no musician. But like her, I am very moved by music. Brinley is very moved by music. And so the opportunity Alex gave me to speak not through words but through art was remarkable. I said things to my sister that I never would have dreamed possible of saying. I expressed things that I never would have dreamed possible of expressing, even if I had used my own words. There is just something about music that heals and inspires and speaks very loudly.

But because of that, it was also grueling. Emotionally. I was speaking through art, not words. And so that means I had to metaphorically grab Brinley's hand and walk her through all the memories and experiences and feelings I associate with each song. I had to relive my deepest pains and deepest longings. And though I couldn't cry like the girls could, it felt like my soul wept.

So hours later, when I run out of steam and tell the girls I'm finished, the car lapses into silence. And we stay like that for a long time. No one speaks and no one breaks the silence. Instead, we all stay quietly immersed in the feelings I created and process our own griefs. I stare out the window, Brinley reclines her seat and traces a finger across the scars on her arms, and Alex keeps her eyes locked on the expanse of desert ahead. In fact, as time passes, Brinley even closes her eyes and begins to fall asleep. Her breathing slows and the sun dips towards the horizon, casting Alex and me in a warm golden sunlight.

I expect her to speak at this point, for Alex to notice that Brinley's asleep and to strike up a conversation with me, and just me. It's been a while since we've had a chance to talk privately, and I long for her to say something. Anything. I'm worried her feelings might still be hurt after our argument, and I want her to talk and assure me that she's ok.

Only, she doesn't. As the evening wanes and Brinley rests, Alex remains silent. No music is played, no gaze flickers to mine. Instead, it's up to me to break the silence I created.

"Hey, Alex?" I finally say, my voice quiet as I lean

forward from the back seat. Her face is illuminated by the lowering sun, casting strange shadows beneath her cheekbones and making her look harrowed. More harrowed than I would have expected.

"What?" she responds, her voice raspy.

"I just...I wanted to apologize," I make myself say, hearing the very words I've been mulling over for hours. "I haven't stopped thinking about how I treated you back at the motel. How I got so upset and yelled at you. I didn't mean to be rude. I didn't mean to overact. I was just so worried. Like I said, I care about you. Like I really, really do, and I—"

"Lucas, stop," Alex says abruptly, cutting me off.

"What?"

"Please, I said stop," she begs, her voice muted so as not to wake Brinley but also strangely distressed. Her tone catches me off guard. It puts me on edge. "Look, I know that we should probably talk things through. I know I owe you an apology too, and I know you probably want to hear my feelings. But can it...can it wait? Please? I'm really not feeling well."

"Oh." My answer is lame. Inadequate. I squint, peering more closely at Alex. Truth be told, she hasn't spoken much in hours. She was quiet even before we played the music. "Alex, are you all right?"

She hesitates. Then, "No," she admits, voice hoarse.

"No, not entirely."

I lean forward further. I put my hand on Brinley's seat, as if to grab it as I move closer. But I forget to focus, and my hand passes right through. Alex, seeming to notice, shudders.

"Alex, what's wrong?" I urgently ask.

But she doesn't answer. She just shakes her head, distress and panic radiating off her.

"Alex, come on," I press. "Talk to me."

"Don't worry about it," she mumbles, shaking her head again. But her voice is choked and getting thick with tears. "I'm fine," she insists. "There's nothing you can do, ok? Nothing anyone can do."

"No way. I don't believe that. Whatever it is, I can help. Someone can help you. So talk to me about it. What's happening? What's going through your head?"

"Nothing," she pleads. But contrary to her words, her shoulders shake and she begins to cry. Clenching the steering wheel, she leans forward and valiantly keeps us on the road, speeding through the desert.

"It's nothing," she finally croaks. "I'm just...I'm just sick, Lucas. My head hurts, I'm light-headed, I've been driving way too long, and my body...I just....I can't. I can't breathe well. It's getting harder every day. And I don't...I don't want to...to die yet, Lucas. I don't want to die."

To my alarm, Alex's breathing speeds up and she starts

gasping in short, shallow bursts, like a rabbit that's been pinned in a corner with no way out. The sudden change in her breathing hurts her. It's obvious, because she lets go of the steering wheel with one hand and presses it against her rib cage, cringing with pain. And her breathing only gets faster. It's like she's starting to have a panic attack or something. Panicking myself, I strain to lean forward even further.

"Alex, pull over. You don't have to keep driving. Pull over right now."

"No," she gasps.

"Alex, listen to me," I say, my voice frightened and warning. "You've done enough today. You've already done so much. For me, for Brinley. Let's just pull over and get you what you need."

"Lucas, I don't even have five months left," she sobs.

"No, that's not true! You do have five months left! The doctors said so. Pull over, Alex. Now." My voice isn't a shout, but it is firm and commanding. And gratefully, unexpectedly, she does as I say. After a long hesitation and more painful, sobbing gasps, Alex starts slowing. She veers the car over the rumble strips and crunches to a stop on the gravel shoulder, parking on the empty desert road. Miraculously, the sound doesn't wake Brinley. She must be sleeping hard.

"There," I say once we roll to a stop. Then I twist to get a better view of Alex's face. Tears are streaking down her cheeks, and when she sees me looking, she squeezes her eyes shut, embarrassed. Her teeth are nearly chattering, and she's still gasping as if she's being strangled.

"Alex, come on," I plead, trying to be gentle despite my growing panic. "You can't keep thinking like this. You're not dying, all right? You're here, you're living, it's going to be ok. I promise, everything's going to be all right." But despite the hope in my words, my voice is scared. And certainly, Alex can tell.

"I...I can't..."

"Can't what? Can't breathe? Alex, do we need to call 911? Do we need to switch out your oxygen tank?"

"No, I can't...can't die yet, Lucas!" she finally bursts out. "Don't you get it? I can't! I'm not ready to leave!" Terrified, Alex rips her eyes open, looking around herself with a wild, animalistic fear.

And her words, said so sincerely, cut deep. They are like a stab to my heart, a literal pain that leaves me staggered. Because I get it. Though I wish I didn't, I know precisely what she means. I know what it's like to not want to die, to feel compelled to live, yet to have no choice in that. I understand, at least to my own degree, what she must be feeling right now. And I want, more than anything, to take it all away.

"I know, I know," I whisper, haggard. "You don't have to

be ready to die. *I'm* not ready for you to die. I didn't...I don't...no one wants you to die, Alex. And no one wants you to live more than I do!"

"But it's going to happen!" Alex wails. "Lucas, I can feel it! My body is giving out! In less than six months, it's going to be in a coffin. I'm going to get less and less oxygen from these crappy lungs, and my body is...it's going to suffocate! It's going to lose oxygen until it can't function anymore. And that's wretched! That's a wretched way to die! And not only that, but...but when it's all said and done, I'm going to be ripped away from my family," she gasps, struggling for breath, sucking desperately at the air. "From piano. From music. From so many things that I...I love. That I care about. And my family? My family, Lucas? They're going to suffer, too, when I'm gone. My death is going to be agony for them!" she cries, squeezing her eyes shut. "And I can't...I can't stand it! Is this really what we're made for? Really? To suffer while we live and then to suffer still when we die? Like you are? Is there really...no greater...p-point to all of this?"

In response, I say nothing. My eyes just grow tight, watching as Alex gulps desperately for oxygen, her teeth beginning to chatter. And truthfully, I don't say anything because she's right. Without a doubt in my mind, I know as I watch Alex tremble that she really is dying. Just like the doctors predict, she can't have much longer to live.

Everything she said about death and its horrible agony? It's accurate. It's brutally and unavoidably accurate.

"And I just..." But here, her sentence strangles off. The tears finally succeed in choking her, and she looks around herself, terrified, at the lonely desert, the setting sun, the approaching darkness. "I just..." She wheezes, teeth chattering. "I just don't know. I don't understand. What do I h-have to look forward to? What's the...p-p-purpose for all of this *pain?* I always thought that heaven would be perfect. Comforting. N-n-nice. But so many of our dreams, our wants they d-d-die too, don't they? And we don't...we don't lose them, Lucas. We don't ch-change! I'm still going to be me and I just...ahhg! Am I going to hurt like this for the r-rest of my...existence? Is that what the point of all this is? To wander without...p-purpose? To hurt without s-s-stop? I just...I don't know what I have to look...look f-forward to. When I die, there's nothing! Nothing good I can hope for! Nothing, Lucas! Except..." Alex grits her chattering teeth. She slams her wet eyes closed, choking, then looks away. "Except, maybe," she chokes, "...you?"

And with that, Alexia Ahmed begins to sob. Shaking, she covers her eyes with one hand while the other goes clawlike against her ribs. She gulps and wheezes for air, hardly breathing, hardly able to get enough.

And me—I'm stunned. Absolutely frozen and stunned.

Because Alex is suffering. She's right about everything,

and she's suffering wretchedly. Yet she just said, just hinted, that maybe *I* have the power to make this moment better. That I can make her future death less painful. *Me.* The lost, imperfect, struggling excuse for a spirit that I am. After all, I was the one who dragged her into all this. I'm the reason she's stuck in this abandoned desert, crying her eyes out, sobbing with broken ribs and a breaking heart.

And yet...she wants *me* to be her hope? Despite all that I am, all that I've done, she wants *me* to be that thing she can look forward to? A light in her darkness, a friend, a support?

And in this moment, realizing that and watching her sob and gasp so desperately for air, my heart almost bursts. Because truthfully, I haven't thought much about what it might be like after she dies. I haven't dared to. I haven't let myself consider where she'll go, or what she'll do, or how long she'll want to linger around me. I just always figured we would cross that bridge when we got there. That all of it would sort itself out with time.

But if Alex needs to know—if she needs to know that I'll be there for her, if she needs to know that I care, and that I'm staying by her side and not intending to go anywhere— then I need to tell her. I need to tell her what I think and what I feel. Right here, right now.

So clearing my throat, my heart wrenching, I finally speak. "Alex," I say quietly, my voice timid and hoarse and trembling. "Alex, I…" I stumble, wincing. She's still crying. Oh gosh, how painfully she is crying. "Alex, can I say something to you?"

Her sobs hitch, and she tries to control them. But she can't. She's gasping and seems dangerously close to passing out. But regardless, she nods dizzily, her eyes pleading, and I decide to shoulder on.

"Ok. I need to tell you this first: I don't have the answers to your questions," I admit. "I don't know if pain ever ends. I don't understand the why behind life, or the reason we exist after death. I don't. I know that's crazy, coming from someone like me who's dead. But truth be told, there are still so many things I *don't* know. But if…if there's one thing that I *do* know, it's how I feel about you. How I feel about life. About death. About family. About…us," I say, my voice growing weak as I look at her, my heart breaking with her pain. "And so maybe you're right. Maybe pain doesn't ever go away. Maybe it doesn't disappear in every form when we die. But you know why that is, Alex? You want to know why? It's because the pain that continues after death is just a result of love. If we didn't love people, we wouldn't feel this terrible when we left them. And so, yes! Hurt continues on after death. But…but pain continues because love continues," I decide, my own voice getting choked. "And I would rather be hit by a thousand semitrucks, I would rather swim through an ocean of needles, than lose the love that I feel for my family. The love that I feel for...for you," I add, my voice sincere and emotional.

"So it's ok to cry. It's ok to be angry, and feel lost, and feel like this existence is so unfair and wrong and *painful*. Because it is. It is! But you know what? *That's* what you can look forward to in death, Alex. You can look forward to keeping your love. And not only keeping it, but growing in it. Because, truth be told," I say, looking over at my sister and her sleeping form next to us, "I love Brinley now more than I ever have before. I understand her better, I see her better. And Alex, I've seen you. And I...I love you. So no matter what happens, no matter how soon or how late you're going to die, I'm not going to let you die alone. Ok? I'll be here. I'm staying by your side, and come heaven or come hell, you and I are going to figure out death and we're going to learn to be happy. Ok? Together, we are going to find joy. I promise you that. Just like you haven't left Brinley, I'm not going to leave you. Not now, not ever. Not if you want me to stay."

I finish, my spiritual heart hammering, my soul rent and raw. At my words, Alex doubles over deeper and continues to cry even harder. But I don't think in a bad way. Tentatively, emotionally, I reach out a ghostly hand and lay it delicately on the bones of her back. I place it there so softly that it doesn't pass through. And I leave it there, tenderly, and murmur kind, reassuring things as she cries.

A lot of time passes that way. A lot. But eventually, the sobbing slows and Alex can weakly lift her head again. I can tell the crying spell has taken a lot out of her. She's still wheezing and cringing in absolute pain, holding a hand to her ribs. But eventually, dizzily, she looks over at me. She's utterly depleted and exhausted.

"Thank you, Lucas," she whispers, her voice haggard but filled with some sort of feeling, some sort of sincerity. "Thank you," she whispers.

And with that, she looks over at Brinley. Wincing, she leans her head back and breathes for a long while more. Then, when she's ready, she puts the car into drive and eases back onto the road, gaining speed as she pushes through the night. I stay close, leaning forward, and silently plead for her like I've never pleaded before.

ALEX

When we finally, finally pull up to the Airbnb in Orderville, I can hardly move. Hardly think. My ribs are splintering, my migraine is whirling, I can't breathe, and every thought is a violent tangle. As I put the car in park, my vision swims and I nearly puke.

"Alex?" Lucas asks, leaning forward from the back seat. Brinley is still curled up, asleep in the passenger's seat. It got dark outside long ago, and the glare from the cabin's porch light cripples me.

"Yes?" I gasp. The world is spinning. I am shaking.

"Alex, let's get you inside. Wake up Brinley, she'll help you in."

But I can't, I don't. The light is excruciatingly painful. Even when I close my eyes, it stabs like a white-hot iron into my skull. So instead of waking Brinley, I do the only thing I can. I bow my head and cry.

"Alex?" Lucas says again.

And then there's another voice. Another person saying my name. "Alex?"

Brinley, rubbing her eyes groggily, props herself up on one elbow. She looks around, then sits up straighter. "Alex, where are we?"

But I don't answer. I just cry. Brinley gasps.

"Alex? Alex, what's going on?"

But I can't. I can't. Blinded by the pain of the migraine and the nausea sweeping through me, I fumble with my cannula, ripping it off. Then, sobbing, I wrench the car door open. I leave the vehicle and stumble into the night, weaving drunkenly, my footsteps crunching in dizzy patterns across the gravel.

I try to head for the front of the cabin. I want to make it to the door. Only, I don't. The migraine is raging. I am pain-racked. And ten feet away, I double over.

Hands on my knees, I vomit.
And finally, I collapse.

CHAPTER NINETEEN

ALEX

"Hey, hey, it's ok. Alex, it's ok. You're all right."

The voice is the first thing I become aware of. It sounds far away, distant. As if coming to me through a long funnel.

The second thing I become aware of is the fact that I'm moaning. Loudly. Once I realize it, I stop. My eyes flutter open, and briefly I see the image of a boy standing over me. Then my leaden eyes sink closed again. My neck turns and my cheek presses against a pillow.

"Hey, Alex," the voice says again quietly, gently. "I'm sorry. I didn't mean to wake you, but...it's been a while. And I don't know your med routine. Do you need any medication right now? Are you ok without it? Brinley brought it in for you, but you didn't take any last night."

Too exhausted and dead, I don't answer. I don't open

my eyes. But something about the words slowly begins to trouble me. My brow furrows and I lift a hand to my face. I can feel a mask there, covering my mouth and nose. Dizzily, weakly, I pry it off.

"Hey there. You coming around?"

"Hmm?" I slur. There's a sharp, debilitating pain in my ribs, and noticing it brings everything into sharper focus. I blink. It's really bright, but I blink again.

"Hey there. It's good to see you waking up. How are you feeling?"

"L-Lucas?" I ask, my tongue thick in my mouth.

"Yeah, I'm here. Just me. Brinley is off on a hike, getting some fresh air. How are you doing?"

I'm trying to process everything he said. Trying to remember where I am.

"Brinley's on a hike?" I eventually mumble.

"Yeah. There was one close by. She, well, kind of needed it. She's been worried about you."

"Worried about me?"

"Yeah. We both are. Are you doing ok? Last night was really rough."

"Last...night?" I repeat, confused. And for the first time since waking up, I really open my eyes and let them roam the room.

The first thing I notice is that I'm on a bed. A big queen-size with an old patchwork quilt. The next thing I notice is that the ceiling is peaked and made of parallel wooden slats. That's really strange. But slowly, I remember. We rented a small, A-frame cabin in Orderville, Utah, nestled in some pine trees away from the main road. It has two beds, a TV, and a kitchenette. And the third thing I notice is Lucas standing over me. His brilliant eyes are bright. Really bright. And they are trained right on me.

"Lucas?" I whisper, feeling dizzy.

"Hi, Alex." His voice is muted and very gentle. There's something kind yet concerned about the way he's looking at me.

"Are you all right?" I mumble, confused.

"Am I all right?" Lucas laughs a little. Then he squats next to me. He moves as if to rest his chin on my bed, his face inches from mine, but I know he's not really touching it. If so, his chin would pass right through. But still, his face is very close to mine. "Yeah. Yeah, I'm fine, Alex. It's you that I'm worried about. Is there anything I can get you?"

His question only serves to confuse me further. Swallowing, brow furrowed, I look around again and try to remember.

We're in a...cabin. The A-frame cabin. I drove us here last night. After...after a panic attack. Lucas had talked to me in the car, saying a lot of things that I needed to hear. Things that helped. But also, after our talk, I *hurt*. My ribs were blazing and I couldn't really breathe. I was dizzy and had a headache. And yet, I drove us. I got the car back on the road.

But the rest of it, what happened after that, is blurry. I vaguely remember getting to the cabin and parking the car in front, doubling over in the driver's seat and sobbing. It had been so, so hard to keep breathing. So painful. Brinley woke up then, and I'm pretty sure I scared her. I remember her own panic, her own worry. But I don't remember much else.

I just remember stumbling out of the car and weaving toward the cabin. Behind me, Brinley yelled something and jumped out of the car too. I remember stumbling to a stop just feet from the door, too dizzy to continue. I remember doubling over, puking, then...fainting?

Brinley, at that point, must have miraculously dragged me inside. She must have cleaned my face, hooked me up to the oxygen tank, gotten my mask for me, and taken care of me. She must have been terrified, yet she'd done it on her own anyways.

"Lucas?" I say suddenly, looking up into his brilliant eyes, my heart hammering with concern. "Lucas, Brinley. Is Brinley ok? She helped me, right? Last night? She got me into bed?"

"Yes, she did."

"And is she ok?" I press. I know all too well what it's like for my mother to help me after a particularly grueling day.

How strong she stays in the moment, how stoic and kind she is as she cleans up all my vomit and drags me into bed. And yet, after the door to my bedroom closes, I often hear her go to hers. And because we share a wall, I always hear the sobs.

Lucas, his expression somber, doesn't answer my question. Not immediately, at least. He's still squatted, his chin still close to the mattress and his face near mine. A small, puckering furrow takes form between his eyebrows and as he stares at me, he sighs. And looks down.

"Yeah, she's ok. After all, that's why I'm here with you, not her."

"But she's not doing well."

"Well..." he hesitates. "It *was* hard for her to see you pass out last night. It affected her pretty deeply. But she'll be all right," he smiles sadly. "She's just grown to love you is all. You kind of have that effect on people, you know."

But I'm too worried, my brain too rattled to respond to his comment. The memories are returning and I am distracted. "But Lucas, she was crying." I look over to Brinley's empty, perfectly made bed. "I remember. I saw her crying on her bed! Did she cut? Did anything happen?"

"No, she didn't cut." When he sees I'm about to argue, he holds out his fingers until they are right above my lips, hovering there as if to shush me. Slowly, I close my mouth again. "She didn't cut, Alex. I told you she was all right.

Truthfully, she did cry for a long time. But I stood by her, and told her I was right there, and that everything was going to be fine. I know she couldn't hear me, but—" he shrugs. "In the end, she didn't cut. And that is progress."

"Oh." I don't know how to respond. The pain in my ribs is meddling terribly with my mind. But the pain in my heart is crescendoing too and growing to an excruciating pinnacle. The thought of Brinley hurting herself is unbearable to me. Especially now that I know her. That I love her.

"Lucas, I...I don't want anything to happen," I confess, blinking fast against sudden tears. "If I cause her pain, if I'm ever the reason she decides to hurt her—"

"Shh," Lucas says, cutting me off again. "Shh, Alex. Don't worry about it. Remember? She didn't cut herself. She may be a little shaken up from last night, but she's ok. You've been doing really good things for her, and overall, she's going to be fine."

"But Lucas, what about when I die?" And at the thought, another surge of panic constricts my throat. I had thought, had naively hoped, that last night was just a fluke. That it was a random burst of anxiety that had to escape from me and wouldn't return. But apparently not. The anxiety is back and it wants vengeance. "What about my death? Won't that trigger Brinley? And just depress her all over again? I didn't think about that before, but I'm just going to hurt her eventually, aren't I? If not last night, then another day. She's still grieving you. And the last thing she needs now is to make a friend like me. One that she's only going to lose."

"Hey, stop talking like that," Lucas begs, giving me a heartbroken look. "Please. You've been getting so focused on dying, so focused on what could go wrong. But...but what about what's going right? I mean, yeah, Brinley is going to be sad when you die. Of course she's going to be devastated. And perhaps it *is* going to hurt her," Lucas says honestly. "Because Brinley loves you, your death *will* be painful to her. But that's not hopeless, Alex. Pain isn't hopeless. And sometimes, it's even necessary. Because even though your friendship may eventually hurt her, it doesn't mean it isn't needed. The kind of love that you show people, that you have for Brinley, it *heals*. I know, because I've felt it. I've benefited from it. And right now, Brinley needs healing. So just don't worry about that, ok? Let the future take care of itself and let other miracles come along when they're needed. But right here, right now, you are the miracle that my sister needs. And no future event, no matter how painful, can change the fact that she needs you. Or the fact that she's being healed by you."

Lucas tentatively reaches his hand out again. This time, it hovers near my forehead, as if he wants to wipe away a strand of dark, sweaty hair. As if he wants to do what my mother so often does. Closing my eyes, I imagine it. I let myself imagine what it might feel like if he could only touch.

"So please?" he whispers, his own voice getting husky. "Don't worry yourself like this. You're doing amazing things, Alex. And you're living your life beautifully."

Emotional all over again, and feeling incessantly dizzy and light-headed, I just nod. And with all my might, I will Lucas's words to be true. I will the universe to send Brinley another miracle besides me, if I really do end up hurting her. And deep inside, I plead with my body to hold on a little bit longer.

"So just focus on that, ok? For today. For right now. Because of you, Brinley knows I'm here. She knows that I love her and I forgive her. And really, moving forward, all we have left is one simple job. And that's to keep loving Brinley. So, think you're up to that? Think you can do that for her?"

Swallowing a lump in my aching throat, I nod again. I open my eyes and my mouth to say I can, but what comes out instead is a cough. Then another cough. Followed by another, barking third.

"Oh," Lucas's eyes go wide. He stands up from the side of my bed and takes a stumbling step back. "Oh," he repeats.

I keep coughing, the pain crescendoing throughout my chest. Unable to breathe, I roll over onto one elbow, hacking over the edge of the bed and into my hand, bright lights bursting across my vision.

The coughing sounds terrible, deep. It also begins to taste terrible.

"Oh crap," Lucas whispers.

Weak, shaking from the exertion of the coughing fit, I finally catch a rattling breath. Blinking at the bursts of light in my vision, I wipe at my mouth with the back of my hand.

And when I do, it comes away wet—smeared with red and sticky blood.

BRINLEY

It shouldn't be this cold in early spring, but it is. It may be because we drove north to Utah. It may be because I'm hiking in the mountains at higher elevation. It may be because it's still morning and the sun has yet to peak and really warm the earth. But regardless of the reason, it's cold. I'm cold. But I don't want to go back. Not to the A-frame and not, especially, to Alex.

Instead, I shove my forearms deeper into the pocket of my hoodie and crouch into a squatting position. It's taken me more than two hours to get here, but finally, I've reached the end of the hike. And cold or not, it is magnificent.

Granted, it's not, I know, as majestic as a view within

Zion National Park itself would be. I'm still on the outskirts, still leashed to the little town of Orderville where the hike began. But that said, I've crested a mountaintop and I can see out for miles and miles and miles. Miles of green-yellow hills, miles of craggy rock, and miles of earth-shattering mountains and valley-scarring canyons. And both the view and the cold take my breath away.

But...not entirely in a positive way. Because as I close my eyes against the sight, picturing it rather than seeing it, I know that I shouldn't be here alone. Under better circumstances, Lucas should be alive and healthy and with me. And so should Alex.

I shudder unconsciously as I think of her. As I remember what it was like to sit in the car, not understanding what was happening, then watch in the headlights as Alex pitched and weaved through the darkness, doubling over to vomit, then falling over unconscious. I leapt out of the car, screaming her name. And for a moment, I thought she was dead.

Dead, just like Lucas.

Yet thankfully, she wasn't. She certainly wasn't alive and thriving, but she wasn't dead. I dragged her then, sagging under her weight, until I got one of her arms over my shoulders and could lug her into the cabin. It wasn't a far walk, but it felt like one. There was a pile of throw up behind us, vomit on Alex's lips, a foreign home in front of me, and nothing from Lucas for me to hear.

Because once Alex is gone, Lucas is gone too. She's my connection to him. And once she finally dies, I will abruptly lose them both. Two friends, two people I love, both lost in a single day.

Unless, of course, I do something about it.

Opening my eyes, I peer over the valley again. And then, very deliberately, I eye the edge of the cliff. I inch closer. Then I peer over.

The drop is long, merciless, and far from any civilization. Even if I don't die on impact, I will die soon enough. The untouched pills from my mother's long-ago ACL surgery are in my backpack, stowed away in Alex's trunk. Maybe I won't need them after all.

But no. No sooner do I think that than I shove the thought away. Roughly, disgustedly.

Because Alex is back at the cabin. As far as I know, she still hasn't woken up. And even though I obviously don't want this life, *she* still does. So I better get my butt back there and make sure I do my part in giving her what she deserves. If she's sick, then she will need me to care for her. If she's dying, then she'll need me to call 911. To keep her alive. To keep her breathing. And my decision to die right now wouldn't just impact me, it would impact her.

So, standing up, I back away from the cliff.

"Lucas," I say out loud, looking forward with tight eyes

across the valley. I don't know if he is here. I can never feel him, and I very deliberately whispered before I left the cabin that I wanted him to stay with Alex. I told him where I was going, then asked that he not follow me. But truth be told, he's my brother. And I can't guarantee that he didn't follow against my will.

"Lucas, if you're there, hear me out. I don't like this. I don't like the thought of losing you, and I don't like the thought of losing Alex, ok? So if things get ugly, if Alex really isn't doing ok, you've got to help me out. Oh please, please, just help me out."

And just like that, this trip has become not about keeping myself alive, but about keeping Alex alive.

And that gives me an unexpected reason to live.

CHAPTER TWENTY

BRINLEY

When I get back to the cabin, I am surprised to see that Alex is awake. And not only awake but sitting on a wooden porch bench outside, delicately nibbling on a peanut butter and jelly sandwich. She is dressed in cutoff jeans and an overly large hoodie. She's showered, her hair is combed, and her oxygen tank is hooked up at her feet. It's one of the large ones in a wheeled rack. Apparently, she isn't going to waste one of her travel-sized tanks if she doesn't have to.

Pausing, I slow my urgent steps and take a deep, bracing breath. I pull in the crisp mountain air through my nose. Then I let it out again and lengthen my stride. When she hears me approaching, my boots crunching across the dead pine needles, Alex looks up. She lifts her hand in greeting. But she doesn't lift it very high. And the closer I get, the better I can see that her eyes are swollen and bloodshot. Almost as if she's been crying.

"Hey," I say, reaching the porch and stopping at its bottom step. I search her ragged face, then hesitantly add, "So you're alive, then?"

Swallowing, Alex looks down at the ground. Her eyes troubled, her face pale. "Yeah, mostly, I suppose." Only, her voice is raspy, croaky.

"Well, that's good," I say. "And, uh, it's good to see that you're eating again." I nod towards her sandwich, not commenting on her tears. Partly because I don't know what to say. But mostly because I've been there. And I know that, at least personally, I hate it when people comment after I've been privately crying. Sometimes the most respectful thing to do is to pretend that someone is stronger than they actually are. "Is there any more left where that came from?"

"Yeah, there is. Want me to make you one?"

"Nah, I'll make it myself. But do you want to come inside? You look kind of cold out here."

Alex looks down at herself, almost as if she's surprised to see goose bumps all up and down her exposed shins. Grimacing, she starts to say something. But then it turns into a cough.

And it's not a good-sounding cough.

"Yeah, let's get you inside," I say immediately. Not giving her a chance to say no, I hop up onto the porch. The wood is old and warped from the elements. It creaks underneath my new hiking boots. The boots that Alex kindly brought for me, the boots I found in my duffle bag. "Need help standing?" I ask, already holding out one of my hands.

Alex seems surprised, her slender brows rising. But then she reaches out and takes my hand. "Yeah that would be nice." She clears her throat. "Thanks."

I nod but don't say anything more. Once she's standing, I look around.

"So, uh, is Lucas out here?"

"Yeah, he's—" Alex pauses, coughing. As she does, she winces and holds her side. "Yes. He's... he's standing right next to us. He and I were talking out here. For a long time."

"So he stayed, then? While I hiked?"

Alex nods and leans heavily against the cabin wall for support. "Yes. He said that you asked him to? That you wanted him to stay and keep an eye on me?"

I blush a little, chagrined that she caught me caring. "Yeah, I did. I kept looking all around myself the whole hike though. I kept faking myself out that he might have been somewhere, that he might have followed me anyways."

Surprisingly, Alex laughs a little. It's pained, but at least it's a laugh. "Well, I'm glad you kept checking. That would be just like Lucas to ignore what you want. But tell you what. What if, rather than having to look all over, you look on your left side next time? Lucas doesn't mind standing on that side of you anytime he's with you. That way, you'll always know more or less where to look. Is that ok, Lucas?"

Alex pauses. Then, "Yeah, he says the left side works."

I nod, then look uncertainly to my left. Presumably, where Lucas should be at this moment. "Left side, huh?"

Alex nods, her lips pursed. "Left side."

I help her into the cabin after that. Well, more so hold the door open for her while she grasps the doorframe and helps herself in. I can't help but notice that she's moving stiffly, as if sore, and that her lips are still pursed, as if trying not to puke.

Once inside, I go straight for the sandwich stuff on the counter of the kitchenette while Alex goes to the closest bed, the one she slept in last night. Rather than sitting on the edge, she gingerly lays herself down, kicking her feet up. Her eyes flicker, then she shakes her head, as if responding to Lucas.

I give her a moment, letting them finish whatever conversation they are having. Then, while smearing peanut butter across the bread, I speak up.

"So, are you doing all right?"

There's not an immediate response. I grab the jelly and smear that on too. When Alex still doesn't answer, I mash the two pieces of bread together and look over my shoulder.

Alex is lying on the bed, fingers laced over her stomach,

just staring at the ceiling. She must feel the pressure of my gaze because finally, she clears her throat and speaks.

"No," she whispers quietly. "I'm not."

"Oh."

"But thank you," she adds, as if trying to change the subject. "For last night. I appreciate you taking care of me. I'm sorry I wasn't very...conscious."

A pang of fear trickles down my neck, but I don't let it show. I just shrug and shove a bite of sandwich into my mouth then walk over. Only hesitating a little, I decide to perch myself on the edge of her bed, sitting kinda close to her, as if we are buds or something. "Don't mention it. What are friends for, huh?" I say, nudging her foot playfully with my elbow.

Alex smiles weakly, but her gaze remains on the ceiling.

"Brinley?"

"Yes?"

She sighs, eyes tightening. Her fingers also tighten over her stomach, clenching it like claws. "There's something I need to tell you."

Slowly, I lower the sandwich from my mouth. I was about to take another bite, but not anymore. "Oh yeah? What do you need to tell me?"

"You know," she begins, speaking carefully, "how I recently had a surgery? A lung surgery?

"Yes. I think you mentioned that. When you visited my

house, didn't you say you met Lucas in the hospital? After a surgery?"

"Right," Alex confirms, coughing again. "Well, the purpose of that surgery was to cut some tumors out of my lungs, but these weren't normal tumors. My cancer is in my bone marrow, which is the part of the body that produces blood. So these tumors, as sometimes happens with myelofibrosis, were made of blood-producing cells. The surgery was supposed to cut them out. To help me breathe and stop coughing up so much blood. But...um...they're back. The little tumors they said they left in there must be growing now. And I coughed up blood this morning."

"Oh." I'm stunned. And suddenly, I don't have an appetite for my sandwich any longer.

"Yeah, it's...well, it's just a part of my cancer. But on top of that, my ribs are kind of broken, right? From our fall? I noticed when showering today that my entire side is still bruised purple and black. So, if you've noticed, I'm getting out of breath a lot more frequently. That was part of the problem last night. Lack of oxygen, you know? Major migraine."

I nod, feeling empty. Alex keeps talking, returning her eyes back to the ceiling.

"And the thing is, my ribs probably *aren't* going to heal. Since the cancer is in my bone marrow, I have a lot of problems with my bones and a lot of bleeding problems anywhere I'm hurt. My ribs aren't going to heal fully for the rest of my life. And my lungs…" Alex has to clear her throat before moving on. Not of mucus, I don't think, but of emotion. "They already cut out what they could of my lungs, so there's not much more the doctors can do for them. Which, I suppose, leaves us with two options."

And now, Alex looks over at me, her eyes deep and sad.

"And what are our two options?" I ask, then clear my own   throat.

"One, we can turn around and go back home. We're behind schedule anyways, and we should probably get you back in time for school tomorrow. If we leave now and don't make many stops, we could have you back in as little as eight or nine hours. That would get you home late, but tonight."

"Ok, and what's the second option?" I hedge.

Alex coughs. Then grimaces. Then she closes her eyes, looking pale and exhausted. "Option two is a selfish option," she says quietly. "I'm sick enough now that I probably won't leave home very much. Not after this. And I've always wanted to go to Abravanel Hall in Salt Lake City. My dad, apparently, played his final master's performance there when he was in college, right before my parents broke up. He was a pianist, just like me. My parents met while attending college in Utah, and I always wanted to be like him. That's why I played piano so much growing up; I wanted to have something I could talk to him about each time he called. Something that would make him proud, that would maybe make him like me more." And at that, Alex grimaces, a sad, pained look in her eyes.

"Anyways," she sighs, "I thought it might be nice to go to Abravanel Hall this week. To feel that connection with him just once before I die. He's been pretty distant my whole life, and...well, I can't exactly explain why this matters so much to me. But it does. So extending our trip to go to Salt Lake City could be our second crazy, ludicrous option. I looked it up, and well, the concert tomorrow evening is a piano concerto. Along with some other songs, they're playing Mozart's Piano Concerto No. 21. Not sure if you're familiar with it, but it's a good one. It's one of my favorites."

I look down at my partly eaten sandwich, turning it over in my hand, and then I look over at Alex again. She's terribly bony, and she's watching me. From her sick, weak position on the bed, she's watching me. "Go to Abravanel Hall, huh? And what does Lucas think about this?"

Alex's response is unexpected. Rather than looking around the room as if to find Lucas, her gaze stays steadily on me. Her brown eyes start brimming with tears. It's as if she already knows and doesn't need to consult him.

"This was his idea," she admits quietly. "Lucas wants this for me. He wants me to be happy before I die."

LUCAS

We don't leave for Salt Lake City immediately. After all, Alex just about killed herself getting us to Zion National Park, and we aren't about to leave without making her sacrifice worth it.

So while Alex rolls over and takes a much-needed nap, Brinley busies herself cleaning the Airbnb and packing the car. I follow her for a while, ghosting along and imagining that my invisible presence on her left-hand side is somehow helpful. Brinley's eyes flicker in my direction once or twice as she cleans, but that's really it. And eventually, pacing back and forth from the car to the cabin gets a little old. So, realizing how unneeded I am, I leave her side. And instead, I sit on the floor by Alex and watch.

The nice thing is, Alex is sleeping and Brinley can't see me. So really, I can watch my sister all I want without being called out for staring. So I do. I watch her walk back and forth, wipe off counters, sort through dirty clothes, and strip mattresses of their bedding. She's still wearing the black leggings and hoodie from her hike. Her blonde hair is in dual French braids and she doesn't really have makeup on. It's a change from how carefully put together and painted Brinley typically is at school, but Alex hasn't seemed to notice the difference. And really, I don't think twice about it either. After all, Brinley's my sister. I've seen her in diapers, for goodness' sake, let alone in braids with no makeup on. And for some weird reason, the look makes her seem older, more mature. Steadier, not less.

I reflect on this as I watch Brinley busy about the room. It's only been five months since my death, and already Brinley is growing. Maturing. Changing. The Brinley I knew when I died wouldn't have been too thrilled about packing a car all by herself. Or taking out the trash. Or pulling up a checklist and making sure she's done everything exactly right. And yet, here she is. Tidying up a home.

My Brinley is growing up on me.

And with a start, I realize that she will only continue to. It's only been five months since my death, but time will continue to roll on. She will continue to grow. And in the long run, Brinley won't really need me anymore. Sure, things are hard right now. They are hard because they are raw. Like the cuts on her arms and legs, the emotions of my death are still scabbed and crusty and cracking. But as long as Brinley doesn't do anything too drastic, they won't stay like that forever.

Time will pass, seasons will turn, and my Brinley will be ok. She will heal and she will learn to move on. She will make her own friends, new friends, and will forge her own path, her own future. She's going to start a career, get married, have kids, and keep growing into an amazing, wonderful woman.

I reflect on what it might be like to watch her years from now, tidying a home, but this time surrounded by little children and a loving husband.

And the thought makes me both sad and immensely peaceful.

Because maybe, at some point, Brinley won't need me anymore. Time is a funny thing, and she will come to find happiness in her own way, totally independent of me. But that doesn't mean I'm going anywhere. I will always cheer her on and watch over her and yearn desperately for the very best to happen. And yet, what if I can mature too, not just Brinley? What if *I* can heal? Grow? And find happiness outside of just my sister?

Glancing back, I look over my shoulder to Alex, lying peacefully on the bed. Her body is turned towards me, her face covered by her oxygen mask. But something about how fragile she is, how beautiful she is, stirs something within me.

Deep within me.

Truthfully, I don't understand what our future could be like together. As I told her in the car, I don't understand how things work in the afterlife. How friendships work, how love works. But I do know that when I'm with Alex, I *am* truly happier. And if she changes, if she becomes a spirit like me, I don't see that difference changing the way I feel. Some things are just so entrenched in the human soul—the need for people, the need for love, the need for a purpose and for kindness and affection—that I don't see it entirely disappearing. Ever. What I wanted in life still feels like the same things I want in death. Only this time, magnified. Hyper-focused. Because material things are gone. Distractions are gone. And all that remains are the wants and needs of the soul.

CHAPTER TWENTY-ONE

BRINLEY

"What the crap, Alex?" I cry. I crane my head further out the window, gawking, not even caring as the wind whips loose strands of hair into my face. All around us are massive, red-rock cliffs thousands of feet high. They tower over us, surrounding us, striated with different shades of red, white, and black, and topped with dark green spurts of spring foliage. It's like we've been transported to Mars or something. But a Mars that is majestic and thriving and alive, not barren and dead. "How on earth did my parents never bring us here before? This is ridiculous!"

Alex chuckles, inclining her own head forward so she can better see the tops of the cliffs through the windshield. "Isn't it? I could come here a million times and it would never get old."

"So, what? You've been here a lot then?"

Alex nods, maneuvering the car around yet another bend. The turn repositions our car so that we're facing directly into the sunlight. Squinting, I pull my head back into the vehicle. We're driving down the main, scenic road of Zion National Park, and I've never been struck by such awe before in my life.

"Yeah, I have. Before I got cancer, my mother and I used to love hiking together. We would come here most summers. Zion was our paradise."

"Well, I can see why," I mutter, shaking my head. "And Lucas, he can see all this too?"

Alex laughs again, making herself cough. "Oh definitely. While you were sticking your head out the window, he was standing up in the back seat. Literally. Standing. His whole torso was sticking out of the roof of the car so he could see better."

Alex's eyes flicker to the rearview mirror. "Also, he says that it was great. Better than any convertible he's ever been in. And he doesn't want me to leave out the fact that he yelled 'I love Zion!' at the top of his lungs."

I grin at the mental image, then roll my eyes. "That lunatic. Did you hear that, Lucas?" I ask, turning to face the empty back seat. "You're a lunatic!"

"Why, thank you. He says he accepts the compliment."

I roll my eyes again, then face forward in my seat. "So,

what? Are we just going to drive through and leave? That feels like such a waste."

Next to me, Alex starts to say something. Then she stops. She looks really uncomfortable. For a while, I don't understand why. Then it hits me.

"Oh," I say quickly. "Sorry, I didn't mean it like that. Hiking, cancer...right."

"Right," Alex agrees, seeming uneasy. "I'm sincerely sorry. I honestly wish we could do more here. I wish I could take you to The Narrows, or Angels Landing, or really any one of these amazing trails. But if you would like, I do know there's a paved walking path. It runs by the river and takes us deeper into the canyon. It's nothing like standing at the top of one of these cliffs, but..." She shrugs. "At least it's something. I'm sure you've seen the wheelchair in the trunk? If you don't mind pushing me..." Alex trails off, turning it into a question.

"Um, yes!" I say immediately. "Of course I don't mind. Where's this walking path? Let's do it!"

"Ok, just keep in mind that it means we'll get to Salt Lake City later. We still have a five-hour drive ahead of us. And I..." Alex purses her lips, seeming not to like where this is going. Finally, she sighs. "And honestly, Brinley, this will wear me out. I don't think my iron levels are doing great, and I'm pretty exhausted as is. Driving afterwards may be tough. I won't be great company."

"Oh." Images of last night flash into my mind. Images of Alex puking, images of her collapsing. "Oh," I say again.

It's quiet in the car as I mull over the scenario. Next to me, Alex is clenching and unclenching the steering wheel. I can tell she's frustrated by her limitations and is probably hating on herself right now. The more I get to know Alex, the more I realize that she doesn't like it when cancer keeps her from doing something. If we don't do this, she's going to be mad at herself for the rest of the day. She's going to be mad that she couldn't give me what I wanted.

Besides, she's dying. And she deserves to see this canyon just as much as I do.

"Alex, I can drive," I suddenly blurt.

She looks over at me, eyebrows raised. "Um, I hate to break it to you, but you only have a learner's permit. That would be illegal."

"So what?" I ask, now getting frustrated at my own limitations. "Come on, I've been fifteen since September. I've already had it for, like, half a year. And besides, this is rural Utah. Not like a lot of cops are going to be patrolling a freeway in the middle of nowhere. I'll be safe. I'll go under the speed limit. And once we get to more urban areas, I'll swap you. Besides, you're practically an adult! I can drive with adults."

"I thought the law says you can only drive with adults twenty-one or older."

I scowl. "So what? Take your age, add it to Lucas's, and between the two of you, we have plenty of maturity here."

Alex lets out a burst of laughter, coupled with a burst of coughing. "Yeah, right. Try explaining that to a cop."

I scowl deeper. "Yeah, well, I won't need to. I'm not going to get pulled over."

"Says you."

"Yes! Says me! Come on, Alex. I hate to use this card on you, but this is probably your last visit to Zion. Do you really, really want to miss out on the river walk?"

Alex hesitates. I've got her there.

Suddenly, her eyes flicker to the rearview mirror. My gut drops. I look away, cursing under my breath.

"Brinley," Alex says slowly.

"What?" I snap.

"Lucas told me how he died that night."

"Yeah? Well, I'm sure he did."

And slowly, carefully, a smile grows across her face. The skin around Alex's eyes crinkles in kindness. "Lucas wants you to know that this is exactly how he felt that night too. He felt like he loved you and just wanted to give you the world. He's asking me to let you drive."

"Huh?" My jaw drops. My head whips around and I stare at the back seat.

"He says"—Alex smiles wider—"that he trusts you. You're a much better driver now than you were six months ago. And he wants me to let you, so you can understand the reasons he wanted to drive that night too."

LUCAS

Truth be told, I'm nervous to let Brinley drive. Just like Alex predicted, the Riverside Walk seems to take a lot out of her. I mean, not to say it isn't beautiful, absolutely beautiful, and she does seem to enjoy it, regardless of the double takes she and Brinley garner as they walk along. After all, the path is somewhat crowded and she and Brinley are an odd pair. One tourist even pulls out his camera and tries to discreetly take a picture of the wheelchaired, balding girl and her even younger companion. Alex ignores him; Brinley glares him down.

But after the hour and a half of exploring, winding through a tree-canopied path and staring up at towering, majestic red cliffs, it is time to leave. Alex is starting to cough a lot, and little specks of red are dotting her lips and hand. So, whipping out her phone, Brinley insists we take one final picture together. With the red walls as our backdrop, we crowd around each other, with Brinley crouched in front of Alex's wheelchair and me bending over the back of it, grinning by her face. Brinley snaps the photo excitedly, though, of course, I don't show up. Even Alex says she can't see me in it. But there is this large, empty spot in the corner where I should be, and that is good enough for me. And Brinley can't seem to rip her eyes away from it.

But eventually, once Alex starts coughing again, she does. Pocketing her phone and taking her place behind the wheelchair, Brinley turns Alex around. And later, with one last, wistful glance at the canyon, Alex lets Brinley help her into the car.

Only Brinley helps Alex into the back seat, not the front. And for the next many hours, Alex sleeps while Brinley drives. And as she drives, she plays again all the songs I picked out for her yesterday.

And by the end of it, she isn't crying. She is, for once, smiling.

CHAPTER TWENTY-TWO

ALEX

There's not much that a good nap and almost seven hundred dollars in your bank account can't fix. For most of my life, my mother awarded me a modest allowance, siphoned from my father's payments of child support. But I was never a needy child. I didn't need many material things besides my piano to keep me happy. So though the monthly payments she gave me were small, they always added up.

So with nearly seven hundred dollars to spend and less than five months to live, I feel like I can get a little spendy. Rather than finding the cheapest motel available in downtown Salt Lake City, I swap Brinley seats and drive us to a place called Little America. There are two hotels notorious for being classy in Utah's capital city. The first one, the Grand America, is a towering, gray-stone structure with an intricately beautiful interior. In my mind's eye, it is the epitome of wealth.

The Little America is just across the street from it and is a much smaller and cheaper hotel. In fact, it is made of red bricks, and the interior of the rooms are a little bit outdated. But regardless, it's known for its classy and breathtaking lobby. So I figure I can splurge. Just a little. Just to feel special. And that's where Brinley and I end up.

After checking us in, she gives me a shoulder to lean on as we shuffle towards our room. I slept for a long time in the car, so I'm not feeling as awful as I anticipated I might. In fact, even though it is after eight o'clock, I decide to stay awake and watch a movie with Brinley. Despite Lucas's exaggerated protests, we settle on a very romantic chick flick that turns out to be as funny as it is swoon-worthy. By the end of it, Brinley is in tears from laughing so much, and I am in tears from trying so hard *not* to laugh, just because it hurts my ribs.

Throughout the whole movie, Lucas watched us giggle, frequently rolling his eyes and making snarky comments. But there was also this giant grin on his face sometimes, and I can only hope that our girls' night did his heart some good. In fact, he seemed to have just as much fun watching the two of us bond and laugh and swoon as we did watching the movie.

But when the credits finally roll and we click off the

television, Brinley still doesn't seem tired. Rather than get ready for bed, she hops over to my mattress and sits herself cross-legged at the foot of it. She prattles on about the movie, drooling over how cute the main actor was, and I go along with it. Truthfully, it's kind of awkward for me, because I didn't think he was all that cute compared to Lucas, but I certainly don't admit to that out loud. Instead, I just blush and shrug a little when Lucas meets my eyes. He laughs and returns the gesture with an eye roll, following it with a wink.

Eventually though, Brinley does, actually, seem to run out of saliva to drool with. And quite abruptly, she changes the subject. She starts asking me about my family, admitting that she feels bad for not asking more get-to-know-you questions before now. So whatever she asks, I obligingly tell her.

As the late-night minutes tick by, I tell her about my mom, Craig, and the way they met at church just weeks before we found out I had cancer. I tell her how much they want to get married but haven't yet, all because I'm sick. And I even tell her about my secret, intense hope that one day as a spirit, I might get the chance to watch their marriage. I long to see them finally unite, move into a nice home together, and be happy, just like they've always deserved. Because if I could give my mom anything, anything at all, to thank her for all the sacrifices she's made for me, I would give her a happy-ever-after. And as cheesy as it sounds, I hope against hope that, even after my death, she'll be able to find happiness again.

I tell Brinley all this and she listens, clinging to my every word as if I am telling her a fairytale. But when it starts getting too emotional for me, I have to change the subject. Wiping at my eyes, I start asking Brinley about her family, and she tells me anything I want to know.

She tells me what her parents do for work, about their life spent in Albuquerque, and about a yearly tradition where her family travels to an exotic location each Christmas. Except this year, she says, they were too broken from Lucas's death to go. They canceled their trip to the Caribbean and all stayed home to cry. Her mother lay in bed under the covers all day, sobbing, and her father left for a long, long drive and didn't come home until dark. Brinley admits that after Lucas left, they all felt lost. Really lost. And her parents haven't been the same since.

At this point in her story, Brinley gets really emotional too and turns her face away from me. She bites her bottom lip and I can tell she's trying not to cry.

"I just..." she croaks, "I just don't think anyone understands, Alex. It's hard to describe how much I ruined my family by going to that party. Lucas is dead. My parents are depressed too, not just me, and I just...I just didn't think. I didn't know..." Brinley stops and squeezes her eyes shut. Her hands fist on her knees and she takes deep, ragged breaths. When she opens her eyes again, her expression is tormented.

"I seriously ruined everything that night. Not just for Lucas but for my parents too," she says, her voice trembling. "Lucas's death has been *terrible* for them. And all I ever do is give them more to worry about. I'm...I'm not...*good* at home. I'm not anything worthwhile. I'm just another massive problem for them to deal with, and I know it hurts them. *I* hurt them. So please. *Please*. When we get back to Albuquerque, you can't tell them anything. You can't tell them why we went on this trip. You can't tell them what I've been doing. If they ever found out I was cutting—if they found out about my letters..."

And with that, Brinley comes undone and starts crying. She's not sobbing, not like I've seen her do before, but the tears are falling fast and her breaths are getting unsteady. Concerned, I lean forward and place my hand on her knee. But I don't say anything. I let her keep talking.

"My parents have so much to deal with already," Brinley moans, burying her face in her hands. "The last thing they need is another problem. The last thing they need is an extra burden like me."

Pained, I purse my lips. Feeling torn, I drop my gaze to the bed sheets and don't look at Brinley.

"So, Alex, don't tell them. Ok?"

I stay silent.

"Alex?" Brinley lifts her face from her hands, her cheeks wet and eyes bloodshot. "Alex, you have to promise me."

Still, I don't say anything. I just stare at the bedsheets. Then taking my own deep, steeling breath, I make my decision. I shake my head. "No. I can't promise that. Not if I think you're going to hurt yourself."

"Alex!"

"I can't!" I repeat, looking up. "Brinley, if I didn't say anything and something happened to you, do you understand what that would do to me? What that would do to your parents? It would be terrible! Your suicide would hurt them in ways you can't even imagine! In ways they could never recover from. And I can't let that happen. I can't promise you something I'll regret."

But that just makes Brinley cry harder. She shakes her head at me, her body starting to tremble. "No," she moans. "Please. No, no, no. You don't understand! They won't take it well, Alex. They'll think there's something wrong with me. They'll try to get me help!"

"What kind of help?" I say, forcing my voice softer, trying to steady my emotions and make it more gentle. "Therapy? Brinley, therapy is a great thing. It's there for a reason."

But Brinley just moans loudly. She drops her head back into her hands, her fingernails curling inward like claws.

Quietly, she starts muttering, "No, no, no, no, no," to herself, over and over again.

Looking away from her, I make eye contact with Lucas, standing at the foot of our bed. His brow is furrowed, his eyes sad and worried. He's been quiet this whole time, but now he steps forward and comes to a crouch right in front of his sister. Slowly and delicately, he reaches out a hand and places it reassuringly on Brinley's other knee. Giving him more room, I retract mine.

"Brinley," I say quietly, eyeing him and the careful touch of his hand. It's soft and gentle, hovering a hair's breadth away from her skin. "Can you feel that?"

Briefly, Brinley's muttering pauses. She doesn't lift her head, but she does ask in a husky voice, "Feel what?"

"Feel Lucas. He's touching you. On your knee. Can you feel that?"

And this time, Brinley's head does lift. Her eyes are bloodshot, but she quickly wipes away the tears. She looks down at herself, brow furrowed.

"Which knee?"

"Your right one."

Brinley settles her gaze there and keeps staring. Lucas gets an intense expression on his face, looking at her with deep, painful longing.

"What if you...what if you close your eyes?" I suggest, sounding hopeful. I'm not confident it will work, but I am curious, and I really, really want Brinley to have this moment. "Like, focus. Really hard. And maybe you'll feel something."

And so, Brinley does. Sitting stiff and nervous, she first looks around herself uncomfortably, then does as I ask, closing her eyes and wiping at her cheeks. She breathes in deeply and breathes out slowly, getting her emotions under control.

"There," I say when she seems to be calming down. "Can you feel it?"

"I...I don't think I can," she admits, worried.

"Then don't focus on how it feels physically," I suggest. "Focus on how it feels emotionally. Can you feel what Lucas wants you to feel?"

Brinley is silent and still. Really, really still. Time ticks by. And then with a dramatic gasp, her eyes fly open.

"*Lucas!*" she cries.

Lucas jumps a mile at his name. Gasping, he jolts to his feet and stumbles backward, passing right through the bed adjacent to the one Brinley and I are sitting on. He gasps loudly again, shudders violently, then stumbles back out of the mattress.

"Alex, I felt something! I felt something!" Brinley cries.

"Yeah, you did?" I ask, getting excited. And truthfully, I'm kind of shocked. Lucas seems kind of shocked too.

"Yes! I mean, I didn't feel anything physical. Of course I

didn't feel anything physical. But I felt *something*. I felt something kind. Something soft and sort of warm in my chest, or almost like goose bumps or a shiver down my spine! Only, it was nice. It was *really* easy to miss if I wasn't focusing, but...but I think it was real! Alex, is it possible to feel love from a ghost, even if they're dead?"

My eyes grow wide. I share a stunned look with Lucas, both of us reeling.

"I don't know," I say truthfully. "I mean, I've felt love when I'm around Lucas. But that's because I can see him and talk to him. So I don't know. But what I *do* know is that Lucas was aware of you in that moment. He was touching you, and he wanted you to know that he was there."

"Yes! And I felt that!" Brinley crows. "I felt love! It was...I dunno. I haven't felt love for myself in so long—*so long*, Alex. And I haven't ever felt that kind of peace. So it couldn't have come from my head, right? Because I don't love myself in my head. So doesn't that mean it had to come from someplace else? That the love had to come from Lucas!"

"I...yeah. I think so," I say, thunderstruck. "That would make sense."

And at both my words and Brinley's, Lucas slowly begins to smile. And his smile grows wider, and wider, and wider.

Looking from his sister, to him, and back again, I shake

my head in wonder and my eyes fill up with tears. "Well, there you have it, Brinley," I say, laughing with the emotion of the moment. "That's how you can stay connected to Lucas. You may not be able to see him. You may not be able to hear him. But you can recognize his love. You know how it feels. And maybe, if you just pay attention sometimes, maybe you can feel that it's still there. Strong and peaceful and real."

CHAPTER TWENTY-THREE

BRINLEY

Alex is one tough nut. She wouldn't leave for breakfast this morning until I promised her, crossing my heart about three times over, that I would talk to my parents when I got home. And also, that I would tell them about things. About everything. My cutting, the suicide notes, the reason for this trip. Yeah. She wants all of it out.

She almost, in fact, made me call them this very morning. But with a little bit of persistence and a whole lot of anxiety, I squirmed my way out of it. Alex called her mom, checking in and explaining that we extended our trip to Salt Lake City, but I just lay on my bed, staring at the ceiling. I didn't call my own parents. I wasn't ready for that quite yet. But I did close my eyes and focus on feeling Lucas. I couldn't be sure, because it was nowhere near as clear as I felt last night, but I thought that maybe, *maybe*, I could sense something. Something little. Something a little bit hopeful and a little bit nice. Either that or I was totally psyching myself out.

But either way, I can't deny that I felt something last night. Something real. And that, at the moment, is good enough for me. Besides, Alex and I are having breakfast together now, we still didn't know our day plans, and it is time to shift my focus from the intangible to the tangible. And possibly, even to the frilly.

"So, what?" I ask suddenly, shoveling another bite of rubbery eggs into my mouth, compliments of the free hotel breakfast. "We're going to the symphony tonight, yeah? So doesn't that mean we need dresses? Like, I thought we were supposed to dress up for fancy concerts like this."

Alex is leaning back in her chair across the table from me, one arm loosely draped over her abdomen, the other holding a cup of milk she is delicately sipping at through a straw. She long ago lost interest in her muffin. She only ate one bite, perhaps two, and I can tell that she's forcing herself to drink the milk. Apparently, she doesn't really want to.

"Well, yes, technically," she says. "But there's always a big variety in what the audience wears. Some people wear dresses while others might wear nice pants and just a simple blouse or something."

"But what you're saying is, our jeans won't cut it."

Alex hesitates. Then, "No," she admits. "I mean, they won't kick us out. But we might look out of place."

"Well, all right then," I say, taking my last bite of eggs and slapping my plastic fork down on the table as if making an announcement. "I've figured out what we're going to do today. You and I are going shopping."

"Shopping?" Alex raises her eyebrows. "We drove ten hours to get here and you want to go shopping?"

I sigh and very dramatically roll my eyes. Alex, for her part, throws a glance at the empty air beside her. I can only imagine that Lucas must be snickering right now. In life, he always used to tease me about my obsession with shopping. "Oh come on, Alex, you're making it sound boring. This isn't just any shopping. We are going *dress* shopping. For a night out at the symphony! Come on. Doesn't that sound classy to you? Fun? Worthwhile?"

Alex just looks at me, raising both eyebrows and slowly shaking her head. "Fun? You really think dress shopping is fun?"

"Of course I do! What? Don't you? Didn't you have fun picking out your dresses for a school dance? Wasn't that the best part?"

"I never went to a dance. Homeschooled. Cancer. Remember?"

My jaw drops. Like literally drops. "Get out. Get out!" I

cry. "You never went to a dance? You've never been dress shopping before?"

"No, of course I have! I go to church on Sundays, remember? I wear dresses," Alex says defensively.

I groan. "Church dresses? Really? That *so* doesn't count. And besides, you didn't bring any church dresses with you on this trip, did you?"

"Well, no. Not exactly."

"Well, all right then! It's settled. You and I are having a girls' day out. We're going to go to City Creek Mall, or whatever the heck that place is called, and we are going to buy you a dress. A *real* dress. Not something you would wear to a church service. And then I'll do your makeup, I'll do your hair even, and then you and I are going to show up as the classiest, most jaw-dropping women who have ever graced that symphony hall with their presence. You hear me? This is going to be epic."

Alex, groaning, drops her head into her hand, kneading her forehead. "Brinley, let's not overdo this. Please. If we do that, we'll stick out like sore thumbs."

"Stick out like sore thumbs? Um, no. That's what would happen if we went in jeans. Instead, we are going to stand out like elegant pearls in a pile of pebbles."

Alex groans again, then looks over her shoulder, giving the empty spot to her right a disapproving look. "Lucas, stay out of this."

"He's agreeing with me, isn't he?"

"No, he's *guilt-tripping* me. He's telling me that you'll be devastated if I don't agree. He says shopping is your favorite thing in the whole world."

"Because it *is* my favorite thing in this whole world. It very seriously is," I say, my voice deadpan with the seriousness of it. "And I truly will be devastated."

Alex groans yet again, now dragging her hand slowly down her face. "Can't we just get skirts or something? Don't you understand how difficult it will be to try on dresses with a broken rib cage?"

"Don't you understand that I'll help you?"

"Don't you understand that this is crazy?"

"Don't you understand that this whole trip has been crazy? Come on, just say yes," I plead. "Please? You need this life experience. Dress shopping is a rite of passage that every girl has to go through at least once in their life. At least once. And I'll make it fun! I promise! So...pretty please? I really want a dress too."

"Oh, you did not just use that card on me."

"Oh, I just did," I say. Then I stubbornly fold my arms across my chest and slowly smirk with triumph. I know I have her now. "You don't get a dress, then I don't get a dress. And I'll be devastated."

"Brinley..." Alex intones.

"Alex..." I intone back.

And finally, she gives in. "Oh, all right," she says, throwing up her hands and rolling her eyes. But also, looking closely, I think I see a small smile tugging at the corners of her mouth. Alex may be throwing a fit about this, but oh, she wants it. She's a girl, and deep down inside, she wants this. "But don't expect me to try on fifty million dresses. I'll try on one or two, three at max. But after that, I'm sure I'll be done. My dying body can only take so much."

"Oh, don't worry, I'll choose carefully," I say with a grin. "And Lucas, by the way, is not invited."

LUCAS

Brinley really wasn't kidding. I am not invited on their shopping trip. And not only is she being adamant about it, but she's being pretty obnoxious about it too.

"So, Alex, you are *sure* he's not coming with us?" Brinley asks for the thousandth time as the girls put on their shoes in the hotel room. "Like, he really did agree to stay back and watch TV? You did explain to him the absolute importance that he does this, right?"

Alex, straightening from her bent-over position and cringing with the movement, sighs. Yet again. "Lucas can actually hear you, remember? He's heard the absolute importance of this straight from your very own mouth.

Repeatedly. He doesn't need to hear it from me."

"Oh, yeah. Right. Forgot about that. Hey, Lucas? If you follow us, I'll kill you."

I burst out laughing at that one, and Alex rolls her eyes. She's not feeling well, I can tell, but she's being a good sport about this. Under normal circumstances, I might have been a little more protective of her. I might have sided with Alex, not Brinley, and done my best to rein in my sister and save Alex from her glitz. But having caught on rather quickly to what Brinley is doing, I don't.

Because though she seems pigheaded about this, I suspect that Brinley is, in her own way, actually being intensely kind. Like me, she seemed surprised that Alex has never been to a school dance before. Like me, she's probably saddened by that. And like me, she must assume that Alex may, possibly, have never even been on a date before. Not, of course, for lack of good looks or a winning personality. But rather because of her circumstances. Homeschool. Cancer. Perpetual puking and hair loss and surgeries. Yeah. Alex, it seems, has not had extensive dating experience.

So what Brinley must be doing is ensuring that Alex and I get to have our very own, classy date tonight. She wants to save Alex's final appearance for a beautiful, surprise reveal for me, right before the symphony. She wants to replicate what it would be like on an actual date, had I gone up to her doorstep to fetch her. And if that is Brinley's plan—if that is her beautiful, brilliant plan—then there is no way I'm going to say no to that.

Instead, I will just obediently stay behind in the hotel room, watch the streaming service they turn on for me, and incessantly fret about the fact that I will be showing up for my date with Alex in jeans, Converse shoes, and a white cotton T-shirt. Not a tuxedo.

Which is a shame, really. A true, bitter shame. Because man, I would look sharp in a tuxedo. And what I wouldn't give to look sharp for Alex tonight.

ALEX

"Keep your eyes closed just a little longer, I'm almost done."

Brinley's face is hovering inches away from mine. Likely, the tip of her tongue is peeking through her lips in concentration, just as it has been all evening. Both she and I are in our dresses, sitting in the bathroom. I'm perched on the counter, facing away from the mirror with feet dangling so I can't see. And she's sitting on the back of a chair, her feet planted on the seat, her tongue sticking out as she leans forward and does my makeup.

"Oh my freak, you're going to love this," Brinley mutters. I don't answer. I know I'm not supposed to. One wrong move and I'm certain she'll stab me through with the pointed handle of her eyeshadow brush. I am under strict instructions not to move an inch.

Until, moments later, I feel Brinley pull back. And then the motion is followed by a squeal.

"Ah! Alex, open your eyes. Open your eyes! You're going to love this!"

I do, blinking awkwardly against the heavy weight of the mascara. I've worn makeup plenty of times before in my life. Of course I have. Just...not recently. It seems that the sicker I get, the less bandwidth, or strength, I have to care for my looks. It's probably been since before the lung surgery that I've worn any degree of makeup like this. And Brinley, I can already feel, has done an excellent job.

She squeals again, beaming at me with self-pride. "Ok, turn around, turn around. You have to see this. Oh my gosh, you have to see this."

Thankfully, my cannula is back in my nose. I had to remove it for several minutes while Brinley did my foundation, some contouring, and light brushes of blush. The time without it just about did me in, and I know she rushed as much as she could. Moving stiffly so as not to jostle my incredibly sore ribs, I slide off the bathroom counter and stand. Brinley steadies me, then turns me around.

And I won't lie. What I see just about makes me cry. I

can't help it. Because for the first time in a long, long while, I actually feel like I'm beautiful.

"Brinley," I whisper, shaking my head at myself in the mirror and swallowing back the thick lump in my throat. "Brinley, I—"

"Look amazing?" she fills in. "Look stunning? I know! Lucas is going to die!" And then she laughs at her own joke. But even though I know she's being funny, she's also got her eyes trained on me, and she's looking at me with extreme pride and a streak of kindness. A kindness I've never quite seen in her before.

"You really, really are beautiful, Alex," she tells me.

I just swallow again, nodding. And then, being tender so as not to hurt me, Brinley wraps her scarred arms around me in a hug. And in a really emotional moment, I hug her back.

"Thank you," I say quietly, my words just a whisper because of the emotion. "Brinley, thank you," I repeat.

"Don't mention it." She pulls back, holding me at arm's length. Then she can't help but squeal again. "Shall I go get my brother?"

I blush. Of course I deeply blush. "Brinley, it's really not that big of a—"

"Nope, nope. I won't have any of that. Not tonight. You, Alexia Ahmed, *are* a big deal." And with that, she dances over to the bathroom door and yanks it open, sticking her head out.

"Hey, Lucas," she says. "You better prepare yourself. Because Alex is going to knock you dead."

"Brinley," I complain, embarrassed.

"Oh, don't 'Brinley' me. Now get out here. Lucas, you in position?"

"I'm in position," his voice confirms from the room.

"He says that he's ready," I relay to Brinley.

"Ok, great," she grins. And with that, she steps out of the bathroom, decked out in her extremely flattering, silken black dress. It's shorter in the front than in the back and is held over her delicate shoulders with two thin spaghetti straps. She does a twirl for Lucas, and I hear him whooping and giving her a catcall whistle. At the sound of it, I can't help but laugh.

"He likes it, Brinley," I tell her with all the sincerity I can muster. "He really, really likes it."

"Well, of course he does," she says, shrugging flippantly. "Though I've got to admit, it feels weird parading myself in front of an empty room."

I laugh again, imagining how incredibly weird this must be from her perspective.

And then Brinley lifts a finger and scrunches it towards herself, beckoning me out with a mischievous look on her face. "Your turn," is all that she says.

And so, sighing deeply and reaching down to pick up my

oxygen-tank backpack, I do as I'm told. And stiffly, limping from the pain in my side and the soreness radiating deep in my bones, I step out. And slowly, I turn.

Only this time, Lucas doesn't whoop. He doesn't catcall. The way he's holding up one hand halfway, it seems like he was about to. But then, it's like he froze in his tracks. And, dumbfounded, he's just gaping at me. Then slowly, he closes his mouth. He gulps. And wrinkles appear around the corners of his eyes and his expression gets very, very emotional.

"Oh my gosh," he finally whispers. "I could kiss you right now."

And at that, my face blushes a burning, beet red. And I look at the ground, unable to meet his riveted eyes.

"What? What did he say, Alex? What did he say?" Brinley demands from behind me.

"I—" I start to answer her. In my shock, I try to. I want to. But at the same time, there is no way in the heavens I'm going to tell her what Lucas just said.

Looking up, I see Lucas wink at me, his eyes still glued intensely on mine. "Tell her I'm speechless," he suggests, and a slow, warm smile spreads across his lips.

"He's...uh...he's speechless," I say, looking back at Brinley. And with that, she squeals. And the face-splitting smile on her lips is almost enough to make this ludicrous, over-the-top moment worth it. Beaming with pride and joy,

Brinley claps her hands in front of herself, her scars visible on her forearms.

"Oh, that's good. Alex, you have no idea how good that is. Lucas? He's never speechless. He's such a motormouth, that's the biggest compliment you could ever get!"

I laugh slightly, then cough, looking down in timid embarrassment. Brinley may have a good point about the motormouth thing, but I think I know of a compliment that was, truthfully, a little bit better.

LUCAS

There is no denying it. Brinley did a remarkable job. Alex is stunning.

I am, of course, a bit of a jock and not really a smart dude when it comes to fashion. So I may not know the names of any of the materials. But Brinley picked out for Alex a pale sage-green dress that does amazing things against her soft olive skin and deep brown eyes. The dress comes to her knees and the shoes she wears are flat sandals, keeping it easy for her to walk. She also has on a long-sleeved, cream-colored cardigan to keep her bony frame warm. Her short, wavy hair is carefully styled, and one side is pulled away from her eyes with a simple, stylish barrette. It isn't an ostentatious look, because Alex isn't an ostentatious person. Nor is it one that would make her stand out like an overpriced aristocrat, because that isn't Alex either. Rather, it is an outfit that brings out her soft side, her gentle demeanor, and her natural, unpretentious beauty.

And for that, I am absolutely, undeniably floored. I am standing in front of someone who doesn't take my breath away because she's trying to. But rather because she's trying so hard not to.

And that is what I love about Alex.

"Well," Brinley eventually says, smug about her handiwork as she looks Alex over. "I don't know about you, but I think I'm ready to show ourselves off to the world. Lucas, would you like to escort this fine lady to the symphony?"

"Don't mind if I do," I say with a flash of aristocratic flair. I puff out my T-shirt-clad chest, kind of like a proper gentleman, and slowly stride up to Alex. When I'm side by side with her, I grin and then jut out my elbow as if requesting her arm through mine.

Alex laughs. That cute, embarrassed blush is still tinting her cheeks, and she looks at me uncertainly.

"Give it a shot," I tell her. "Loop your arm through mine. It doesn't require touching."

She raises one eyebrow at me, unsure. "You're kidding me."

"Nope, not at all. Alexia Ahmed, may I have the exquisite privilege of escorting you to Abravanel Hall?"

And at that, I've got her. There's a light in her eyes as she laughs and slowly, hesitantly loops her arm through mine. At first it is, admittedly, awkward. Our arms don't touch and I'm sure to the outside world, we look ridiculous. I'm invisible and Alex's arm is held away from her body at a skewed, unnatural angle. But we are arm in arm. I'm actually escorting Alex. And though I won't take her all the way to the symphony like this, I do get to accompany her to the car to grab her wheelchair. And that is enough for me.

"Thank you for this honor," I murmur, looking up from our arms to meet her eyes. A thrill courses through me as our gazes lock, and I really, truly, can't help but smile. Alex, whether she meant to or not, has permanently found a place in my heart, in my very soul.

"Well, aren't you two cute?" Brinley says, her look smug as her eyes pass back and forth from Alex to where she assumes I must be. "Two lovebirds headed to the symphony with their fashionable third wheel, Brinley. How could the night possibly get better?"

CHAPTER TWENTY-FOUR

ALEX

It is a distance of one mile from the Little America Hotel to Abravanel Hall, which would have felt too far for me to walk even before spending a whole day shopping. So rather than make me lug my fatigued body all that way, Lucas escorts me to the car and Brinley pulls my wheelchair from the trunk. She gingerly removes my backpack from off my shoulders and loops it over the back of the wheelchair, then has me take my seat. She even crouches down in her dress, popping down the wheelchair feet to make sure I am comfortable.

"Thank you, Brinley," I tell her, for what feels like the millionth time today. I get emotional as I realize there is so much I've come to owe her for.

"Don't mention it," she says with a shrug. Then she

turns to her left side. "Hey, Lucas, under different circumstances, I would let you push Alex. But seeing as you can't actually touch anything, I'm going to push her myself. That savvy?"

Lucas grins. "Of course. That just means I get to walk side by side with you guys and stare at Alex the whole time. I'm happy with that."

Embarrassed, I roll my eyes and relay the message to Brinley. Well, at least most of the message. And then, together, the three of us are off. It's not too late in the evening, so the sun is still up but low to the horizon, causing streaks of soft sunlight to slant across the city. We maneuver through the crowded streets of downtown, and I find myself transfixed by the sight of Lucas dodging all the people. They can't see him, of course they can't, so they repeatedly try to walk through him. Most of the time, he is able to get himself out of their way, but occasionally, he isn't.

It's baffling to watch this take place and realize just how oblivious we humans are to the spiritual. It makes me wonder how many times I may have passed by a spirit, or even walked right through one myself, without even knowing it. And since seeing Lucas, it's made me wonder how many other spirits I may have glimpsed in the past month without realizing it. After all, besides the brightness of his eyes, Lucas looks no different to me than an actual human. So could any number of these strangers actually be a ghost that only Lucas and I see, but Brinley can't? The thought, honestly, is a little bit eerie.

What I find reassuring, though, is watching just how respectful Lucas is, and I admire how much he honors the space and autonomy of the living. He doesn't take cruel advantage of the fact that people can't see him. He doesn't get in their bubble, or play pranks on them, or mess around by passing through their bodies. He interacts with the living as if he himself were alive, with a considerate aloofness to strangers. And as he walks by a cute infant or sees a sweet family, he even reacts the same way I do: he smiles affectionately.

In fact, if all spirits were as good and kind as Lucas, I don't think we as a species would have come to fear the dead. Instead, I wonder if we would have come to pity them. Or appreciate them. Or honestly, even welcome their company. It's a sobering thought, how good a spirit can be yet how frequently we are taught to fear them. It's not fair because they are, after all, just the echoes of people who once lived, of people who once were loved. And whether we want to admit it or not, spirits are what each of us, eventually, are destined to become.

"You still doing good down there?" Brinley asks, yanking me out of my revelry as she leans over to speak in my ear. With a little shove, she pushes me forward into a crowd of people waiting to cross at an intersection. Lucas, for his part, lingers behind us. There isn't enough room for him to follow.

"Doing great," I confirm, giving Brinley a thumbs up. Brinley nods and then straightens again. She saw me cough up a bit of blood during our shopping trip today and it unsettled her. So I'm not surprised that she's inclined to hover tonight. In fact, she insisted on buying tissues and a little purse while we were at the mall, just so she could give me something to wipe my mouth with during the concert. It was a small thing, but also an incredibly thoughtful thing, for her to do.

We walk for another fifteen minutes, enjoying the sights and sounds of downtown Salt Lake City until, finally, the symphony hall looms into view. The building is situated across the street from the historic Temple Square and is parallel to the city TRAX line that runs through the streets of downtown. The front side of the building is all made of glass, letting us see into the ornate lobby with its fancy dark carpeting and beautiful gold balconies. Near the center of the lobby is a massive, thirty-foot-tall, red-glass sculpture that looks like octopus tentacles stacked on top of each other, reaching out and up for the ceiling. Just looking at it, my heart tightens with excitement.

"There she is, there's Abravenal Hall," I say, sounding like an excited little kid.

Behind me, Brinley gives a low whistle. "Dang. I'm glad we bought the dresses. That place is fancy."

I nod. Then I close my eyes, briefly imagining my father in a dark suit and tie, walking in through the doors and seating himself on stage behind a piano. The thought gives me goose bumps. For the first time in my life, I've finally made it here.

"So, uh, how expensive did you say these tickets were?" Brinley asks, still eyeing the ornate sculpture in the lobby as we draw closer. Behind it, nestled in a corner underneath the swooping stairwell, I spot a gorgeous Steinway piano, sectioned off with velvet rope. I stare at it, heart speeding, my fingertips tingling at just the sight of it.

"Not too expensive," I answer as I stare longingly at the piano. Brinley's brought us to the front doors now, and a kind, older gentleman in a pullover sweater holds the door open. I nod at him politely and he nods back. "They were just fifteen dollars. The symphony has really good discounts for young students like us, and our seats are close to the front. I also made sure to buy seats that touch the aisle, so Lucas can stand close by."

Brinley nods. "Ah, smart. That was smart of you. So, uh, where do I go from here?"

I point. "See that desk? That's will call. That's where we'll pick up the tickets."

I guide Brinley through the process, then once we've got

the tickets in hand, we take our time admiring the lobby. Brinley takes out her phone, snapping pictures of us and our incredible surroundings, then she pushes me towards the sculpture. Having spent most of the afternoon researching all I could about Abravanel Hall, I admittedly begin to geek out about it. After all, I love this place and am completely in my element now.

"Ok, so you want to know something cool?" I ask, grinning over my shoulder with excessive enthusiasm, first at Brinley then at Lucas. "This sculpture was created by Dale Chihuly for the 2002 Salt Lake Olympic Games. It's called *The Olympic Tower*, and he sold it to Abravanel Hall for a discount because he wanted the public to be able to admire it without having to attend an art exhibit. If you don't know Dale Chihuly, you should. He's one of the most renowned glass artists in America. Only, he was in a bad car accident a lot of years ago and lost vision in one of his eyes, so he has to wear an eye patch. And I don't know, I just love that. A glassblowing artist with an eye patch?" I grin. "What a legend."

Brinley raises her eyebrows, then looks up at the sculpture, nodding her approval. "No joke. What a legend indeed."

"And that piano behind us," I say, turning in my wheelchair to point at it. Brinley, following my cue, takes us over to look at it. "It's a Steinway. I'm sure you already know, but oh my gosh, Steinways are like the sports car of the piano world. And a concert hall model like this one probably costs over $200,000. I mean, just look at it! It's so gorgeous, I'm drooling! The company, Steinway & Sons, was started by a German immigrant who came to America in the 1800s. But before that, he built his first piano in the kitchen of his house in Germany. Can you imagine that? Building a piano in the middle of a kitchen? My mom would have killed me!" I laugh. "Anyways, since then, Steinways have been the piano of choice for the majority of concert pianists. I've never played one, but...what I wouldn't give to," I say wistfully.

"Then do it. You should! Go for it!"

"What?" I crane over my shoulder, giving Brinley a crazy look. "What are you saying? You want me to play this thing *now?*"

"Well, yeah. It's only roped off. You could step over that easily. From everything you've said about your piano skills, I'm assuming you're good enough to get away with it. It's not like you would play 'Twinkle, Twinkle, Little Star' or something."

I snort. "Well, maybe I would. Ever heard of Mozart's Twelve Variations on 'Ah, vous dirai-je, Maman'?"

"Huh?"

"Never mind. Great thought, Brinley, but I would never."

"What? Never play a piano in public?"

"No. Never play a *roped-off* piano in public. Big difference."

And then Lucas speaks up, making me jump. "Well, I highly doubt you would regret it," he says, sizing up the piano. He's looking it over with his hands in his pockets, his brow raised as if he's impressed. "I mean, you have how long left to live? And you've never played a Steinway before? This could be your chance. Your final, one-and-only chance. So live a little." He shrugs. "Do something reckless."

"Right before our concert? No way! I'm not going to risk getting us kicked out of Abravanel Hall right before Mozart's Piano Concerto No. 21. Are you crazy? Not a chance!"

"All right, then play it after the concert," Lucas says, shrugging again. "Doesn't matter if they kick you out then, does it?"

And with that, he grins at me. Then he turns on his heel and starts walking casually towards the concert hall, leaving me with my mouth hanging open.

Because Lucas's idea, no matter how well-intentioned, is ludicrous. Ludicrous. I wouldn't hijack a concert piano in the middle of Abravanel Hall. And I definitely, definitely wouldn't do that to a Steinway as beautiful as this gorgeous one is.

I would rather die before being such a rebel.

315

Wouldn't I?

LUCAS

Ok, I seriously wish I had a thousand lifetimes to spend going to the symphony with Alex. Because not only is the music more entertaining than I thought it would be, but Alex herself is absolutely entertaining. The moment we stepped into Abravanel Hall, it was like a whole new side of her came out. Her typical modesty, her typical reluctance to focus on herself, her quiet selflessness and unassuming demeanor all just melted away. And instead, she was gushing. And watching Alex gush about music has to be my new, absolute favorite thing in this world to watch. Ever.

Because for a while, as she talks about pianos and music, she actually seems to forget that she is sick. She just prattles on and on and on about legendary concert halls, incredible concertos, and outstanding composers and musicians. After she and Brinley take their seats and before the concert starts, Alex rushes to share with us everything she knows about Wolfgang Amadeus Mozart. She tells us all about his prodigious childhood, his years spent as a freelance composer and piano soloist in Vienna, and the mysterious disease that took his life at the young age of thirty-five. She seems especially heartbroken by the fact that he died an early death and keeps musing about what else he would have written, had he lived longer than he did.

She keeps telling us all about Mozart, music, and the upcoming piano concerto right until the moment that the concertmaster steps onto the stage. When he does, the whole audience erupts into cheers. And no one claps as loudly or as enthusiastically for him as Alex does. Then, the concerto begins.

The pianist, a young man with flowing, shoulder-length hair, sits at a black piano, probably a Steinway, I'd guess. It's positioned at the front of the stage, the entire symphony orchestra arranged behind him. The dude is decked out in a really great tuxedo and absolutely tears apart the keyboard, movement after movement. Alex is sitting closest to where I am positioned in the aisle, and I keep stealing glances at her, thoroughly enjoying the expressions on her face as much as the concert itself. She's pinching one of her thumbnails tightly between her teeth, gnawing on it, while the other hand keeps twitching as if wanting to mimic the pianist's motions. I watch as her keen eyes dart across the keyboard, understanding every minute movement the musician is making and analyzing it at a level that I will never comprehend. Alex, I'm coming to realize, is secretly brilliant. She is really, truly brilliant. And it is remarkable to see her become so enthralled by the concert and so immersed in the music. She's at her happiest here, she honestly seems to be, and I feel it an immense privilege to stand by and watch her soak in every moment with rapt and passion-filled attention.

In fact, the moment is so perfect, so exquisite, that it feels like nothing can possibly ruin it.

Nothing, that is, except cancer.

Because it's during the final piece of the concert that Alex's coughing begins. It starts out as just the occasional, small, closed-mouth cough that no one would think twice about. But as the music picks up speed and intensity, climbing to a climax, so does her coughing. Her occasional coughs start taking on a deep, guttural sound that makes me cringe, and it gets bad enough that Alex winces and doubles over in pain each time it happens. She has one coughing fit, gets control of it, then another one starts. The people in front of us start looking over their shoulders. The people next to her start subtly sliding farther away from her, and one older woman seated directly behind us actually leans forward, her white hair spilling over the seat as she lays a hand on Alex's back.

"Sweetie, are you all right?" she whispers, keeping her voice low. "Do you need water? I have a bottle here if you want it."

"No, no," Alex desperately gasps, her eyes watering. I can hear it in her voice, she's really struggling to breathe. "I'm...fine. I'll go...to the fountain...outside."

And with that, still hacking up a lung, Alex grabs the seat in front of her and painfully pulls herself to her feet. Brinley quickly stands too, grabbing Alex's elbow to steady her. I scramble out of the way as Alex stumbles into the aisle, still coughing. By this point, most heads in the audience are turning, and I can tell she hates the attention. She hates being a distraction.

"Let me grab the wheelchair," Brinley whispers in her ear, carrying Alex's backpack in one hand. We folded the wheelchair and left it at the bottom of the aisle when we got seated. It's in a large open space next to the door.

But Alex, shaking her head and continuing to hack, doesn't answer. Red is starting to appear at the corners of her mouth, and she's gagging. I can tell she's trying not to open her mouth with blood in it. Not here. Not in public. So she doesn't wait for Brinley. Stumbling, she lunges forward and lurches for the door as best she can. The attendant, seeing her coming, quickly opens it.

Brinley shadows her every move, keeping a hold of Alex's elbow, and rushes with her out of the concert hall. They run, fleeing the concert, and head straight for the girls' restroom. As they burst through the door, I hesitate, locking my knees and grinding to a halt just outside. Moments later, the sound of deep, hacking, painful vomiting emanates from within, making my spirit run chill. The sound is deeper, more desperate, and more violent than anything I've heard from Alex before. Cursing, I whirl from the door and run a hand anxiously through my hair. Behind me, the hacking and vomiting only grow louder.

CHAPTER TWENTY-FIVE

BRINLEY

"You're sure that you're ok?" the usher asks for the millionth time, crouching in front of Alex. She and I just spent the last ten minutes together in the restroom, as I held her up while she puked into the toilet. Nonstop, Alex had hacked and vomited and spewed blood and bile from her mouth, knees on the tile floor and shaking hands grasping the bowl. It was a terrible thing to watch, and truth be told, I want to scream at the usher that, no, she's not fine. She obviously isn't fine. "Give me just one word and we'll have an ambulance here immediately."

But rather than scream at him, I lock my lips, letting Alex answer. She's seated on the carpeted floor just outside the bathroom, her head leaned back against the brick wall, looking as gaunt as ever with deep, exhausted bruises under her eyes.

"No, I'm...fine," she says weakly, her head lolling slightly on her neck, her voice raspy and faded. "It's normal...for me. Just the cancer."

The usher raises his eyebrows, seemingly not convinced. He looks to me for confirmation.

"She has tumors in her lungs," I explain, sounding mechanical and numb even to myself. After witnessing what I just saw in the bathroom, I swear I am going into shock or something. Behind us, music continues to emanate faintly from behind the closed doors of the concert hall. "They're blood-producing tumors, so I know it looks scary, but it's not new. She has only a few months to live," I add, gulping. Those words have never felt as real as they do just now. A lump forms in my throat and I look away from Alex.

"Oh," the usher says. He looks at Alex again, a new expression taking over his face. "I'm sorry. My mom just died of cancer this year. I...I'm so sorry."

Alex weakly meets his eyes, raising both eyebrows. "It sucks, doesn't it?" she rasps quietly.

"Yeah, it definitely, definitely does."

We don't say anything for a moment after that. It's quiet, the mood heavy and somber. Then the young man asks again, "Really? No ambulance?"

"No ambulance," Alex confirms, coughing and shaking her head. "I don't want one. I'll be fine if I just...sit for a while."

"We've got a wheelchair," I add. "We left it in the concert hall by the door. I can get it and take her back home as soon as she feels well enough."

"Ok. Then tell you what, I'll go grab it for you," the man says. Standing, I see that his golden name tag reads *Roger*.

"No, don't," Alex says quickly. Wincing, she straightens up further against the wall, holding her ribs. I see her hands are shaking. "Please, not yet. The concert is almost over. We've disturbed the audience enough already."

"Oh, it won't disturb them, ma'am. All I'm going to do is open the door."

"No," Alex repeats, shaking her head. "No, not so close to the ending. Let the musicians have their moment. Brinley, can you...help me up? We can go wait on the bench over there. We'll leave after everyone else clears out. I need some...time to breathe anyways. To catch my breath. It...it really hurts," she admits, grimacing.

"Um, yeah. If that's what you need." I throw a look at Roger, not totally convinced that I'm doing the right thing but not knowing what else to do. I loop one of Alex's arms over my shoulders, then Roger, jumping forward, gets the other. And together, we carefully, gingerly, pull Alex to her feet. As she stands, she squeezes her eyes shut and cries out in pain. Both of her knees buckle.

"You ok?" Roger asks immediately, worried. Alex opens

her eyes and looks directly ahead, at what I assume must be Lucas. She grits her teeth, then nods discreetly. Slowly, she straightens and pulls her arm off Roger's shoulder. More of her weight slumps against me as she does, and I stumble just a little.

"Yeah, I'm fine," she pants, shaking and looking pale. She's still cringing painfully and holding that side of hers. "Thank you."

"Ok, I'm going to call an ambulance."

"No!" she says. "No, don't! I can't afford it. The three of us are from New Mexico and your hospitals are probably outside my insurance network. Or at least, they could be. Please."

Roger cocks his head. "The three of you?"

"Two. Sorry, I meant two. Brinley and I."

"Ok, well..." Roger hesitates. "Let me take you to a back room, then. We can sit you down somewhere more private than a bench. The crowds are about to come out at any moment."

And that's when the lightbulb goes off in my head. And before I know it, I'm speaking, blurting out my thoughts in a desperate, intense plea. My grip tightens on Alex. "Hey, Roger, what about that piano over there? Can Alex sit and catch her breath at your Steinway?"

"Huh?" he asks, confused.

"That piano in the lobby," I say, nodding my head

towards it. The lobby is mostly empty except for one or two workers at concessions, who are watching us with anxious expressions. "Alex is a pianist. A really, really good one. Classically trained. It would mean a lot to her."

"You're a pianist, huh?" he asks, seeming surprised.

"Yeah, she is. A phenomenal one. She wants to be a music professor, but she's never played a Steinway before. Never in her life. So please?"

"Brinley," Alex says in a low voice, trying to get me to stop. Only, she starts coughing again and can't say any more. Panic floods my chest as she slumps against me further.

"No, I'm serious!" I say, only getting more desperate. "Just let her sit there and play. Just this once. She'll play real quietly, just until the concert is over. Please, Roger."

Roger looks at me, lips pursed. Then he looks over at Alex. And finally, he jerks his head towards the piano. "If you want to, go for it. It's all yours."

"Oh my gosh, thank you! Thank you! You're the best, Roger! You really are!" I cry. Then, "Come on, Alex. Here's your chance. Let's go knock the ivory off that thing!" And before she can say no, I start dragging her away in that direction, anxious to make her dream happen. Anxious, desperately anxious, for her not to die.

"Brinley," she whispers, wincing as we stumble forward across the lobby together. "Brinley, I...can't. I'm in so much pain. Please...my lungs..."

"Yes, you can, Alex," I almost growl. "Yes, you can. Don't tell me that. Don't tell me that you can't. This is your dream, your moment."

Alex looks up, her eyes tight and deep and pained. They're starting to grow unfocused, almost like she's about to pass out or something. "Brinley," she whispers.

"You can do this, Alex. I've never heard you play before. We are in Abravanel Hall and you need to play the piano. It's just you and me and Lucas. Let us hear you play."

And with that, I drag her sagging body over to the piano. Using my free hand, the one that isn't supporting Alex, I move aside the velvet rope. Then I lead her to the bench.

"There you go," I say, helping her ease onto the cushioned seat. "A concert hall Steinway, just for you. And in your favorite place, even! Can you believe this is happening?"

Alex's head dips forward and she just grimaces, her face looking pale, her forehead beading with sweat. This time, rather than clutching at her side, she clutches at her heart.

I step back, then gesture at her and the piano. "Alex, here's your moment. Play for us, will you?"

Looking up at my face, Alex's eyes tighten. I try to force a smile at her. But instead, tears are brimming in my eyes. Seeing them, Alex's expression changes. Her lips purse and tears form in her own eyes. Then, cringing in pain, she turns herself on the piano seat. Lifting her shaking, bony hands, she places them on the keyboard.

And rather than pick out a classical melody, she instead starts to quietly, softly, play an intricate arrangement of "A Million Dreams" from *The Greatest Showman*. The longing in her tremulous playing is so haunting and so heart-wrenching that a sob escapes and the water spills freely from my eyes.

I watch her, transfixed, as her hands fly elegantly around the keyboard, tears streaming down her own gaunt cheeks. Then moments later, she cries out. Alex's hands slip off the keyboard, causing a dissonant chord, and they clutch desperately at her chest. She doubles over, gasping, gritting her teeth in agony. And next thing I know, Alex tumbles off the piano bench and is on the ground, collapsed.

I scream her name. I scream it for all to hear. But it does no good. Slowly, her eyes roll up and her eyelids slide closed.

One bony, talented hand is left curled by her tear-streaked face.

CHAPTER TWENTY-SIX

LUCAS

Pulmonary embolism. The doctors explained it was a pulmonary embolism. It's when a blood clot gets lodged in the lungs, blocking blood flow through the major arteries there, preventing oxygenation throughout the body and leading, in the worst of all cases, to tissue death and organ failure. They said risk factors can include cancer, recent surgery, certain medications, injury, and long periods of sitting, like driving for hours on a road trip. Symptoms include anxiety, feeling light-headed, difficulty breathing, intense chest pain, and coughing up blood. A pulmonary embolism is fatal if it's not caught and treated quickly. It's life-threatening even under the best of circumstances. And Alex's circumstances are certainly not the best. Her organs were already shutting down long before this happened.

I sit next to her, collapsed on the ground of the hospital room, hands knotted in my hair and head between my knees as I stare vacantly. There are scuffs and mars all across the white tile floor. Alex wasn't the first one to be in this room. She won't be the last. But never again will there be someone in this hospital room who matters as much to me as Alex does.

She's above me, above my spot on the floor, lying unconscious and hooked to a ventilator. There is a tube shoved down her throat that's breathing for her, forcing air into and out of her dying lungs. She's sedated right now, but the doctors don't know how long that will last. They don't know how long *she* will last. It's only been a few hours since the incident, but already her body is intent on shutting down. Her mother and Craig are on a plane right now. My parents are scheduled only one flight behind them. Brinley is in the lobby, not allowed into the ICU. And I am here alone, sitting with Alex's soon-to-be corpse.

Though I don't have a body, though I don't have tear ducts to cry with, a lump forms in my throat and tears threaten to choke me. To kill me. Because I can't do this. I can't handle this. I can't play a role in my best friend's death.

So standing, I look down with despair at Alex, her fragile form donned in a hospital gown, her face covered by the ventilator. And as I look, a sob tears through my soul. I bite my fist, feeling nothing. And just like I did all those weeks ago, I turn and flee her hospital room.

This time, not because I am a chicken and am scared to watch her die. But this time, because I am a soul, and I can't bear to see her suffer.

I flee, walking quickly and blindly out of the room, my body ravaged by sobs. I tear down the hallway, half running, half stumbling. My eyes are on my feet. My eyes are squeezed shut.

And then...I run into something. I *hit* into it. My spirit grinds to a halt, coming to a physical stop. I have tangibly hit something solid, and my spirit didn't pass through.

Gasping, I stumble backward and open my eyes. There, standing in front of me, is a woman.

She's small, barely five feet tall, and has a dark complexion with copper skin. Her short hair is rather curly, hugging close to her scalp, and there are threads of pure white weaved among the dark. Her frame is slight but her eyes are large, bright, penetrating, and warm. Her whole being, in fact, is luminous.

"Hello, Lucas," she says quietly. Her large chocolate eyes bore into mine.

I open my mouth, intending to speak. But I don't. The lump is still there. I'm still being choked.

"Do you know who I am?" she asks. And as she does, she raises both eyebrows. Something about that look is familiar. And still, she looks at me.

"Uh...no," I finally croak. "I don't." Then I look down, away. I swallow. My thoughts are running wild, all stampeding in circles around Alex.

"I am Alex's grandmother."

Abruptly, my head snaps up. The woman's eyes smile, her lips barely perking.

"Excuse me?"

"I am Alex's grandmother. My name is Halima Sharifa Ahmed. You may call me Halima."

I stare, my eyes bulging, my jaw dropping slightly. Finally, I stammer, "H-hello, Halima."

She inclines her head at me, accepting my greeting graciously.

"Your grandfather is in the waiting room. He's sitting with Brinley right now, but he wants me to tell you that he would like a moment to speak with you."

"Excuse me?" I ask, my mouth falling open. This moment is getting more surreal by the second. "My grandfather? He can't be. He had a heart attack. He died almost ten years ago."

Halima just raises her eyebrows further. Something passes between us. I shudder, not quite knowing what just happened. It was almost like she was impressing an idea on my mind. Like she was communicating with her spirit, not with words.

331

But as she did, I felt something. A calm, a peace, images of Alex, the face of my dead grandfather, and a curious sense pulling me towards the waiting room. It was fleeting and quickly vanished. But it was real.

"H-h...how did you do that?"

Halima just smiles. "Your grandfather is waiting. Now if you don't mind, I would like to spend some time with my granddaughter. She needs me."

Before I can say anything further, Halima nods politely then steps around me. I whirl, stunned as I watch her walk peacefully away down the hallway. But then, a thought hits me. A sudden sense of dread clutches through me. And down the hall, I shout, "Don't! Don't you dare take her, Halima!" I plead. "Don't you dare take Alex!"

The woman stops in her tracks, back stiffening. Then she slowly turns around.

When she looks at me, her eyes are bright, penetrating, and absolutely captivating. There is something special about this spirit, and I can't quite place it.

"If I take her, Lucas, it will only be because she is ready and she is willing. Now please, go and join your grandfather."

And with that, Halima turns and disappears around the corner.

My grandfather's name was Harrison Blair Prowley. Just like I told Halima, he died ten years ago of a sudden, debilitating heart attack. He and his wife lived in Florida, so I didn't see them very often. But the few memories I have of him are fond, filled with vague impressions of childhood happiness and love.

The problem is, though, the last time I saw him, I must have been six years old. And I don't feel those things in this moment. Not anymore. As I get closer to him and farther from Alex's dying body, those cheerful memories could not feel more distant or foreign to my breaking heart.

When I reach my destination, I pass numbly through the door into the waiting room, shuddering as the atoms split my spirit. And though I don't remember his face well, my eyes immediately fall on him. He is crouching in front of Brinley, hands on her knees, and stands as I come in. Our eyes meet. A shiver runs up my spine. And I know that it is him.

Just like I see in all spirits, there is an innate glow about Harrison. It's not an aura, just a characteristic. Light is imbued within his soul. His eyes are as blue as mine are and as blue as my father's have always been. His chin and his nose have the same narrow angle as mine. With a lurch, I realize I look far more like my grandfather than I ever realized. He was fifty-seven when he died. But, standing here, looking at me, he appears as if he could be younger. There is a vitality in his stance, a wellness in his demeanor, that contrasts with the mature carving of his face. He is still my senior in age, but feels to be my equal in mind and soul.

"Lucas, my boy," Grandfather says. He smiles widely, and his expression takes on a look so tender and longing, it sends spiritual chills racing through my spine. "My, how you've grown. And how magnificent you've become."

Then in three large bounds, he is in front of me, wrapping me up in an embrace that I can *feel*. An embrace that is like nothing I've experienced since death.

At first, I don't speak. I can't. I just freeze, every particle of my being locking itself in shock. Over his shoulder, behind him, I see Brinley. She's seated on a waiting room chair, her knees pulled to her chest, her face buried in her hands. Exactly as I left her.

"What are you doing here?" I finally ask, speaking slowly. I pull away from the hug, and Harrison, seeming to sense my discomfort, lets his arms drop. "I thought you would be in Florida."

"I was," he tells me, looking at me with earnest sincerity. "I don't stray far from your grandmother very often, especially now that she has Alzheimer's. But today, I came for you. And I came to be with your sister." He turns and waves a hand at Brinley's devastated form. His expression, again, softens with that deep compassion.

But for some reason, that look, that love, triggers me. Because no matter how real it seems, no matter how sincere he is acting, none of this can be real. That compassion can't be real. My mind reeling, I realize that my grandfather, all this time, has been dead. All this time, he had the capacity to travel from Florida to Utah. And all this time, he's been aware of us. And yet, he never came? He left me lost and stranded and dead and *alone* for nearly six agonizing months?

As if reading my mind, Grandfather takes another step back and slowly grimaces, a real sorrow emerging in his blue eyes. "That wasn't part of the plan, Lucas," he says quietly.

Startled, I jump. Violently. *Can* he read my mind?

"Perhaps I can, but perhaps I can't. There's still so much you don't know, so much you have to learn. There are reasons for why things had to happen this way."

He pauses, looking at me expectantly. But my mind whirling, my heart wrenching, I can't respond. I just look at him, glare at him, my emotions unstable and roiling close to the surface. Quietly, he sighs.

"You're suffering," he acknowledges sadly. "I know you've been suffering. And I know that your sister is suffering too. But all of this is, and has been, part of a larger plan. Pain, as your friend Alex once so eloquently asked, does serve a purpose. And though I understand why you may hesitate to believe that, I ask that you please trust me."

But still, I say nothing. I stare at my grandfather, my jaw working angrily, my mind lurching desperately. And finally, I ask my burning question.

"So if my death was all part of some great plan, and if you knew all along, then why didn't you come for me, Harrison?" I nearly yell, clenching my hands on either side. "Alex's grandmother came for her. Her grandmother recognizes that she needs help, that she needs her. I mean, call me crazy, but I had always figured that, if there really was an afterlife, that family members would be there for me. That they would help me, welcome me. But there was no family, Harrison," I say, spitting the words. "There was no you. So why are you here now? Why have you finally come? Is it because you've decided I've been through enough already? That I've hurt so badly that some...some stupid *purpose* is met now?"

Slowly, his eyes searching mine, Grandfather drops his gaze. He looks away. First at Brinley, then back to me. "No, Lucas. It's because your sister needed you, didn't she?" he says, his voice soft but his eyes bright and striking. "Believe it or not, Brinley's pain *is* serving a purpose. Yet it was becoming too much. And what you've accomplished for Brinley would not have happened—could not have happened—if I had first come," he says, his voice thick with sincerity. "So though it was difficult for me to stay away, I did. That was my role to play. However," he adds, holding up a finger, "like Brinley, you have grown through this. You are more ready now, and because of that, I have a different role to take on."

"Ready?" I cry, hearing an echo of what Halima said in his words, my mind tripping and spinning incredulously. "I've grown? I'm more ready? Ready for what?"

"Ready to discover. Ready to be taught."

"Ready to be taught what?" I shout, clutching at my hair. "Quit playing games with me, Harrison. What are you talking about?" My voice, magnified by emotion and distress and love and confusion and anger, reverberates around the room. But no one hears me. Brinley doesn't hear me. Only my grandfather does.

"To be taught about the most important things," he answers quietly, calm as an afternoon sun. "There is so much you don't understand, so many whys you still need to learn."

"Oh yeah? No joke!" I yell again. "No joke! Because yeah, you're right! I don't understand any of this! I don't understand why I had to die. Why Brinley has to suffer so desperately, so innocently. Why Alex is sick and dying and why she doesn't get to live her extraordinary life any longer. She deserves to live, Harrison! Alex deserves to live! And don't any of you, *any* of you spirits, care about that?"

My grandfather only looks at me, searching. Then with a soft, chilling whisper, he admits, "Yes. Alex does deserve to live. But have you ever considered that she might also deserve something better?"

"Better? Better? What about this existence could possibly be better?"

"More than you know," he intones, his eyes flashing, dancing like fire. "There is more to this existence and more to our purpose. Lucas, there are reasons why things happen that are deeper than coincidence and more precious than you can imagine. If your friend leaves this life, it is to claim a reward. I promise," he says, looking at me intensely, "we each get better than we deserve here. Alex will get better than she deserves. She just first had a role to play in this life, and she played it marvelously. Now if you don't mind, we are ready to start teaching you. And, if I'm not mistaken, your dear friend would rather like to join us."

"What?" I shake my head, spluttering. "What are you talking about? What are you even saying?"

And then I feel it. My entire spirit tingles, my dormant heartbeat speeds, and I sense *something*.

Whirling around, I turn. And there, standing in front of the closed door from which I just came, is Alex. Standing tall and with no oxygen tubes. No gasping. No pain.

Then, slowly, she smiles triumphantly. And the magnificent light that is imbued within her takes my breath away.

EPILOGUE

BRINLEY

My feet throb, my back aches, and my scrubs severely need a wash. But regardless of the exhaustion, I am happy as I push open the door. Because when I do, a tiny voice calls out to me.

"Mommy!"

The cry is a shriek, a squeal of happiness and joy. As I step into our home, closing the door behind me, little Ethan Lucas comes barreling for my legs. Reaching down, I scoop him into my arms, smothering my face into his little neck. In response, he squeals and wraps his tiny arms around me.

"Mommy, Mommy, look what Daddy helped me make!" He pulls away from me, pointing into the room behind him, where Jonathan lies on the carpet. In front of him is sprawled an overturned tub of Legos and a giant, uneven-looking tower. It's apparent which side Jonathan made and at which parts Ethan contributed.

"Oh wow!" I say enthusiastically, looking my little boy in the eyes. They are blue, as piercing blue and happy and excited as any boy's could be. "You made that? I can't believe it!"

"I did, I did, I did!" Ethan cries.

"Oh my word. And what about your sister? Did Ella help you?"

Ethan's little four-year-old face scrunches as if he's tasted something unpleasant. Then he points to the bassinet in the corner, where Ella must be sleeping. "No, she just lay there. It was Daddy who made the tower. And I helped him!"

"I see. Well, I am so impressed, Ethan. That is one big tower!"

"I know!" he squeals.

Laughing, I plant a kiss on his little, dimpled cheek, then set him on the ground, letting him speed off. As Jonathan heaves himself off the floor, joints cracking, I walk over to Ella and peer into her bassinet. Sure enough, she is fast asleep, her little hands curled into little, perfect fists.

Behind me, Jonathan comes up, looping his hands around my waist.

"How was your shift?" he murmurs, his breath warm

against my ear. I shudder.

"Good. It was good. Just long," I sigh. "But do you want to hear some good news? My little three-year-old patient, the one I keep telling you about, got released today."

"Oh really?" Jonathan sounds pleasantly surprised. "Does that mean he's in remission?"

"For now it does. We're hoping it stays that way."

"It will," Jonathan reassures me. He buries his face in my neck, giving me a kiss. At my feet, Ethan is tugging on my scrubs again, demanding my attention. In his hands, he holds a misshapen pile of bricks to show me.

"You're such a good nurse," Jonathan whispers. "Your patients are so lucky to have you."

For a moment, I soak in his words and let myself feel loved. Then I carefully extricate myself from his arms and turn my attention to Ethan. The moment I look at him, he begins prattling at a million miles per hour. I know, at this stage of the night, that he won't stop talking until he's tucked into bed, his favorite Spider-Man doll wrapped tightly in his arms. I listen, mostly, like I always do, and help Jonathan get the children into bed.

Then when the house is quiet and Jonathan is sitting on the couch, his feet propped up and his glasses illuminated by his laptop, I steal outside.

I go out onto the porch and let the chill, crisp darkness envelop me. Taking a deep breath, I close my eyes and slowly let it out.

Then, opening them, I look to my right. Then to my left. A small shudder runs down my spine and a soft peace blossoms in my heart.

And tonight, I swear I can feel them both.

Acknowledgements

When I first began to write, I had no idea what a monumental task it is to publish a novel. In my beginner's mindset, I assumed that most of the work could be accomplished on my own. All I had to do was write a good story and sell it.

Fast forward to now, and I've grown a little bit wiser. I now understand that writing a story requires a team, and publishing it takes a village. *When Breath Is Taken* never would have become reality without the support of many amazing people.

To begin, I would like to acknowledge the many individuals who helped craft the story through their invaluable feedback. Jade, Athena, Amina, Courtney, and Madi each read the manuscript in its earliest, incomplete stages. They guided my approach to the second half of the novel, and their enthusiasm gave me hope to keep writing.

I would also like to acknowledge my beta readers—those who read the complete manuscript before publication. Athena, Bruce, Darci, Josh, Mom, and Dad each spent hours of their life reading this story, voicing their insights, and helping me identify the final improvements to be made.

I am also indebted to the paid editors who perfected this book in beautiful ways. To put it simply, Jana Miller was a godsend. The developmental and line edits she suggested were precisely what this novel needed, and her influence can be felt in almost every page. She loved Lucas, Alex, and Brinley, and her belief in this novel supported me through many difficult months of burnout. It is because of her edits and her words that I came to believe this novel was worth publishing.

In addition to Jana's help, I also received wonderful proofreads from Meghan, Bruce, and Nancy. Each of these editors are fantastic, and I would recommend their services to anyone in need of an expert.

Though I never shared the full manuscript with them, I am also grateful for the influence of my critique group. Cassie, Eli, Fisher, Lauren, and Sophie have all been instrumental in helping me improve my writing. Their regular advice makes me a better author, and their feedback on the cover, blurb, and first several pages of *When Breath Is Taken* was so valuable to me. They were the team that helped get this novel across the finish line to publication.

And above all, I need to acknowledge my greatest supporter, my husband. More than anyone else, Josh helped me through every late night and tearful breakdown, bringing me chocolate, hugs, and words of encouragement when I needed them most. His love for me extended into a love for this story, and it is because of him that the audiobook and book trailer were created. If every husband were as kind and good as Josh, then this world would never cease to be a breathtaking place. I am so thankful for him and the endless ways he cheers me on.

About the Author

Morgan Hadden graduated from Utah State University with a Bachelor of Science in Health Education and Promotion and a Master of Public Health. When not writing, she can be found pinned beneath a purring cat, going on a long run with an audiobook, or attending symphonies, ballets, and plays with her husband.

Let's Connect!

Facebook: @morganhaddenauthor
Instagram: @morganhaddenauthor
TikTok: @morganhaddenauthor

Email: morganhaddenauthor@gmail.com
Website: www.morganhaddenauthor.com